DARK V

By Tommy

Contents

Chapter 1 The Third Estate

Chapter 2 The Battle of Mouffetard

Chapter 3 The Wolf Band Legend of the Dog Soldiers

Chapter 4 The Defiance

Chapter 5 Four Claws

Chapter 6 Ramone Rodriques

Chapter 7 Morning Star

Chapter 8 Blood and Bones

Chapter 9 The Reunion

Chapter 10 Twice the Slave

Chapter 11 The Company of the Indies

Chapter 12 Sishu

Chapter 13 St. Catherine

Chapter 14 Stones of Gold

Chapter 15 Grand Soliel (The Sun God)

Chapter 16 Des Natanapalle (The City of Slaves)

Chapter 17 The Giving of the Shield

Chapter 18 The King Is Dead

Chapter 19 The Gathering

Chapter 20 Awakening

Chapter 21 Sweet Medicine

Chapter 22 Broken Promise

Chapter 23 The Death Song

Chapter 24 Invisible

Chapter 25 Captive

Chapter 26 Riders in the Sky

Chapter 27 A Battle Cry For All

Chapter 1

The Third Estate

Pierre DeBois flew along the narrow cobblestone streets. His band of men clung to the four corners of the carriage as it careened past large groups of patriots gathering in the streets. His cousin, King Louis the 16th, had summoned Pierre to the Louvre. He was truly loyal to the King and didn't hesitate to perform gruesome duties no one else would. Pierre kept his hand close to his sword because he was well aware of the dangers he faced passing through the center of the city. Groups of men with red sashes and blood stained swords lurked at every turn. His men cleared the way allowing the carriage to run the many blockades leading to the gates of the palace. As he climbed from the carriage, he could still see the smoke rising from the Bastille. Earlier he had seen the rebels take the old armory and Governor DeLauney. All the captives were marched into the city square. DeLauney, along with his men, had their heads cut off and placed on pikes, blood streaming down all sides. He grimaced at the recollection as he began to jog into the palace to see the King.

King Louis was pacing back and forth before the great windows facing the Rue St. Antoine. He, too, had seen the Patriots running towards the great plume of smoke and heard the reports of the Bastille falling.

"So, it's begun, young DeBois," Louis said with a great sigh. "Are the reports true? Have we lost the Bastille?"

"I am afraid we have, Sire. The men have been killed and the weapons taken from the armory. DeLauney's head has been placed on a pike in the square. I've seen it. It is true. The Third Estate calls for change."

King Louis responded with anger in his face. "What is the Third Estate of the common man? They believe that they are everything! What have they been thus far? Nothing! What do they demand? To be something! The common people cry for their freedom and equal rights. And what is the cost of this freedom? It won't be a loaf of bread or 5 acres of land this time. It will be a painful freedom!," the King shouted as he turned his back on the chaos unfolding outside. "A dark wind is blowing over my country and the First Estate of nobility will be the blood that gives these commoners their freedom."

Shots were heard somewhere in the city as great fires burned all around. The King winced as if in pain. Pierre glared at the insurrectionists running along the palace wall and then asked, "What do you desire of me, Sire?"

Louis said, "Come, walk with me. I have little time before the real change comes. The people of the Church and the National Assembly will not give into the murder of their king. I have sent for Marquis DeLafayette. With the help of the Assembly, I plan on putting him in charge of this rabble they call an army. I must get safely out of the city until he arrives. I commission you 'Council to the King'. Take this seal and do what you must to move us to the castle at Versailles."

Pierre had been waiting for an opportunity like this one his whole life. He already knew how he could use Louis's fears to his advantage. He accepted the position by bowing before the King. It appeared almost comical.

"Your wish shall be my command. Be ready to move at a moment's notice, Sire".

He pivoted suddenly, sending his black cape spinning out as if he was flying away. He called out, "The common estate calls for my blade, Sire," and then he disappeared. He left the Palace from a side entrance without the carriage. It was not a good idea to be riding through the city as one of the First Estate. Many nobles had been dragged down from their coaches that day to their deaths. His plan was to slip out of the palace on foot. Pierre was a chameleon. Two steps outside the palace walls, Pierre disappeared with his men down the steps to the river into the dark underworld he controlled.

Pierre had ordered a boat to be at the Louvre. It was the easiest way to traverse the city. Their destination was the Latin Quarter where Pierre controlled a 3-mile square. Patriots blocked all the Rues, but they seemed to have overlooked the river for travel. The boat was a 20-foot fishing boat with a small cover to hide the cargo. These boats were common in the river and no one would pay any attention to it slipping through the turmoil. They moved from one bridge to the next using the large block arches to hide under when danger was near. The contents of the Justice Building had been dumped in the courtyard by hundreds of men from the Third Estate. It was burning and the flames lit up the river like daytime making it dangerous to pass. They were just about to abandon the boat when Chief Magistrate Bonnet was dragged from the building to the cheers of the crowd gathered there. The whole crowd moved away from the river, allowing the boat to just slip past unnoticed in order to get to the Cathedral of Notre Dame. Pierre couldn't believe that just 200 yards beyond the Palace of Justice and all the noise, the cathedral sat calm, its stonewalls casting an eerie peacefulness over the city. The towering windows were like dark eyes that surveyed the chaotic city below; a giant waiting its turn to live or die. *Only God would know,* he thought, as they went by.

One by one Pierre and his men passed under the 12 bridges controlled by the Third Estate until they reached the Rue De Ravioli. They abandoned the boat and slipped down the narrow street towards safety. The Rue DeRavioli crossed a large street called Boulevard St. Germain. The Boulevard was blocked near the corner by a barricade of wagons with several men standing guard close to a fire that burned in the center. Pierre nodded to his companions. The black figures left him, and then slithered along the shadows cast by the light until they were close enough to strike. There was a fat man telling a story as he faced the others and they were laughing at him. When the blade came out of his chest, he looked down at it for just an instant. Then as his smile disappeared, the blade vanished and he fell dead. The head of another man was severed from his shoulders and rolled along the gutter as the Dark Wind descended upon the group. In a few seconds, it was over. Pierre then flew past the dead men and turned into Rue Monge, a dismal, narrow street heading away from all the activity of the river. The street continued for a mile, and then it narrowed once again as it ended at Rue Mouffetard. Pierre turned to the north and in a few steps was within the safety of the empire he alone controlled.

Since the early years Rue Mouffetard had been the home of many Gypsy clans banished there by the ruling classes. Sabotha, fortuneteller of the clans, was a ruthless old woman, five foot five with a wrinkled face. Sabotha had placed him in charge of his tribe. Her eyes looked like white pearls set deep in the dark, tanned face. She had several scars across her cheek and nose lending her features

8

an evil look. Pierre had stumbled across Sabotha one evening outside a tavern near the river. As he passed, she asked him if he wanted his palm read. Pierre had a fascination with palm reading and so he consented. Sabotha grabbed his hand and rubbed across it a few times. She began to tremble violently; her eyes rolled back in their sockets and she fell on the ground, mumbling, "The darkness, darkness." He helped her up on her feet again.

"You are the one," she said as her eyes opened.

Pierre said, "I am the what, old one?"

"You are the one we've been looking for."

"To do what?"

"You're the one to bring the Gypsy clans together. I have seen it. A legend says one will come to us and organize us into a great clan. I have seen it in your hand and the hands do not lie. You are the one." With that she slipped into the darkness of the street.

After that first meeting, she arranged many more with him and soon he took control of the Sinti tribe at Rue Moffetard. The tribes accepted Sabotha's visions about Pierre being the new leader and joined under his authority, but one group, the tribe led by Coureur de Calonne, did not. Calonne had long proclaimed himself the sole King of all Gypsies and he vowed not to let Pierre take that away from him. Calonne controlled the Gitanos; they lived along the river and were responsible for most of the black market items entering the city from central Europe. Calonne hated Pierre because Pierre used his influence with the King to take over portions of the city once controlled by Calonne. The crown often arrested or condemned Gitano men and at the same time released Sinti men for the same crime. Calonne still lived in the shadows of his underworld while Pierre walked the street in daylight unafraid of any government intervention.

Pierre slammed the heavy oak doors and entered the Vista; he turned the corner, and then hurried down the steps to Sabotha's room. It was a cold, damp, dark place that fit her personality. The room was littered with bits of bone, smooth stones and foul-smelling bottles filled with things Pierre didn't recognize. He relied on her visions to tell him what moves he should make. Since their first meeting, she had never been wrong and he attributed his success to her.

"Sabotha," he called and kicked a frog away from his feet as he marched in. "Sabotha."

She appeared from behind a curtain that separated the room. "I see the King has made you excited, DeBois. Is he so afraid of his own people, he calls on the hated Gypsies for help?"

"He calls on his cousin for help and I will help if it suits me to do so."

Sabotha picked up her bones and stones. "And I'm the one to tell you if it suits you."

Pacing restlessly Pierre answered, "You often predicted the day would come when our tribe would rule over others. Look at the bones and tell me what they say."

She tossed them down on the wooden table, snatched up the frog, chopped it in two and splattered the blood over the bones. She began to shake and wave her hands up in the air still holding the bleeding frog. "Daba tee, Daba tee, de tourano ---I see the King floating on the river. Black arms and hands grab at him." Her flailing arms knocked the candles from the table. Pierre jumped away from her, his eyes wide. "You stand above on the bow of the boat chopping away at them as they reach for the King. The arms are cut off, but the fingers keep pushing the arms toward him." She spins and falls forward catching herself on the pole holding up the curtain, her spin causing the dripping blood to splatter across Pierre's face. "The boat breaks free then floats away, but the arms in the boat keep coming. You fly away and people of different colors bow before you in a strange land. Ahh… Daba tee." She slid into a chair by the table, her energy gone, her mind fatigued.

DeBois wiped the blood from his shocked face; he had seen a lot of Sabotha's visions, but this was the wildest one yet. He leaned towards her and asked, "What does it mean, Sabotha?"

She replied, "You will rescue the King from Calonne, but the patriots will keep coming for him. He will stay in danger; death will stalk him from this day forth. You on the other hand, young Prince, will be granted a great wish. The wish will make you king of a distant land. It is your destiny to accept what the King offers. Your survival will depend on it."

It was a hot July and the city burned, making it seem hotter than it really was.

Pierre knew from the fear in the King and the increasing bravery of the patriots that it was just a matter of time until they took control of the palace. The street vendor spies had already told DeBois that Calonne was preparing to do anything possible to stop the King from leaving.

The safety of the King could not be trusted just to anyone. It would have to be his guards of the Dark Wind who ushered him from the city. His most trusted man, Bebai, was called the Wolf of Fulani because he was a fierce killer who used the night to stalk his prey.

"Bebai," he called, as he entered his private quarters.

"Yes, Lord DeBois."

"It's time! Call for the Sinti to meet us tomorrow night at the lower gates of the palace. Be prepared." The Wolf of Fulani evaporated from the room; it was almost daylight and time for rest.

Calonne, the gypsy king, had spent the night watching the streets of the Rue Monge and DuBois's visit to the palace hadn't gone unnoticed. Calonne knew it wouldn't be long until Louis tried to flee the city. This would be the time to settle with DeBois and capture the King. He smiled to himself at the thought of giving Louis to the patriots. If there were any doubt about his future this one act would insure his place in the new government. He hurried back because earlier that day he had summoned the Gitano leaders to his fortress beneath the Arwan warehouse.

"Gitanos," he said, holding his hands high asking for their cheers.

"The time has come for us to reclaim our city." They mumbled and shook their heads in agreement.

"I have observed the Sinti planning to move the King to safety. I believe tomorrow night will be the time to get revenge on our enemies for the years of injustice." The mumbles of agreement were louder.

"We must take the King alive! What you do with the Sinti is up to you, but leave DeBois to me." A great roar exploded from the tribe leaders.

"Now go and prepare to meet me on the Rue De Mouffetard tomorrow night." The room emptied and Calonne took refuge in the arms of his women.

The faint cries of the burning city were not the only sounds the men heard as they left the presence of their king. The moan of a starving people made the air hang thick. The outcome of the seemingly inevitable battle had no importance to the common man starving in the alleys of Paris, but to the survival of the gypsy bands it was the only reason for life.

Chapter 2
The Battle of Mouffetard

King Louis's wife, Marie Antoinette, ushered the children into the great hall.

"The hour draws late and Pierre is not to be seen. I trust he hasn't been bribed to deliver you to the rabble that slithers along the rues of the city."

The King was in deep thought at his desk. "All things are possible, but to doubt Pierre's loyalty to me is preposterous. We have had too many dealings to start doubting him now."

"I told you my brother would help us. His army stands at the border as we speak."

"To ask help from the Emperor of Austria would make things worse. He already thinks I have no control over this tyrannous bunch and to have him use this situation to possibly take over my country is too much to risk. We will wait for DeBois."

Marie moved to the balcony. The screams from the city below worried her. Just yesterday she had stood in this same place the day before addressing a group of peasants who had come to petition her for bread. How could things have changed that much in one night? Her thoughts were interrupted by the sound of men coming through the hidden doorway behind a large bookcase. It was Pierre entering and he had four men with him. They seemed to float on air, their legs hidden from sight by the long black capes they wore. Their faces were the only things she could see and even those were covered with strange markings of the gypsy clan.

"It's time, sire. The Third Estate is busy burning the National Assembly Hall," Pierre said as he ushered the King and his family towards the doorway. He paused in front of Marie to give a lustful little smile. "My Lady," he said, letting her pass in front of him. Her movement caused a wave of strong floral perfume to explode into his nostrils.

Coming out onto the Rue De Mouffetard quickly rewarded the group's serpentine flight down the stairs as they met with the rest of Pierre's men.

The street was filled with black figures carrying weapons of all shapes and sizes.

"Let's move," Pierre said to his group.

The King, with his family and protectors, moved along as if they were pushed by a dark wind towards the river. The group moved towards Boulevard St. Germain where they met several patriots blocking the road. Pierre's men swept over them leaving their bodies strewn like rag dolls. The Louvre was in sight for a moment, and then the Rue came alive from all directions with the movement of men filling the street. It was the Gitanos, the clan of Calonne, blocking their escape route.

A deathly stillness came upon the city, as the two groups of mortal enemies faced each other. Pierre caught himself staring into the face of Coureur De Calonne, his face wet with great beads of sweat. Pierre noticed a particularly large droplet clinging to Calonne's nose. Five, six whole seconds it clung to its perch. It was as if time was waiting on this one drop to fall before it restarted. Then, as if it could wait no longer, the drop came free, descending towards the cobblestones of the street. Calonne's wild eyes opened wide as he pulled his blade from its hiding place and led the charge towards DeBois.

The first line of men on both sides fell beneath the blades of the onrushing men behind. Both groups became entangled and some killed their own comrades in the confusion. Calonne pushed towards DeBois and the King's family, but the flashing knives of the Sinti kept him at a distance. The battle was brutal, but the Gitanos were no match for the Dark Wind whose brutal and relentless hacking finally punched a hole through the Gitanos, clearing a path to the Seine River where they descended the stairs to the boats. Calonne could see them on the move and pushed closer, leaving the battle raging on behind him. Waves of mutilated bodies were pushed into the river by the sudden shift in the battle, turning it as red as wine. Calonne stood on the stone bank cursing and barking orders to his men, who in turn moved down the bank to their boats.

"Don't let them get away; hurry, fools, to the boats!"

Movement from St. Germain distracted Calonne for a moment. Some of the patriots who had escaped earlier mustered their fellow comrades and returned to attack the fighting clans. The battle spilled into the national courtyard. No longer was it a battle to capture the King, it was a fight to simply survive. The Sinti, realizing DeBois was safe on the boats, scattered into the night. Seeing Calonne abandon them, the Gitanos fought their way back to the Rue Monge then disappeared themselves into the shanties all along the French quarter. The patriots cheered wildly as the gypsy clans retreated. In their glee, they failed to realize their King was escaping along the river.

Pierre's plan was supposed to be simple, but now he and his men must row for their lives because somewhere in the black waters behind them, Calonne was hunting them. Once again they pushed their boats past the Justice Building and in the burnt courtyard hung the headless corpse of Magistrate Bonnet. He was the only witness to the cruelty of the previous night. The Cathedral Notre Dame loomed in the distance. Pierre marveled that the Third Estate hadn't found fault with the church and decreed the death of all its servants, but he knew these times were not meant to be understood. One by one they passed by the bridges. No time was spent worrying about being seen by those standing on the shore. The gypsies pulled at their oars with a purpose.

Pierre moved the group Southwest towards Meudon and shortly before dawn landed at Barles swamp. Horses and a carriage waited for them there. Swiftly they transferred their cargo into the carriage, and then sprang towards the Château De Versailles.

Pierre had sent word to Lafayette and the Flanders Regiment. All 20,000 of them stood guard as the King arrived at the Palace.

The Chateau had been built for entertainment, not safety. There were no actual walls to defend the buildings, just lavish gardens, banquet halls, dressing rooms and sleeping quarters.

The courtyard was a stream of activity. Several hundred fearful nobles had fled to the Chateau hoping to find safety from the mobs in Paris. Luckily they found the Flanders Guard to protect them.

The crowds, startled at the arrival of the King, began falling to their knees before him.

"Lafayette, my friend, it's good to be back under your protection." The King grasped his hand with a firm grip.

"Sire, I'm at a loss for words and must apologize for not coming to your aid myself in the city," all the while eyeing the gypsy clan as they were surrounding the King. "The Regiment has been on the northern border and has since marched day and night since we heard the revolution had started."

"Not to worry, General. My cousin, Pierre DeBois, has seen to my safety this day, and what a day it has been."

Pierre stepped forward. "Monsignor DeBois," the General said, extending his hand.

"General."

The King was then ushered into his private quarters.

"Pierre, stay. I have matters to discuss with you."

The General excused himself and closed the door behind him.

"My cousin, you have been a great service to this King tonight and I suspect you know that service will be rewarded."

"My King, I expect nothing in return." It was just a formality. They both knew the deeds of Pierre must be rewarded.

"I have to raise an army to defeat this infection that plagues my country and that doesn't come cheap."

DeBois was intrigued.

The King continued, "I have a plan. You, my cousin, will become the Governor of the port of New Orleans. As governor you may use your influence to levy taxes or raise money by any other means you deem necessary. At this point, I have no cares as to how you do it, but this must stay between you and me. There is no time to waste; my war ship the Defiance stands ready to take you and your men as we speak." The King pulled a parchment from his coat.

"This makes it official, Pierre. What say you?" he asked, slapping the seal of wax on the parchment.

By now, word of his helping the King flee the city was being passed down every alley in Paris. There would be nothing for Pierre to go back to.

"I would consider it an honor, sire." Retrieving the parchment from the desk, Pierre said, "I'm sure there will be ways to help raise money for your cause."

"All is not well for you in Paris, my cousin. Word has come that the Gitano has joined forces with the patriots and all that was yours has been taken or destroyed. I've taken the liberty to move the Defiance to the mouth of the river for your convenience."

"I will not disappoint you, my King."

Anxious to be on his way, Pierre spun suddenly around, his black cape unfurling as he turned, and smirking, he darted out into a new world.

Sabotha had foreseen the events that were to come and already had everything important to Pierre moved to the ship.

Pierre was overcome with a feeling of power. Few people came to a defining moment in their lives when their own destiny was within their grasp. This was his time!

The road to the ship was made short by the thoughts of what he could do and for many weeks to come his thoughts were consumed by what he would do.

Chapter 3
The Wolf Band
Legend of the Dog Soldiers

Summer lasted longer than it should have making the Wolf Band think winter wasn't coming at all. Stories circulated around the camp that winter had passed them by, but Sweet Medicine knew that wasn't true. He felt the crisp air and saw the geese flying south on this dark, cloudy day.

Here on the upper Missouri River the Cheyenne had become used to trading with the Mandan and Hidatsu. Once a year the upper tribes on the Great Plains would travel many miles to trade their pelts, blankets, and weapons at the great gathering of the Cheyenne. As the chief looked at the sky with his pale eyes, he knew the time was drawing near and soon all the others would gather.

In his heart, something told him this fall was going to be different. It dug at his soul deep inside. This feeling had plagued him since the day he had seen several men on the Missouri River, strange men. He could not tell their tribe, but they traveled with a Kiowa warrior and even now he did not understand their presence here. No men such as these had ever been seen in the land of the Cheyenne. Stories of strange-tongued hunters had been told to him before, but from his first sighting he was bothered by it.

The Wolf Band was a warrior band of the Cheyenne tribe and on this particular day Sweet Medicine was planning a raid into Lakota Sioux territory. The Lakota had been pushing closer and closer with their hunting parties and he thought it was time to give them a show of force. The warriors in the Wolf Band were known for their fighting abilities, but often they didn't have to fight at all. They just scared their enemies to death. Armed to the teeth with several knifes, hatchets, bows, and feathered lances, the proud and haughty warriors would give chilling war cries and then whip their ponies through the field of battle giving the impression they simply rose from the ground. Impressed with their power, some tribes would choose not to fight at all and simply give up horses or some other offering.

A covey of quail suddenly took flight at the end of the canyon wall and the breaking of the stillness caused several warriors to look in that direction. Sweet Medicine ordered them to gather their weapons and horses and then ride to the base of the bluff.

Running their ponies up and down the canyon floor, they gave out their war cries. A white puff of smoke appeared in the distance knocking Little Hawk from his horse next to Sweet Medicine. They could see the bleeding wound in his side and for the first time in their lives they were afraid of this new magic.

Frozen, they looked at their dying friend and then to the bluff where the smoke had appeared only to see several other clouds of smoke curl up from the sagebrush. Tall One, Plenty Hair, and Dull Hatchet were thrown from their horses to the ground. Sweet Medicine seeing this jumped from his horse.

"Take shelter from this magic." His men in return jumped to the ground and gathered behind the trees and rocks.

"Great Ones, tell me what to do. Let me lead in honor to save my people," he prayed, all the while little puffs of smoke pelted at them. Some of the shots reached the tee pees behind him injuring some women and children.

"Give me your help. Give me the magic of the Great Spirit."

The spirit heard his cry and the clouds broke behind him sending blinding rays of sunlight straight at the bluff.

Dividing his men, he sent Talks Too Much to take the women and children to safety while the others gathered close to him for battle.

"Grab your ropes and picket pins," he called, tying his rope to his leg then driving the pin into the ground. "The spirit is with us and we stand together until no one stands at all."

They all got their ropes and picket pins, tying themselves and driving the pins into the ground. Fifty Cheyenne met the charge of over 200 Kiowa and the strange tongued warriors. Hatchet and blade in each hand flashing death with every wave of their hand, they battled on mortally wounded. They fought lying on the ground. Sweet Medicine threw his hatchet which struck the head of a Kiowa, then glanced into the chest of a white man. He replaced the hatchet with his other knives, wielding them right then left until the blades were broken. He retrieved his war club and fought on. Standing in the gaps between his men, he could see the spirit warriors fighting toe to toe with the invaders.

"Hu-na-na Hu-na- na -to- ki," he sang. Sixty, eighty and then a hundred invaders fell to the Wolf band.

Then a shot through his breastplate stopped the singing. Sweet Medicine fell to the ground. Even as he lay dying, the Kiowa began their retreat up the hill and out of sight. The spirits rose above the dead Cheyenne warriors like tiny figures seen in the distance, and then bigger and bigger they grew until they covered the sky, dancing the dead Cheyenne into the spirit world.

Sweet Medicine's body, along with his weapons, was laid in a cave at the edge of the river. The ashes of his men were placed in an elk hide pouch and the story of Sweet Medicine uniting with the spirits to save the Wolf Band was told over and over around many Cheyenne campfires.

A great legend grew among the Cheyenne about the braves who stood their ground that day and fought like dogs. The legend of the dog soldiers was born.

"That was a good story, Father," Manez said as he stirred the sparks in the flames.

"I should hope to tell that story as good as you around the fire someday."

The old Cheyenne Chief smiled. He was pleased the boy had liked the story about Sweet Medicine. Onotsa was the Chief of the Hotamimasaw or Crazy Dogs. They lived in the northern territory of the Cheyenne Nation.

Manez wasn't really the Chief's son. Onotsa had found him in a burned out village close to the Missouri River in the south just after the Lakota Sioux wars, but he treated him as his real son. No distinction was ever made between Kanan the chief's real son and Manez; they were raised as real brothers.

Even though they were raised as brothers from the beginning, the tribe could tell something was different about the new little boy. He often dressed warm before the weather changed; made ready to catch raindrops before a cloud appeared in the sky. He could sense when the hunting would be good or danger was near, but most of all, it was his physical powers that amazed the tribe. They had never seen a 10-year-old run down a jackrabbit nor had they ever seen a boy that young pull a bow to kill his first deer. In games of hide and hunt, he was never found, even when hiding right in front of the others. His abilities elevated his worth in the eyes of the elders, but made the other young boys jealous. Even so, Kanan stayed true to his brother taking great pride in his abilities.

It was fun being a young brave of the Hotamimasaw. Every day was filled with hunting and make believe adventures against the warring parties of the Sioux.

"Why are we still here, brother?" Kanan said. He was tired of being quiet, waiting for some game to cross the path.

"Just a moment more," Manez said.

"A moment more! For what? The sun is too high. No deer will pass this way till dark. See, nothing!" Standing, he gazed through the forest.

Manez let the arrow fly past the leg of the standing boy before the buck stepped between the trees. The arrow caught the mighty beast in the chest just above his heart killing him instantly.

"You must show patience, brother," he said, tripping the boy with his bow, then dashing towards the kill. "Last one there has to skin him."

The boys took off running, but halfway there Manez tackled Kanan and they tumbled into a clump of ferns. As they fell, Manez grabbed Kanan's mouth. "Shh," he gestured. As still as they could, they lay in the shadowy underbrush. Kanan trusted his brother's ability to know that something was coming. A slight rustling of leaves and a few small twigs snapping close by announced the arrival of what Manez had sensed.

"Back! Arikara," he whispered. The two boys eased back close to the fern above them. Manez easily recognized them by the three large red tail hawk feathers fanned out at the back of their heads.

"Arikara?" Kanan asked and Manez shook his head. Four warriors appeared from the underbrush in full view of the two boys.

The warriors paused, listening, smelling the breeze. Then as quickly as they appeared, they disappeared into the green underbrush.

Frozen stiff the boys lay perfectly still until the birds began to sing again.

"A scouting party all the way down here? I wonder what the Arikara are up to?" Kanan asked.

"Let's follow and find out." Manez was full of adventure and the fact it could be dangerous never crossed his mind.

"If they catch us, we will be killed," Kanan said softly.

"Trust me, brother, they won't know we are even here." Manez moved into the brush.

"Trusting you is like trusting trouble. You can't touch it, but it bites you." He complained a lot, but he followed his brother.

Hours passed as the boys followed the signs just close enough to not be discovered. The Arikaras moved south until they hit the breaks near the Platte River, then they turned west until dusk. They must have killed some game along the way because by the time the boys got close to them again, they had built a small fire in a stone cut along the bank. You could barely see the fire concealed by the rocks; only small puffs of smoke told you they were there.

The sunset faded quickly turning the strange shadows around them into black shapes. A large cluster of slow moving clouds blocked the moon. When the moon was at its darkest point, Manez stiffened with fear.

He grabbed Kanan's arm pushing him towards a large cottonwood tree.

"Climb for your life." Kanan didn't hesitate because when Manez was afraid he was sure to be in danger. Manez scrambled up the tree behind him.

"Higher, much higher," he said.

The two climbed as high as they could until the limbs began to bend with their weight. At this height they could see the shapes of the warriors sitting close to the fire below and then something directly below them moved. It wasn't quick or noisy, but sneaky. Slow, like a cat on the prowl. It paused, as if it was looking up at the boys trying to decide if they were worth pursuing. Then it moved forward towards the unsuspecting braves.

With a rush of breaking limbs, it sprang on the Arikara tossing one then another into the air; crushing and clawing at them until there were no more screams. The monster then turned its fury towards the fire knocking hot chunks of wood in all directions. Hot coals from the wood started other small fires and each one met the same fury as the Arikara until it was completely dark.

With each passing cloud, a spray of light from the moon teased the boy's eyes as to what had happened below them. These bits of light fueled their imagination and kept them hugging tight to the tree until the morning sun came up.

Manez was the first to stir. Holding his hand to his lips as if to say, "Shh," he started slowly down, pausing on every limb to check for sounds or a sign of the monster until he reached the ground. Kanan was then quick to follow him.

A short walk away lay the four broken bodies of the Arikara.

"It didn't eat them," Manez said. "It wasn't for food; the way he clawed at them, he was mad."

"Mad at what?" Kanan asked.

Bending down looking at the pieces of firewood Manez said, "Mad at the fire. The fire, it made him crazy." He saw something in the dirt and flicked at it with his knife. "A bear claw."

"This is bad medicine," Kanan said, as he took his pouch from his neck and began to chant. Manez placed the bear claw in his bag, then moved the bodies onto some fallen limbs protruding from the riverbank. He waved his hand above the bodies of the dead Indians.

"May the old woman find favor with you when you try to cross the lake. That will have to do, we must go."

After what they had seen, the frightened young boys ran all day in the direction of home and when night came they slept in a tree. They would never feel safe in the dark again.

Chapter 4

The Defiance

It wasn't easy for Pierre to slip back into the city past the watchful eyes of the patriots, but he had to make sure everything he needed would be taken to the Defiance, now anchored at the mouth of the Seine River.

His usual lookouts were not where they should have been, and the further they traveled down Boulevard St. Germain to Rue Monge the streets became very busy with combatants dashing here and there. The gypsies were attacked almost at every turn by bands of marauding gangs of patriots and on each occasion the Dark Wind cut through the enemy like they were little children at play. Just before St. Germain ended, the group slipped through a wooden gate between the tall buildings facing the Rue Monge and made their way out onto the street. His Sinti had barricaded both ends of the great street and the battle of the previous day with the Gitanos was still raging.

At the sight of Pierre, a great shout rose from the men manning the wall of carts that blocked the street and they pushed forward driving the Gitanos back into hiding.

"Jacque, how long have we been fighting?"

"Since you left us at Moffetard, sir. Street by street they grew in ranks as the patriots joined them."

"How long can we hold them?" DeBois asked.

"Two hours and they will overrun us."

"Use the alleyway to start moving the wounded and the women and children to the river. I have boats waiting there. Be sure and take Sabotha."

"Yes sir."

Pierre walked to the center of the street and turned in a slow circle making certain the enemy saw him.

"We will hold until our families escape, then we will charge the St. Germain entrance together cutting a path to the boats. My weapons, Bebai."

The black capes moved and a large musclebound slave must have read his mind because he appeared with DeBois's pistols and his sparat. All the Sinti appeared with their sparats. Some were shaped out of horns with spike points; others were made of metal and had knife blades imbedded in the handles. Pierre's sparat was about four feet long and had two hatchet blades attached under a spear point. The weapon was unique to the Sinti clan. Bebai had introduced it to them soon after Pierre had bought him at the slave sale. The weapon had come from his country, Fulani; somewhere on the west coast of Africa. No matter where it had come from, it had changed many a battle in the hands of the Sinti. The African slave was some sort of king in Africa, whose people rose up against him, then sold him into slavery. He was a scary looking man with scrolling tattoos around his eyes, nose and lips.

It took a long time for the wounded to slip down the alley and make their escape, but they slowly moved secretly street by street to safety.

Coureur Calonne appeared at the barricade on the west end and began to mock DeBois by calling him names.

"It is time we end this," DeBois said. "Once and for all we will leave the indentions of our weapons on them." Then with a great shout the Sinti rolled open the barricaded wagons and charged the Gitanos and the patriots. The attack was so fierce and brutal the cowardly patriots immediately turned and fled, confusing the Gitano Clan.

There were so many men running towards them, the Gitanos began killing their own men. The sudden shift towards them made it impossible to stop the advance of the Sinti. Not knowing friend from foe, Calonne, wielding his sword, cut down anyone close to him until Pierre appeared in front of him. His wild eyes finally recognized a real enemy, but before he could raise his weapon Pierre was driving the edge of his sparat into his skull.

All grew still and quiet as DeBois stood over the dying, self proclaimed Gypsy King. It was a disturbing calm that made their ears ring.

Then as quickly as the battle had stopped, it started again. With a great heaving, the Sinti pushed forward into St. Germain leaving piles of broken bodies behind them. Pierre and his companions moved hurriedly along the empty streets, their black capes flowing along behind them making it look as if the wind had a color. Families hiding along the way knew the Dark Wind was passing; they passed unchallenged towards the Defiance.

The fog of night had settled in by the time the last of the clan arrived at the docks, but despite the fog, DeBois could see the galleon floating proudly in the fading light. The Defiance was a four masted warship built along Spanish galleon designs. She was 150 feet long with a hundred foot keel; a beam of thirty seven-feet. Defiance weighed five hundred tons and carried thirty- eight guns; twenty- two culverins and sixteen demi-culverins. Her crew numbered 320 sailors and there was room for all of them on this occasion. Having more than one deck allowed the ship to have guns mounted on several decks giving them much more firepower.

DeBois stepped up the gangplank. He was looking forward to meeting Captain Trouin. At a young age, Duquay Trouin had impressed the King with his privateering. His reputation and captured treasures made him a well-known French hero.

"Captain Trouin," Pierre said as he extended his hand.

"Pierre DeBois. At your service, sir."

Captain Trouin took his hand. "From the looks of you and your men, you've had a considerable fight just to get here," he said as he looked at the bloody sparat in DeBois's hand.

Pierre tossed the weapon to one of his men. "Yes, I fear the city will never be a place I can call home." He looked almost sad for a moment. "But, about the King's business, yes?"

Captain Trouin said, "The King's business." Turning to the first officer, "Put her out to sea, Mr. Fuquay."

"All men on deck; loosen all lines. Shove her hard, men! Drop the main sails." All kinds of orders came spewing from the officer's lips and the ship became a sea of moving figures. It seemed to Pierre he had stirred an ant's nest to have this much activity around him. It didn't take the experienced crew of the Defiance long to break away from the protection of the sea wall into the open sea. DeBois looked back at the lights of the city until the pitch of the sea prevented it, then he took shelter below decks.

A typical galleon had a number of decks: forecastle, upper or weather deck, main deck, lower deck, poop deck, and quarter deck. The crew's quarters were in the bow, while the officers and passengers lived in cramped cabins in the center section of the ship. Provisions were stowed near the galley.

The captain lived in the great cabin in the rear; earmarked by large windows, greater space, and more comfort. Pierre was guided to a moderate sized cabin. The pitching of the ship might have sickened him, but the hour was late and exhausted from the day's battle, sleep quickly overtook him.

The gentle rolls of the big ship cutting through towering waves and the sounds of the sea awoke him early. A ding of a bell, an occasional yell, and the constant crashing of waves on the hull gave a welcome distance to the events of the day before.

Pierre made his way to the top deck. It was a bright, sunny day and the wind was quite blustery. He noticed several large birds weaving in and out of the rigging tied to the main sail.

He was taken by surprise. Another ship was in full sail close by.

"The Ark Royal," Pierre read aloud.

Trouin noticed DeBois staring out at the battle ship and said, "It's the Ark Royal. An English built ship flying under French colors. Her Captain is Jean Bart."

"Is this the same Jean Bart who escaped the English and fought his way across the English Channel in a row boat?" Pierre exclaimed.

"Yes, that's him."

"How in the world did he come to possess an English battle ship?"

"She was anchored in a cove near St. Thomas. Most of the crew was on shore trying to scavenge for food and supplies. He simply sailed in behind her, cannons blazing, tossed the Captain and remaining crew overboard, then sailed her away."

Trouin's thoughts were lost. A cry came from the crow's roost.

"Sail, ho! Straight out on the horizon, Captain."

"What is she, Mr. Fuquay?" he asked.

"Looks to be Spanish, sir, and she's riding low in the water."

"Call all hands to quarters; prepare the forward guns."

The crew scrambled in all directions very excited. The captain, turning to Pierre, called out,"It's a treasure boat and if we take her, all hands take in a share in the bounty."

A hundred yards away the Ark Royal struck her colors acknowledging the treasure boat being sighted.

The two ships closed in fast on the fleeing Spanish galleon. So fast, that after Trouin fired a shot over her bow, she realized escape was impossible, dropped her sail, then made ready to be boarded. With the Ark Royal perched on one side and the Defiance on the other, the crew of the badly damaged Spanish galleon had no fight left in them.

The Captain of the captured ship stood at her helm, hat in hand, ready to surrender when the two pirates came aboard.

"Don Louie Fernando Vaques, senors," he said, bowing to the two men.

"I willingly surrender the San Felipe and hope you will remember this gesture when you deal with my men and officers," he continued. "If you have a doctor on board one of your ships, I have men in need of help. A great storm overtook the fleet we were sailing with. Eleven ships and the only doctor were lost."

Jean Bart turned to his first mate. "See to it, man." The man hurried away as he continued, "We will willingly deal fairly with you and your men if you continue to tell us the truth about your cargo and destination."

Captain Trouin shook his head in agreement. "What's your cargo?"

Don Louie took the manifest from his clerk. "Fruits, sugar, silks, ivory, two hundred pounds of jewels and precious stones, eighty pounds of gold and twenty-six tons of uncoined silver." The two pirates almost shouted out, but the men closest to them did all the cheering. The Spanish Captain continued, "Then, there's the twenty-five African slaves."

"Slaves!" Trouin said. "Since when do the Spanish deal in slavery?"

"We don't usually, but we took them on in Rio de Janeiro to load the silver aboard in Santo Domingo and had planned to use them to unload it again in port."

Bebai had been prowling around the cargo hold and through the deck grating he could see the black men. They could see him too as they began to chant "Mani Bebai Fulani, Bebai Fulani."

The disturbance from below brought the attention of the two Captains.

Trouin turned to Debois and asked, "Your man there. What's he up to?"

Pierre asked Bebai, "What is that they are saying to you?"

"They are calling me King of Fulani." Bebai broke open the lock holding the prisoners inside and they spilled out onto the deck groveling at the feet of Bebai. The stature of the man suddenly appeared tall, strong, and kingly before his unlikely subjects. He helped one of the slaves to his feet and turned to the group of Frenchmen watching him. The same spiraling tattoos that Bebai had flowed all around the eyes of the slave.

"I am Mani Bebai, King of the Fulani, sold into slavery and these are those that were sold into slavery with me." He paused and dipped his head, as a king would do.

DeBois almost fell over. He had never noticed how elegant the stature of the man he called Bebai was until that moment. He really was a king. He looked out towards the deck of the Defiance. In all the excitement of the day before, he had neglected to make sure Sabotha had been taken care of; but as he gazed at the ship, he saw her standing in the doorway. Debois's eyes met with hers. He could tell she had foreseen this and approved of it; then as quickly as she appeared, she slipped back into the safety of the silhouetted decks below.

"It seems we have a King on board," Jean Bart said.

Pierre turned to Jean Bart and Trouin. "I know I have no say in the spoils taken at sea, but these men," motioning to the slaves on deck, "these men of Fulani. What say you to turning them over to me?"

"With a treasure of jewels and silver, I don't care what is done with these men. He can take them, for all I care," Trouin said looking at Jean Bart.

Jean Bart said, "Fine, take them."

Pierre motioned to Bebai and after a quick discussion, the slave King took his men to the Defiance.

Several hours were spent with Trouin and Jean Bart discussing the fate of the captured ship and her crew. It was finally decided to take her back to St. Malo, or as the English called it The Wasp's nest, a pirate's haven, and sell her cargo to the highest bidder. The Captain and crew's lives were to be spared as long as they helped sail the ship to port, then their fate would be decided based on their conduct during the voyage.

The crews of the three ships banded together and over the course of the next two days made all the necessary repairs to the San Felipe. A few men from each ship boarded the San Felipe along with Mr. Fuquay.

"Mr. Fuquay, don't fly your colors until you know who you're dealing with. Speed to you, man," Jean Bart said.

"Here are your commission papers, Captain Fuquay." Trouin saluted the man.

"Yes sir," Fuquay replied.

"Cut away all lines, make ready all sails, prepare to come about." They slipped forward one hundred yards, turned into the wind, and quickly all three ships were at full sail.

St. Malo was three days away and the appearances of Sabotha with the tattooed slaves, now and then on deck, had the crew spooked. Rumors of being damned and sailing off the edge of the earth ran rampant among them.

Pierre was unhappy about not being able to share in the great wealth the ships had captured and his thoughts turned to where the gold and silver had come from. While talking to Bebai, he had learned the silver and gold was being shipped steadily from Santo Domingo in the Dominican Republic. The slaves said great quantities were being hoarded there, waiting transportation to Spain. DeBois conceived a plan and one night at Captain Trouin's table he decided to put it into action.

"What's the largest treasure you have ever taken, Captain Trouin?"

"Ah, this one, I believe. This one will make me rich," he replied.

"What would you say if I could give you a treasure five, maybe six times greater than this one?"

"Six times greater? I didn't know the King's relatives had money enough to give away."

"I don't have anything to give away, but the Governor of Santo Domingo does."

"Oh, I see. Now that we have three ships, you want to blast your way into a heavily fortified harbor, battle troops street by street to the treasure and then take it," Trouin said.

"We don't have to take the harbor; we just have to take the Governor,"

DeBois said, chuckling. "If the Governor were to be invited on board a Spanish galleon by visiting a sick dignitary, then set upon by pirates, he might give you the city after he peed his pants."

Trouin's chuckle turned to laughter. Pierre joined in.

"DeBois, I like the way your mind works. That is a good plan."

"Of course, I would only want a third of the profit."

The two men tipped their glasses in a toast to their coming venture. DeBois' mind was already working on the exact plan of how he could keep even the King's share.

The stop in St. Malo was a nuisance to Pierre. He had bigger fish to fry and he was irritated at the time the two Captains spent in port. The stop was profitable to Jean Bart and Trouin. They sold all the goods on board and sent Louie his share. The men restocked all three ships for their next voyage and after a few days of revelry, they finally set out.

Like sharks hunting for another bloody feast, the San Felipe, the Ark Royal and the Defiance turned their attention to Santo Domingo.

Chapter 5

Four Claws

Fall was fading fast and it was just a matter of time until the land would be lost in the white of winter. Fall was a soft, quiet time for Manez; he loved the change of colors and the crisp air in the mornings. Much was to be done. Kanan and Manez spent most of their time hunting and putting up furs for the spring tribal trade. Once a year the Mandans, Hidatsa, and Arapaho met the Cheyenne on the banks of the upper Missouri to trade goods. The great pow-wow was a high point in Cheyenne life. To most, it meant a celebration of new life, a new birth of Mother Earth. To Kanan and Manez it meant the ceremony of the Dog Warrior would be soon. Since they had returned from their deer hunt and told the story about the beast that destroyed the Arikara warriors, their induction into the society was a much-discussed topic around the fires at night. The boys knew this would be the year they would be asked to participate in the ceremony.

Manez had poked a hole in the big, black claw he had found lying next to the dead Arikara warriors. He put a rawhide strip through it and wore it around his neck. Time and time again, he was asked to tell the story and the legend of "Four Claws" was born.

It was around such a fire one night as Manez told the story that Onotsa spoke.

"A good story, my son. You said once you wished you could tell a story as good as mine, but yours is a better story about this Four Claws. You must be cautious; the claw you have taken from the beast and hung around your neck connects you to his spirit." He turned his head slightly, as if he was trying to feel the air. "I can't tell if the connection is a good thing or a bad one. I just cannot be sure of these things, but I know your paths will cross again. Respect the beast, but don't fear him." All around the fire they shook their heads and passed the pipe.

"There is another matter, my son," he said, staring off into the air and then beginning again. "I found you, took you in to live as my son, but things must be told to you that you will be wanting to know soon."

The bobbing of heads began again. Manez just sat quietly. He knew the Chief didn't want him to answer.

"I never found any of your people, not one human being. It was as if they and all their possessions had been devoured." He paused until all the agreeing grunts had stopped.

"I searched in the river thickets, the tall pines, and among the cottonwoods, but your people were not to be found. That was quite disturbing because I take pride in reading the signs and my ability to track." The old braves shook their heads in agreement once again.

"I wondered on this thing a long time, and then I wondered on it a little more." Rubbing his chin, he said, "What could be the truth in this matter, when it came to me, is that the spirits sent you to us." The pipe was passed to Manez; he took it, then passed it on.

"We have seen you run down the deer and the antelope. We have also seen you sneak up on the bobcat. You seem to appear and disappear at your will. These things are not natural. I have long known this, but have chosen this time to tell you because I feel a strange wind blowing in the south and soon this wind will turn into a dark wind for our people." Onotsa was known for his prophesies among the tribe. They all stared into the fire. "You may be the one to bring us out from this darkness." He stared into Manez's eyes and the boy could tell he had seen something that had stirred a great fear for his people.

"Think on these things, my son; we will speak of them again another time."

He took his turn at the pipe and nothing more was said. The fire burned low and one by one the elders left the lodge. Manez himself retired to his teepee. After all that was said, he felt he needed to be alone for a time.

It wasn't unusual for Manez to go out hunting for long periods of time and after the events of the night before, he arose early, took his weapons, and set off into the woods on horseback.

The leaves that covered the ground were damp, making it easy to move silently along without telling the forest he was passing.

He felt like taking a long ride and the Piney Creek trail north of camp offered a good opportunity to hunt big game. The trail wandered back and forth across the creek for two miles, then the stream dropped over a ledge making it impossible to follow, so Manez turned to the west. Deeper canyons and rocky cliffs slowed the travel. He wished he hadn't brought a horse. It would be easier traveling without it.

The wind picked up. He knew a storm was blowing in, so he made for a place called Round Springs. There was a cave cut deep into the stone behind the springs that would provide shelter for the night.

He had time to gather wood and build a small fire before the storm broke. Thunder boomed and lightning pitchforked across the sky and with the noise he soon became indifferent to the sounds around him. He opened a small pouch, produced some jerky and began to consider the things Onotsa had said at the lodge. The steady rhythm of the rain soon caused sleep to overtake him. Small puffs of smoke spilled out of the entrance of the cave and he dreamed. He dreamed of great battles against darkness and the Great Spirit standing with him in battle.

Crack. The sound of a branch breaking started him from sleep. Something fell close to the cave entrance. The horse broke from the back of the cave and almost trampled him as it fled into the rainy night.

Crack. "Grrrrrr."

He froze for an instant; he sensed something standing in the dark staring into the cave. He quickly put dirt on the fire and made his way up a steep wall about twenty feet where a small ledge protruded from the cavern.

Manez knew he was far from safe balanced there, but it was the only place to go. With his bow pointing downward, his every muscle was ready for battle and he waited for whatever stood in the opening.

"Aarrh-grr." The large shape charged into the cave and with one sweep of its paw tossed the smoking twigs into the rocks.

A great growl came from the depths of the animal. The empty cave surprised the bear and he stood on his hind legs sniffing the air. Then with a sudden charge he leaped at the ledge throwing Manez back against the wall. Rocks crashed down as the bear repeatedly jumped at the ledge above.

He wandered back and forth beneath Manez and as the boy's eyes adjusted to the dark, he could see his attacker clearly. It was a grizzly bear. At least, it seemed to be, but it shouldn't be here. The big bears usually stay at higher altitudes. The animal had all the fur burnt off its right side and lower leg. One of its ears was severely burned, along with part of its face. This was the same bear, Four Claws.

From the looks of the beast, Manez could understand why it attacked. It was the fire that drew him and the men who controlled the fire. The animal finally settled down somewhere in the dark blocking any possible hope of escape. Manez tried to stay alert, but occasionally he dosed off only to jerk his eyes open and look down for the bear below him. Time and time again his eyes closed until it was impossible to stay awake and he fell asleep.

Near first light, Manez turned in his sleep and rolled off the ledge. He came fully awake as he fell, hitting the ground hard. Hearing the bear moving in the back of the cave, Manez came up from the floor running; his legs drove wildly into the dirt causing him to almost explode from the entrance of the hole. All seemed quiet for an instant as he looked back over his shoulder. Maybe he was safe. He almost stopped, but at that moment the bear broke into the morning light at full speed. Manez was fast, faster than any of the braves in the Crazy Dogs camp, but he had never raced a bear and it was soon evident he wasn't faster than the 1200 pound animal.

Darting back and forth along the creek he ran with the animal nipping at his heels until it seemed it was useless to run anymore. Would this be his end, his final battle? Perhaps his father's dream was a mistake and the spirits wished him to die at the grip of the giant bear. He thought about giving back the bear's claw.

The trail he was following ended. It happened so fast there was no time to even stop running, so he went right off the ridge and plunged into the creek below. The bear stood at the top of the cliff and stomped the ground with his giant paws. Manez pushed himself to the muddy shore of the stream and came out running again. Now was the time to put some space between the bear and himself. It would be several minutes before the bear found his way down the cliffs and Manez wanted to be far away by then.

He ran westward. He had hoped to circle back towards home eventually, but even that wasn't going to happen. The walls of the canyon he had been following grew too steep and rocky. Trying to climb them would slow him down too much, so he kept pushing himself along further and further west into Crow territory. He wasn't sure which would be worse, fighting the bear or fighting the Crow. He had to find a way to turn back east.

The canyon suddenly split allowing him to turn and the rock walls flattened enough for him to get off the trail and head east.

He realized the sun was setting and that he had been moving west most of the day away from home. If the bear was still after him, he would need a safe place to stop.

"No fire," he said to himself. "The bear will have to find me without my help."

He chose a large oak tree with small lower branches that a big bear couldn't climb, swung himself up to a fork in the great tree and watched the sun set. The evening stars filled a clear sky. He was safe for the time being and he slept.

Chapter 6
Ramone Rodriques

The plan was simple as far as Jean Bart and Captain Trouin were concerned. They were to anchor up the coast a little ways and allow the San Felipe time to sail into the harbor. Then, after the Governor was on board, they were to sail into the harbor and load their share of the gold.

They wouldn't be pirates if they weren't a little suspicious of DeBois, but Captain Fuquay would be on board to watch over him and that seemed to satisfy their concerns about the plan.

The weather held and it was a glorious morning as the San Felipe, with its banners flying in the wind, glided into the harbor.

Word was sent to Governor Ramone Rodrigues that Don Fernando de Latorres, the King's nephew, was on board. He was seasick and he had an urgent message from the king to be hand delivered.

Governor Ramone Rodrigues made his way to the dock and at the sight of the French soldiers disguised in their stolen Spanish uniforms, dismissed all but two of his guards. They boarded the small boat and soon found their way to the deck of the San Felipe where Pierre and Fuquay stood waiting.

"Excuse me, senors. Please escort me to Don Fernando."

"Don Fernando? Oh yes," Fuquay said.

Pierre stepped forward. "Governor Rodrigues, I'm afraid I have deceived you."

Bebai stepped in behind the guards escorting the Governor and disarmed them.

"What is this; what is going on?" Rodrigues said as he scuffled with the men grabbing him.

"You are being held hostage by French pirates and it would be wise to cooperate or else."

At that moment, the French flag was raised setting off alarms ashore and sending soldiers scurrying in all directions. Cannons on fortified walls were rolled forward. Grabbing one of the Spanish guards, Pierre handed him a ransom letter.

"Take that to your captain in charge. You have four hours until we hang the Governor from the main mast."

The two guards made their way back to shore.

Pierre noticed the weak little man nervously rubbing his neck.

"Isn't this exciting? Does the captain do what we say, or does he blow us out of the water with you on board. Do we take your gold and hang you anyway? The next two hours will tell."

The Governor screamed over the rail of the ship, "Hurry, men!"

"Secure him!" The Governor was placed below decks.

An hour went by and every man on the ship stood ready for battle until wagons started appearing on shore.

"Prepare to load cargo, men." Captain Fuquay looked relieved.

A cheer went up from the crew as they scrambled to work and another four hours passed. The gold was stacked ingot by ingot below decks until no more could be taken.

The Spanish captain of the guard knew the ship was almost loaded and had come out in a small boat to get the Governor back.

"Senors, you have loaded until you can't take any more. Give the Governor back and we let you sail."

"On this day, we decide the rules, Captain. You will not get the Governor back until our ship clears the harbor out of range of your guns. Then we will put him in a boat and you can get him."

"How do I know I can trust the word of a pirate? What's to keep you from keeping him?"

"We will put him in a boat trailing behind us and as soon as we drop full sail, we will cut it loose."

The captain could see it would do no good to bargain with the pirates.

Under his breath he cursed, then he pushed away from the ship.

"Let's take her out," Captain Fuquay said. "All hands on deck; make sail, and turn her into the wind."

Pierre was pleased the loading had gone so fast." Well, Captain, we should be far away from here long before Jean Bart and Trouin realize they have been fooled by us."

"I don't want to be caught in this harbor. Move men, move along fast!" he yelled at the top of his lungs.

The huge ship began to move at the winds command and as it cleared the breakwater, a huge gust of air filled the sails; the ship moved forward out to sea. Suddenly a great stream of profanity came from behind the ship.

No one had cut the Governor loose and the sea was tossing the small lifeboat almost upside down.

Pierre grabbed his axe and chopped the rope." So long my Spanish friend."

The crew laughed as Captain Fuquay slung a paddle in the direction of the little boat.

Two cannons on the fortified wall rang out, but the metal balls fell harmlessly short of the fleeing ship.

"Head her for the Gulf, man," Fuquay yelled at the helm. Then turning to Pierre, said, "Keep a sharp eye out. This works or it could get bad, real bad."

"Battle stations men, run out the guns."

The men jumped in every direction. Ropes, pulleys, and fear convulsed as if one organism was engulfing the ship.

"Battle stations and keep an eye out," was repeated all along the deck until it ended in dead silence.

In the fading light great clouds of fog began to close in on the ship. All aboard knew this might be the only way they would escape the sharp eye of Captain Trouin.

Not far away, in the small bay, Jean Bart heard the blast of the two 20-pound cannons and quickly made ready to sail.

"Signal Trouin to make for the harbor," he commanded.

"Aye, aye, sir; getting under way."

From the bridge, Trouin could see the Ark Royal breaking open their sails and heading into the breeze. He could also see the white fog blocking their path.

"Bring us in slow; keep us away from the Ark Royal. We don't want to ram her in the fog."

The two ships slipped out into open water, then headed in the direction of the city.

Nothing could be seen because the fog had settled in as thick as molasses and all was quiet except the sound of the boat being battered by the constant swells crashing on the bow.

Fuquay had chosen his course well; the San Felipe quietly slipped between the two ships coming into the harbor.

They were almost clear of the two pirate ships when a small space opened in the fog allowing you to see a portion of the upper mast but as quickly as the sun appeared the hole closed.

Trouin had been watching the blurred fog dead ahead of the ship roll past, but the sun made him look out at the tiny hole in the fog and he had caught a glimpse of the upper mast.

"What see ye, sailors?" he called to the watch. "Did ye see the sail yonder?"

"Yo, Captain," was the cry back.

"Where's the Ark man; was that sail the Royal?"

"She shouldn't be that close, sir."

Trouin suddenly realized the San Felipe was slipping out to sea between them.

"Turn her starboard hard, Mr. Freeman. Come about." The ship dug into the water and started to swing around, but at that exact moment, the Defiance broke out of the fog directly in the sights of the cannons on the city walls.

Trouin was shocked that they had broken into the clear, but not as shocked as Governor Ramone Rodriguez when the ship appeared directly behind his tiny row boat.

"Pinche cabrones putos," Ramone screamed with all the might his lungs could force.

He swung one of the paddles in a mute effort at the battle ship cutting across his tiny boat. The paddle just bounced off the war ship. The ship had barely missed him as he stood in the tiny boat spewing more profanities at them.

"Besi ma cula pindayhos."

He continued to curse the ship as it quickly pivoted away from him and headed back into the fog.

A shot from the walls of the city fell within a few feet of the Governor's boat.

"Idiots, not me! There is the target!" he cried, pointing at the escaping ship.

Another shot fell even closer to the tiny boat.

"Are you stupid? How could you miss a large thing like that?" He held the other oar up trying to signal his position, but just as he

48

held it as high as he could another shot from the wall split it in two tossing him into the bottom of the boat.

He stood and shook his fist at the cannons on the wall.

"You will pay, you will......" He was cut short by the sound of the Ark Royal bearing down on him from behind.

Jean Bart had turned the Royal causing the galleon to cut almost the same path the Defiance did towards the safety of the fog.

Once again, Ramone screamed in terror at the ship bearing down on him.

He dove into the bottom of the boat then hid his eyes as the great ship knocked the rowboat a few feet away.

The Ark Royal had manned their guns and as she swung into range, she let loose a twenty two-gun blast that was deafening to Ramone.

Chunks of the fortified walls crumbled as the crew rushed to reload the guns.

A large wave almost swamped the rowboat as the Governor stood to poke his fingers into his ringing ears. The gunners on the wall had found the ship's range and sent a volley of cannon balls at the fleeing ship. One struck the topsail snapping it just below the cross mast and it crashed to the deck.

Governor Ramone cheered at the sight.

"Bravo, muchachos, bravo!"

No sooner than he had spoken, one last blast at the French ship erupted from the top of the wall.

"Ondelay, go." He could see it was going to be a close call.

" Ah, no, no." A huge chunk of steel fell through the bottom of his tiny boat.

"Short. How could you be short?" he yelled towards the walls. "Short!"

Then in disgust, he spat, " Cabrones."

Still standing, he slowly sank into the bay.

On board the San Felipe, Pierre listened intently to every cannon shot. He hoped the cannons on the walls could hit their targets well enough to cause some damage to the two warships and slow them down.

"Fuguay. That last round hit something; keep her slow and easy along the coast."

"Man the bow, get a man on the sounding line, call her out; we don't want to run her aground," the captain barked at the crew.

"Crows roosts, keep a good lookout. Call out anything you think you see, anything."

"Aye, aye, sir."

The ship slowly eased along the rocky coastline until the fog began to break up.

"The fog is a lifting, sir," was the cry from the crow's roost.

"As soon as you can, make full sail men," cried Fuquay.

The crew scattered like ants in a great battle and soon the great ship plowed through the sea at full speed with its heavy cargo.

Far away, the crew of the Ark Royal worked frantically trying to clear the deck of debris caused by the final cannon shots. It was evident to Jean Bart the only hope they had of eluding any possible Spanish ship that might pursue them was to turn into the thickest fog and head out to open water. He knew he couldn't stay up with the Defiance and pursue the San Felipe. The game was to stay alive and fight another day. Several small inlets were close at hand and so the ship slipped into the fog.

Trouin, on the other hand, knew if he guessed correctly at the game the traitor Fuquay would play, they could catch the San Felipe and make them pay for their deception. The fog was still present, but there were large open spaces between the patches of clouds making it easier to sail, but still dangerous. The hours passed and several times the lookout thought he could see the galleon straight away, but each time he was set to cry out, the fog buried his view.

Pierre was leaning on the side rail below the wheel peering out at the fog that seemed to smother even the light of day. He knew the loaded gold made them an easy catch for the swifter Defiance. He was deep in thought when movement behind him made him quickly turn to stare directly into the black eyes of Sabotha. Her sudden appearance made him push back in surprise.

"*Ta sendi mata do,*" she whispered as she waved her hand in the air. Wisps of fog spun away with every twirl of her hands.

"The Defiance comes." She pulled him close to her.

"I see a safe place there," she said, pointing into the fog in the direction of shore.

Then as quickly as she had appeared, she disappeared leaving Pierre wondering if he had really seen her at all.

Fuquay, who had been at the wheel and was just as surprised at her appearance, asked, "What did the witch say?"

"She said danger is coming. We must turn into the shore where it is safe."

"There is no safe place here. The shore is rocky and it is shallow," Fuquay said." These islands are bewitched by strange happenings."

"I know it's hard, but trust her; she knows things, things we will never understand. Besides, if that's true, who else would you trust but a witch."

With a futile look of disbelief, Captain Fuquay reluctantly gave the orders to head towards the shore.

"Throw that line, men. We must know where the bottom is," he called.

"Eighty deep," was the answer.

"Seventy and coming up."

"Fifty-three, coming up; forty-two and up, forty-one, forty, thirty-eight, and thirty-five," was the call.

Tall rocky cliffs began to appear on both sides of the ship. The ship's hull began to rub against the bottom making all the men hold their breath. They slowed.

"Thirty-eight, forty-five, fifty, she's going down, sir," was the cry.

"Fifty-five, sixty, deeper yet, sir."

The ship had entered a narrow waterway that jogged sharp to the left. Trees covered the cliffs and in turn the hanging vines covered the trees made a green invisible backdrop to the entrance of the small bay hidden there. The San Felipe dropped anchor hoping the other ships would pass. If Trouin knew of this hiding place, they surely would be hung along with the vines. Dusk settled in and all distinguished shapes disappeared.

Chapter 7

Morning Star

A small stub on the large branch Manez had been clinging to poked at him. Trees were never as comfortable as his teepee along Piney Creek, he thought, as he stirred.

To ease his discomfort, Manez rolled over to catch a glimpse of the sun coming up. One bright star stood in defiance of the sun on the horizon, but soon faded away. The morning star, he thought; tomorrow will be the full moon and a sacred time for all tribes.

He was very cautious as he climbed down, making sure there was no danger from the bear.

I must be a two-day walk from any familiar country, he thought, as he pushed through the low clinging brush that whipped at his legs. Two days of this and I won't have any legs left. I must find a deer trail.

It didn't take long and he was moving down a path he had found through the brush. Surely at this rate he would be home before the next noonday.

The trail soon split and he chose the higher trail that stayed up along the ridge. It seemed to be the less traveled of the two and it gave him a higher advantage to see from.

He hadn't gone far before he began to sense that he should be very cautious because danger was near. His intuition paid off, because a short distance ahead he could see a Crow lookout almost invisible to the naked eye in the underbrush.

Manez moved slowly from the trail and slid in behind a clump of mulberry trees. If there was a Crow guard, there must be a Crow village close.

Manez stared through the morning sunlight until far below he caught sight of smoke curling its way to the top of the trees.

The bright light of the morning sun finally climbed off the horizon high enough that he could make out a cluster of teepees below.

It was a large Crow band and as he scanned the village, his eye caught an area close to the center of the camp where a large post was being planted in the ground by several young braves. A group of old women were gathering bundles of wood and piling them around the post. This foretold a painful death for some unlucky captive, especially with the full moon tonight.

The Crow were known for the festival of the full moon, a gruesome observance practiced in secret. Manez had only heard stories about how each member of the tribe would shoot an arrow into a captive tied to a post. Then the Shaman would cut out the heart and hold it high overhead while the whole tribe would celebrate the coming of the full moon.

"Ugh." He shivered just thinking about it. Gruesome as it was, this wasn't his affair, he thought. He must move on while everyone was busy getting ready.

Some young boys had moved up the hill gathering willow sticks to make their arrows and if he didn't move soon they would discover his hiding place.

Manez crossed the trail and started up over the top. He would just have to find a different way home, bear or no bear.

A sudden scream from below made him look back before he disappeared down the other side.

The boys who had been gathering arrows were running down the hill towards the camp.

He focused in on an Arikara being pulled through the camp by Crow guards.

"What kind of Arikara warrior gets caught by the Crow?" he said to himself.

Straining his eyes. *A girl!* He stopped in his tracks and fell on his knees behind an oak tree. *A young girl.*

He felt like he was battling some unseen force deep within.

"What is it to me? The Arikara were his enemy and this would be a better place without this one."

He turned to leave, but the young girl screamed as the women hit her with sticks.

Manez fell to the ground again. He could clearly picture the arrows being shot into the young girl and her heart throbbing even as it was cut from her chest.

"Only the Crow would think there was honor in this thing. Arikara or not, I will not dishonor my family by walking away."

His mind quickly pieced together a plan. It wasn't a good plan, but it would have to do. If he could endure the girl's screams for the day, he would wait until the Crow had whipped themselves into a frenzy. Then, with the cover of darkness...*Hmmm, it's going to be a full moon,* he would use his great stealthfulness to slip down the hill in the light of the moon, cut a hole in the back of the teepee, and hope to get away with her in plenty of time.

"Well, it might work," he said out loud.

It was a long day and to make things worse, the wind that had been blowing over his shoulder to the south suddenly shifted to the north. It was a stiff, cool wind; the kind that could bring in a storm.

Leaves, dirt, and all kinds of debris battered his hiding place. The Crow guards even took shelter from the beating winds. Manez looked back to the south. The chill in the air made him consider where the bear might be and the adventure he had been sharing with the creature. Maybe his father was right about Four Claws being connected to him. His thoughts slowly scattered into tired eyes and turned to dreams.

In his dream, he stood facing what seemed to be a host of dark spirits. Mighty, they stood on a ridge above him and the night wind blew through them. He wasn't afraid, but he was puzzled by the strange glow of his body in the darkness. The bear stood with him in the light of his body ready to fight.

The host leading the charge screamed.

He jumped awake. It was the girl from the village below screaming. It was dark and he could see the great fire burning. The drums pounded as hard as his heart was pounding. He was having second thoughts about his rescue plan when all of a sudden a subtle movement behind him caused Manez to turn, only to suck in the hot breath of the great bear right in his face.

He leaped from hiding and threw himself down the hill with the bear in pursuit. There would be no time for his great stealthfulness, only a run for his life towards, perhaps, a certain death.

The drums beat harder and the Crow village was so focused on each other's wild dancing that the breaking of tree limbs and falling rocks wasn't even noticed at first.

A few women and some children in the back of the ceremony gazed up the mountain at the commotion. Covered by the red oak trees, Manez exploded from the thick cover directly into the dancing warriors. Running wildly into the center of the camp, he saw a large brave bent over next to the fire and he ran up his back, and then leaped over the flames of the fire, landing at the top of a teepee.

The Crow grew quiet and a fierce looking warrior stepped forward and said to the tribe, "That's one crazy Indian up there."

They all laughed as the brave pulled his knife, pointed at him, and then started towards the teepee.

Manez didn't pay any attention to him. His pale face kept looking towards the red oak trees and that caused the others to notice the noise coming down the hill.

"Crack, snap."

A large limb went flying as Four Claws ran into the clearing.

The whole place went crazy. Women, children and even Crow braves scattered in all directions.

Some didn't escape the bear's fury. He tossed them in crumpled heaps in every direction. With the help of two warriors, the fierce looking brave tried to fight the bear by swinging the tiny knife wildly at him, but the large fire drove Four Claws into a crazy rage. He slashed the tallest Indian across his legs cutting him to the bone, then as he fell forward, grabbed him by the neck with his powerful jaws and tossed him away like a child.

Another brave thought the bear had turned away from him enough that he could drive a large knife behind his shoulder, but the bear suddenly turned back around catching him with the back of his giant paws and sending him directly into the fire.

There wasn't much the other Crow braves could do, so they ran away.

Four Claws unleashed his wrath on the fire scattering it all over everything.

Manez was in a daze watching the embers fly into the air. How terrifying, but also beautiful, was the scene being played out in front of him.

Something was burning; the teepee below him lit up like a dried cattail.

He jabbed a knife into the buffalo hide and rode the handle to the ground.

Everything was burning around him as he dashed to the teepee where he had last seen the girl. Hot embers had ignited the tall grass close enough to catch the bottom of the teepee on fire. It would be only a matter of seconds before it burst into flames. Manez ripped open the deerskin, but the room was full of smoke.

Someone coughed, but before he could move an old squaw charged at him. He deflected the hatchet with the blade of his knife and then clubbed her on the head with the handle.

The girl was there. He quickly cut her loose, then he cut a hole in the back of the smoldering hide and yanked her through at a dead run.

Chunks of fire were still raining down as they sprinted through the burning grass towards the cover of the reeds. They were lucky the whole village was in hiding from the bear and they made it to the river undetected. Manez turned north still running. He was surprised at how easily the girl kept pace. She was a tall, muscular girl. He wasn't an expert on the subject, but perhaps she was 15 years old. Until now, he hadn't had much to do with girls. He tried to take a look back at her, but a branch whacked him across the forehead making him stumble.

Focus on what you're doing, he said to himself.

The girl took the lead. She ran like no other girl he had ever seen. It was two hours before she collapsed into a clump of ferns close to a giant pecan tree.

The moon was gone; it was totally black beneath the tree. Manez fell to the ground beside her and for the longest time he listened to her breathing until the great gasps of air turned into what sounded like sleeping.

What a day, he thought as he lay back in the soft ferns. The girl pulled close to him and laid her head on his arm.

The morning star appeared from behind the clouds as if by magic and in its light he examined the beautiful face of the girl.

"I will have to thank the bear someday," he said, just before falling asleep.

Chapter 8

Blood and Bones

The crew seemed at ease hiding in the small bay. They drank until the late hours arrived. Pierre was staring at the strange shapes made by the small amount of light reflecting off the water. It wouldn't be easy getting away from the other Captains and word of this day's adventure need never be brought before the King, even if he wasn't going to be King very long.

Sabotha appeared suddenly, close enough to his face he could smell her bad breath. Pierre pushed back, so startled he had to grab on to the rigging to keep from falling into the water.

"My God, woman, why must you do that!"

"Do what?" she replied.

"Be so sneaky. You startled even me."

"No one could be as sneaky as you, Pierre."

"Well, perhaps I am a little bit sneakier," he said dryly as he turned.

"Come," she said, then she was gone; evaporated into the night.

Pierre seemed perplexed.

"What a liar that witch is. She disappeared right before my eyes."

"Oh, you're the sneaky one, master."

He started clomping for the stairs, then realizing the noise he was making, he eased up on his tiptoes and slithered down the stairs.

"I haven't lost my touch."

The old woman had made camp in DeBois's cabin and it reeked of rotten things she had brought with her. He hated to go in the place, but he had to.

"This isn't going to be one of those blood splattering sessions is it?" he asked.

She didn't answer, but grabbed him and pulled him close.

"Ta tome neo, Ta tome neo, DeBois, Ta tomeee shama," she chanted as she threw the bones on the table. Then, one by one she placed them in his hands and with each placement she let out a different disturbing noise until she came to the last one; all was quiet.

By now she had backed Pierre into the corner and once again she was in his face whispering in his ear.

"Shh." Her rough voice was soft.

"The one called Fuquay has been plotting against you. Even now he schemes for the gold."

Pierre frowned as she continued, "Sacrifice him and offer tribute to the other captains and when the time comes, they will not tell of this to anyone."

"Sacrifice, as in hang him from a cross? That would be a great spectacle, but I'm afraid it's already been done."

"No, just kill him and all his men with him."

" Ah." A thought crossed his mind. Lure him into the cave pretending to split the treasure, then leave his body there with the gold. If Trouin and Jean Bart catch me, I still have some hidden treasure. Good thinking. He shook his head because he was pleased with himself.

He turned to leave, but Sabotha grabbed him once more and whispered to him. "Beware of the African. He has great power with his men. I see in his eyes there are more ambitions for him than to be a slave."

Pierre pulled away and left the cabin and retraced his steps back to the main deck where Fuquay was peering out at the strange lights.

61

"I saw the witch take you below. What's she up to?"

"She sees the future and says we should hide the treasure. It will give us bargaining power when we're caught."

He turned slightly, white in the face.

"When we're caught? She said *when* we're caught?"

"We have the two greatest pirate captains in the world searching for us. It's only a matter of time till they find us."

"Trouin will hang me for this."

He rubbed his neck with his dirty hands.

"How do we have bargaining power?"

"We hide the gold in the cave and when we're caught we strike an agreement, our lives for the treasure. If the witch is wrong, we still know where the gold is."

Fuguay rubbed his chin in thought.

"Just in case she's wrong, let's keep a little touch of gold on board."

Pierre laughed. "Agreed, captain. Shall we?"

Pierre motioned that Fuquay should go first.

"At first light then, Captain."

They each retired to their quarters, but not until Pierre had made a stop or two along the way. He wanted to secure his plan before daylight.

Bebai was aware that at any moment Pierre could lose interest and need of him. He also knew his owner wouldn't hesitate to kill anyone for any reason, especially for the treasure stacked just below his feet.

Knowing this, Bebai and the natives kept to themselves, out of the way of the other pirates and gypsies. Bebai had been trying to plan a way to escape from the ship and his ability to speak to the tribesmen gave him the slight opportunity he needed. The group had made their home on the third deck next to the powder storage. Other than the fact it was the most dangerous place on the ship, they felt safe because no one ever bothered there.

Bebai was surprised when DeBois came tapping on the hull just beyond the group.

As he gazed around the room at the strange group of slaves huddled here and there, he said, "I've noticed, Bebai, that you've taken a keen interest in how to sail this big beast, barking orders to your men in that strange language you have. You have them take on more duties than they have to."

"It's a fine boat, master. I have paid attention to the sailors."

"Could you sail her with just the help of your men there?"

"I believe I could sail her just fine." He knew to ask no more of DeBois. It was never a good thing to ask too much. Bebai had realized a long time ago how to read Debois and this was a time when greed made him grow tired of sharing anything with Fuquay.

"Good then, good."

With that, he turned and moved to the stairs. He then turned to say, "Don't get ambitious, King of Fulani. Ambition for you is a foolish choice."

Then he was gone up the stairs.

Bebai ambitious? If being ambitious was wanting to walk through hell to get home, then DeBois read him like a book. How much time had passed since his capture by the slavers? How long since Pierre had bought him from the slave sale in Paris. Too long, he thought. It had been so long, he had stopped counting the days. Now he could tell he was moving further away from home. Ambition was his key to his dreams of the tall grasslands of home. A time will come, he thought, my time will come.

The wet fog hung onto the water of the bay as the sun tried to pick its way over the cliffs surrounding the ships hiding place. All hands were busy trailing loads of gold like ants to the shore. A human snake wound its way steadily up the cliffs for two hundred yards, then it turned abruptly to the left and seemed to dead end against the sheer cliffs. A group of banana trees had formed a curtain in front of the entrance to a small opening. Without light or an adventurous heart, most men wouldn't have fought the cramped space very far, but these pirates pushed deep into the cave until it opened into a large cavern. DeBois had placed Fuquay in charge of overseeing the placement of the booty.

The Captain wasn't stupid and he knew he couldn't trust Pierre, so the ship's men labored with one eye on the job at hand, the other eye on the gypsies.

Fuquay and four of his most trusted men had positioned themselves on a large rock above the floor just across from the entrance, feeling safe.

Pierre waited until the last of the gold was off the ship. Then he started to follow the last group of men.

Sabotha stood on the deck chanting as DeBois left, "Blood and bones fall on the stones, Blood and bones fall on the stones."

He gave her a look that could kill, then wound his way up the hill.

Fuquay and his men grew tense while waiting for DeBois. So tense that the air grew foul from it.

As always, Pierre's appearance before the group was a grand one; his cape swirled out dramatically as he moved into the large room.

No sooner had he appeared through the opening when two men grabbed him by each arm and held him tight at knifepoint. Weapons appeared in all the pirates' hands.

"My dear Pierre, I fear for your safety from these blood thirsty pirates. They have the fever for gold and I'm helpless to stop them. You see, I'm mad with it too. Ha, ha, ha." The room laughed.

"I must admit, Captain, you sometimes surprise me. Touché," DeBois replied.

Looking quite confident, Fuquay placed his hands on his hips as he talked. "You should never underestimate anyone, especially me, Pierre."

"I didn't say, monsieur, you surprise me. I said you sometimes surprise me and this is not one of those times that I'm surprised."

The two blades came from under his cape in a flash catching the first man across the throat. The other he stabbed in the heart as he spun away snapping the blade off.

Fuquay didn't have time to move before the steel that the shadow threw at him came bursting through his chest; he just looked at it, then at Pierre. Blood mixed with spit slowly dribbled from his mouth. The blade disappeared and he fell dead.

The pirates tried to react to the killing, but the shadows in the cave came alive from all directions. It was the Dark Wind that had been hiding there all the time.

Pierre produced a sword and one by one he laid the rebels open.

"Blood and bones on the stones."

It wasn't much of a battle for the gypsy warriors compared to the fights in Paris and soon they had killed all the surprised pirates.

No words were said. Pierre turned, throwing his cape out after him and taking the torches, the clan left the Pirates in the dark with their treasure.

Chapter 9
The Reunion

The light of day penetrated the small ferns Manez had taken shelter under. Sharp beams stabbed at his eyes every time the breeze moved them. The girl was standing over him waiting for him to wake up. She could have slipped off by herself, but he had the feeling she had no interest in traveling alone.

He rose to his knees pointing at his chest. "Manez, Manez, Cheyenne, Wolf Band," he said proudly. She turned her head slightly at an angle as if she was trying to comprehend what he was saying.

She in turn touched her shoulder and responded, "Neesuunu Sahnish" (Dawn Arikara)

"Neesuunu Sahnish, Manez Saahe," she said pointing at herself then at him.

"Yes Saahe, Cheyenne."

"Tuhkaaka" (Crow) She slapped the back of her hand into her palm and spit on the ground.

"Tuhkaaka xanis." (Crow urine)

Manez had no idea what xanis was, but he was pretty sure that she was talking about the Crow who had taken her captive.

Standing there in the morning sun she was even prettier than she had been in his arms the night before.

She began a great explanation, gesturing this way and that. Then she would fluctuate her voice and begin all over again.

"Nooxini na tsaapis huukataahpiinaahn, wakau Tuhkaaka, wakau…

Manez watched with great curiosity as Neesuunu went on and on.

She must have realized he had no idea about what she was saying because she stopped, took a big breath, then in a much calmer voice started again.

"Katahakut tatataat hunaahkoohaahkat." She pulled at his arm and motioned to the north.

North was ok by him for now. Part of him wanted to flee for home, but he had committed to her safety and his pride wouldn't let him abandoned her when she needed him.

The Arikaras belonged to the Caddoan language family, specifically related to the Skiri Pawnee. Some things she said had a familiar sound to it, but for now he was just guessing at her meaning.

His father had told him the Arikaras lived south of the black gold area and the big river. They had fallen victim in recent years to raids from the Crow and their numbers had decreased enough to leave only three villages of any size along the river.

Manez jumped into the lead; he planned on heading to the river and there he knew of several abandoned villages where he might be able to find a canoe and some food.

The morning was consumed by the two of them winding along partial deer paths and some human trails. It wasn't until Manez started to see the trail widen and the brittle clumps of reeds appear beside the trail that he knew they were getting close to the river.

Neesuunu pulled at his arm slowing him down and causing him to become very cautious.

"La hoo Sahnish." She waved her hand in a circle around the area.

A few more steps and they were on the edge of a clearing that held 17 earthen houses in various stages of collapse.

She peeked through the branches. "La hoo," she said again.

He held her back and they sat hidden while he listened, looked, and smelled for a long time.

As soon as he was satisfied they were alone, he led her into La hoo.

He had no idea what it meant, but it was nice hearing her say it.

The girl scurried here and there around the houses while Manez's attention was drawn to the sound of the river's rushing water.

He spotted several canoes on the bank, but upon closer inspection all of them had either holes or rotted hide bottoms and were partially submerged in the water. He was about to give up when he spotted buffalo hide draped over something resting above the ground on the limbs of a cottonwood tree.

To his surprise, the hide had preserved a beautiful, two-man canoe, which he promptly freed from its hiding place and slid into the water. It didn't take long to find two paddles that were in good shape.

Neesuunu arrived and for the first time; she had a huge smile on her face.

"Sapane." She rubbed her stomach and held up a squash. "Wahux"

Wahux is squash, sapane is stomach, he thought.

The girl dug a hole in the sand and began to carry wood. Manez could tell she needed a fire.

"Anaxka." That word registered; it sounded like cook in Mandan.

He found a flat rock and placed it in the center of a small fire, then turned to her and said, "Anaxka" (cook in Mandan)

She blushed and repeated, "Anaxka." She too recognized Mandan.

Neesuunu had also found a small amount of corn and with the two ingredients made a feast of flat bread covered in sliced cooked squash. Manez had forgotten how long it had been since he had eaten and the food made him tired. It wouldn't hurt to spend the night and see what else they could find for their trip up stream.

"Iscipi," (sleep) he said in Mandan; she responded, "Iscipi" with a nod of her head.

Manez found a nice place in the closest house for them to spend the night, and then he excused himself for a look around the camp.

The Arikara had left here in a hurry. He found blankets, baskets, rope and several kinds of corn and squash. He loaded all he could in the baskets and carried them to the canoe.

He wasn't surprised that Neesuunu was fast asleep when he returned. It was the first peace she probably had since being taken captive. He placed a blanket over her and she pulled it close around her. Then, he too went to sleep.

He was up early and ready to go by the time she had groomed herself and arrived at the canoe. She was also eager to be going and she automatically took her place in the front of the canoe.

It was Fall and the river was running slow, making it easy to go against the current. Manez found Neesuunu a strong rower and they seemed to be making easy work of the paddling together.

Four miles upstream they passed an adjoining river about 90 yards wide. Neesuunu informed Manez it was the Sur-war-kar-ne. About noon, they passed two Teton braves making their way along the east bank. They acknowledged the passing with only an inquisitive glance.

By late in the evening, the banks of the river narrowed and Manez sensed a village close by. He wanted to put into shore to make sure it was safe to pass, but Neesuunu convinced him it was a place she knew well. The village of Chief Ka Kawissassa (Lightning Crow) sat quietly on the west bank of the river. It was positioned on top of a twelve-foot ledge that ran along side the water for one hundred feet. It was a well-fortified village having only two unrestricted ways to the top of the hill.

"This is the southern boundary of my people," she said in Mandan.

The language barrier had been broken when both of them realized they understood most Mandan words.

"It will be all right, Manez." She tried to comfort his uneasiness.

Manez reluctantly pushed the canoe forward, aware that they were being watched from the tress beyond the sand bank and no sooner had the canoe touched the sand bar, than a host of braves appeared from the bushes.

All was quiet until one of the braves yelled out, "Neesuunu!" All attention turned to the river.

"Neesuunu Pia he to," the brave yelled again and the whole village came running down the path to the water.

The young maiden was whisked away with shouts of joy, leaving Manez alone staring into the eyes of the untrusting warriors.

The Cheyenne and Arikara had never been allies, but they had never been at war either. They had just always looked on each other with distant distrust.

He could hear the cheers in the village for the girl, then all the noise stopped for a long time. The braves on the bank began to nervously fidget with their weapons.

Manez's thoughts were of throwing his tomahawk at the closest man, then diving into the water.

A loud cheer came from the hill above, causing him to almost jump out of the boat.

"Raahukoosu Manez."

They cheered that brave Manez had returned her home.

"Raahukoosu Manez" (Brave Manez)

With that, the braves on the bank engulfed him with loud cheers and carried him up the hill.

He was swept past the waiting crowd and into a small house at the center of the village.

He wasn't sure what was going on, but when the hot bath water arrived, he didn't complain; he was in need of a good scrubbing.

Manez took off his buckskin shirt, then tossed it over a lodge pole. He had one leg out of his pants when four old women came in. He hopped three times on one leg trying to jump back into his pants, but on the fourth try they charged him, throwing him to the ground. It was no use to fight them. They removed his clothes and plopped him into the buffalo skin bathtub.

The water hid most of his private parts and after turning five shades of red, he relaxed.

One old toothless squaw kept scrubbing a little close to home which made his face flare up red again. He slapped her hand away as the others giggled like little girls.

The honey suckle smelled sweet in his hair and even embarrassed he enjoyed it.

Another squaw appeared at the door with clean buckskins.

"Rihuun nut?" (Big snake) she said and they all died laughing. As they picked up and began to leave, he replied, "Kariwii nut." (Wrinkled snake)

They were in shock. He knew what they had said and amid the shock of it all, they began to run out of the hut with muffled laughter and Manez splashed water at them.

The Indian drums pounded loudly and by the time Manez had made his appearance outside, Neesuunu was on the opposite side of the large fire that was blazing in the center of the camp.

Neesuunu hadn't fared any better. She also was scrubbed from head to foot.

He had to move his head back and fourth to get small peeks at her, but the parts he could see were beautiful.

What was he thinking? He couldn't let this girl enchant his mind, but he couldn't keep his eyes off her.

The chief seated him and the party began. A man wearing a bear's head danced into the firelight chasing a boy around the fire. A young girl was placed in his path dressed in white skins. The boy stopped and the bear danced around him. Then he turned on warriors wearing elk skull masks chasing them around and around the fire. The boy, in turn, untied the girl and escaped into the darkness while the bear held the warriors at bay. Then with a wave of his claws, the warriors fell down defeated.

The Indians cheered wildly as they lifted Manez up on their shoulders and carried him around the fire.

Suddenly Chief Ka Kawissassa spoke. "Bring in the Suunaaxu" (young women).

The wall of humanity parted and out stepped four very pretty young girls.

Suunaaxu? Manez thought, He means young woman. No, young wife.

Wife! A bead of sweat broke out across his forehead. How would he get out of this without insulting the chief? He looked at

Neesuunu for help, but she just smiled and nodded her head towards the girls as if to say pick one.

"Great Ka Kawissassa. I'm humbled at the thought that you would think me such a brave warrior that you would give me one of these pretty, young maidens." He paused, grasping for the right words. The old chief gathered something was wrong and had put a scowl on his face.

"The truth is, chief, I don't think I can honestly take the Suunaaxu."

Before the old man could say a word, Neesuunu stood up before the chief.

"I'm not one to say what would be right or wrong in your village, Chief Ka Kawissassa, but perhaps it should be my father who gives the bride to the man who saved me from certain death." She couldn't help but have a red glow to her face. After all, she had begun to care for the young Cheyenne warrior a lot.

The chief thought about it a little while and noticed the glow on her face and then said, "She is right. Pia he to (Grey Eyes) should give his daughter's rescuer a wife."

He passed the smoking pipe to Manez and smiled. It was a nice pipe, not anything like the pipes of the Cheyenne. Instead of having a flat, wide bowl for the tobacco, it had a tall cylinder. Large, eagle feathers dangled from a beaded leather harness and carvings adorned every square inch of it.

The fire light dance continued deep into the night. Manez waited until most of the villagers were gone, and then he told the chief he must be on his way early and excused himself.

Early the next morning as Manez made his way down to the canoe, he was met by the Shunuwanuh medicine man. Somewhere in

73

the distance a dog barked. A bone chilling wind had come in during the night and it nipped at the shoreline. Winter was coming and much sooner than Manez needed it to come. By the time he made the trip up river to Chief Grey Eyes's camp and then return home, snow would be deep in the valleys.

Neesuunu (Dawn) was already there waiting with two older braves as he arrived.

"Good morning, did you sleep well?" she asked.

Of course not, he thought. *Who could sleep while thinking of you.* "Oh, yes, good enough, considering the fright of waking up with a wife that I didn't want."

She laughed as he pushed the canoe into the water.

Two of Chief Ka Kawissassa's men would travel with them until they passed through an area controlled by the Kiowa.

The wind continued to be very high all day causing their travel to be very slow at times.

A canoe carrying three squaws piled high with meat passed them on the other side of the river. The two men hailed them, but they quickly passed on downstream.

"Pawnee," Dawn said.

He had never seen Pawnee women before.

In the middle of the afternoon, the two braves turned their canoe downstream and cried out, "Ut asista Neesuunu." (Look out for Neesuunu.)

It wasn't long until they had disappeared.

"We are getting close to home. It's just up ahead." Pausing she pointed suddenly up river. "There, where the hills flatten out next to the big oak tree."

Manez pushed the paddle deep into the water driving it forward in the direction she had pointed out and it wasn't long until his strong motion at the water brought them to the bank. A buckskin canoe belonging to the Taroxpa tribe was stuck into the soft mud on the bank. The old chief must have sent word ahead to Grey Eyes that the daughter who was lost had now been found. They started up the trail and with every step taken Arikara warriors stepped from hiding and followed them up the path. The trail soon widened and then it jogged to the left only to reveal to their surprise that the whole village had lined the way.

Far ahead Dawn saw her father and for the first time, Manez saw the little girl, not the brave warrior, as she began to cry, and then run towards him. She collapsed in his arms like a rag doll to the cheers of the Arikara people.

Grey Eyes was a stout, serious-looking man about forty years old. After a few minutes of holding his daughter, Chief of all Arikaras, turned his attention to Manez.

"Today, warrior Manez brought back the most precious thing in my life." He pointed to eight large posts with the decaying bodies of what Manez assumed to be Crow braves that hung on them, obviously in retaliation for taking his daughter.

"Killing these Crow did not bring her back. Only Manez could bring her back; I saw it in my dreams." The village cheered wildly as they were escorted to a place of honor. He leaned forward and whispered to the boy. "Sometime, you must tell me why the bear haunts you so." Then he turned again to the people.

"I am reasonable. I try to make peace with all the Arikara enemies, but there is no peace with the Crow. Today the earth gave my only child back to me and we celebrate."

The drums pounded and a feast began to unfurl before them. Manez noticed most of the servers were slaves from other tribes. He saw Sioux, Kiowa and Wichita, but one particular captive caught his attention. He was a white Indian who had hair on his face. Manez had never seen a white Indian before and no tribe known could grow hair on their face. He thought of the story Onotsa had told about the white warriors and the magic they had. Then suddenly, he thought of home and he peered past the celebration into the evening sky. Small flakes of snow began to fall. Winter wasn't coming, it had arrived; his chance to get home was gone. Everyone around him rejoiced about the lost one returning home, but his emotions teetered on a great crevice. His heart ached as his eyes followed the snow down, spinning, floating along until it landed on her cheek and he captured her eyes in his.

Chapter 10
Twice the Slave

Bebai wasn't surprised when the gypsies returned without Fuquay. He didn't question what he already knew. His many years as the slave of Pierre told him all he needed to know. Ugly Sabotha stood with her patchwork hair blowing in the morning wind awaiting Pierre's return. "The danger has past; it's time to go," she said and then she slipped below decks once again.

Pierre turned to Bebai. "Let's see how much you've learned, King of Fulani. Make way and take her out." The tall, black king barked orders to his subjects and soon the ship began to make its way out of the hidden harbor into the open sea. "I trust Sabotha's visions, but keep an eye out for any ships. Trouin will be on the prowl now that we have tricked him." Pierre, tired from his bloodthirsty activities, also retired below decks.

What a sight they made scurrying around the big ship. Who would have thought he would ever be this far from home. Tears flooded Bebai's eyes as he thought of his family. Only the presence of the Dark Wind kept him from turning the ship towards home. With images of home in his mind he vowed once again, "Soon, I promise. Soon."

Below the deck Sabotha sensed the promise Bebai made to the wind as he said it and she would remember it. A certain fear of the King chilled her body and she cast the bones once again trying to find an answer in them. It disturbed her that the bones flipped away from death every time they were thrown down until she tried to place them with her hands, only to have them fly off the table. There was a power about him and the spirits revealed to her they had another use for the African king. She regained her composure then began to laugh as she mumbled. "It will be soon, oh King, very soon."

The wind was good and the days passed. No sail behind them had been sighted to Pierre's good fortune and the closer they came to New Orleans the Gypsy women and children ventured onto the deck of the ship more often. It was interesting watching them practice their individual crafts. The knife throwers, pick pockets, shell games and magicians all began to work diligently at their chosen fields. A small group of musicians gathered with their instruments and began creating melodies that seemed to draw the group into a sea of chaos. All the activity on board didn't distract Bebai from noticing the sea gulls that had come to shadow every move of the ship. *Land is close*, he thought.

"It seems we are to have good fortune, old one. See the birds? They know," Pierre declared to his witch.

"Yes, the bones have told me this also."

Pierre pulled her aside to whisper, "I fear the ambition of our black captain. Perhaps I should relieve him of his commission before we reach land."

"No." The goose bumps appeared once again on Sabotha's pasty white skin and her voice cracked as she continued. "Death is not yours to give, but I know another way to rid you of him that will not disturb the spirits' will."

She leaned forward to whisper in his ear, but her thoughts were broken by a cry from the crow's roost. "Land ho!" All on board moved towards the rails to get a glimpse.

"Land is off the starboard side," the native called out to Bebai.

The crew shifted to the starboard side. "Land it is, Pierre," Bebai repeated to him. "We will follow the shoreline until we find our port."

The water soon turned muddy brown from a river close by and small towns on the shore began to appear. Occasionally they could see a sail appear on the horizon giving Pierre a lingering fear, but the feeling would pass as the ship would disappear. The water became cluttered with boats of all sizes and all in the bay began to pay attention to the Spanish warship as she sailed into port.

An empty berth was spotted and Bebai put the San Felipe against the dock with the skill of a sea hardened captain. It was amazing the precision of the slaves scurrying about the ship.

Pierre had waited for this day all his life and with the King's papers in hand, he sprang down the gangplank escorted by the dark brotherhood. Bebai stepped into his usual place along side his master only to have Pierre stop suddenly.

"Bebai, my friend, it would serve me best if you saw to the unloading of the ship."

He had been at Pierre's side for two years and every battle he had shared, but even Bebai knew his life could change in an instant. After all, he was still a slave bought and paid for from the cages of Paris.

"I will see to it, Governor," he said with a bow.

"That has a nice sound to it, doesn't it?" Pierre replied as he sprang forward towards his destiny.

The familiar sound of whips and chains could be heard coming from behind a walled courtyard and Bebai winced with every crack of the whip snapping the air. All the slaves stopped what they were doing to endure the cracking sound. It seemed like an eternity that they froze to the familiar sounds of the slave masters beyond the walls.

Pierre waltzed through the city streets as if he were on a holiday or perhaps a small boy planning to grab all the candy he could before he got caught. No matter how giddy his actions were, it didn't keep him from peering into the large courtyard of the slave prison. Galleries filled with slaves of all ages surrounded the courtyard. His ears caught the same snapping sound of the whip Bebai had heard from the ship. He peered at a stone table in the center of the yard. A rather large, pompous white man in a tailored suit was watching while a black man was being whipped and with every lash, he demanded another lash for the slave's insubordination.

Without batting an eye to the depravity of the situation, Pierre turned away from it. "I may really like this place after all."

Jean Baptiste Le Moyne sat in his mansion just a short walk from Canal Street. The two-story, whitewashed house stood on a raised portion of land that allowed it to overlook the bay and the lower part of the city. Jean Baptiste had taken his time getting around; this day to him was just like any other day. His midmorning brunch was about to be served on the veranda overlooking the port. He took his normal gaze at the masts of the ships lining the harbor. He wasn't necessarily fond of his Governorship. It was a well-documented fact he preferred the King's court to this rabble of feeble-minded bumpkins. He had often longed for the day when he would be called home again to France.

"I can tell by the masts a Spanish galleon has come in during the night. She's a big ship." He rubbed his chin as if he was thinking. "A 200 gun warship can only mean we should expect an important guest today, Jonathan." He settled himself at the table, but before he could take a bite, doors began to bang and the sound of a scuffle came from downstairs.

"Your grace, it's a Pierre DeBois and he says he has an urgent message from the King."

"I tried to turn him away until later in the day, but he insisted on now."

"DeBois," he repeated to himself. The cousin to the King here to see him? Perhaps this was the day he had been waiting for. "Bring him here, Jonathan."

As glad as he was to have the relative of the King enter the room, DeBois's companions gave the Governor a start. The black-hooded swordsmen filled the room. It wasn't impossible to imagine that perhaps he had done some grievous thing to the King and this was his sentence. Louie wasn't very stable at the moment and he knew that.

Pierre broke the shocking silence embarrassing the Governor. "Jean Baptiste." Pierre stepped forward and announced himself, "Pierre DeBois, the King's cousin."

"Yes, yes. I remember you from that nasty business at Des Ternes." Jean knew it was a slip of the tongue when he said Des Ternes, because it was that day that sent Pierre into hiding. He had tried to use his influence against a local official and when the man refused to cooperate with him, Pierre killed him.

"I know that day was a bad day, but as you can see I have recovered from it quite well, monsieur."

"It is good to have those things put behind you and I'm glad for you." He felt as if he was recovering from a fatal disease. "What brings you to us, sir; perhaps good news of the King and France?"

"All news falls on an ill wind, sir. The King has fled Paris. I escorted him to Versailles myself. Lafayette has taken control of the

King's guard because his life is at jeopardy on all turns. It was he who bid me come to New Orleans. His wish was to raise money to hire the Austrian army to guarantee the defeat of the rabble infesting the Third Estate."

"This is ill news, sir; ill news all around for me because of my love for our country. What does the King wish from me?"

Pierre was just waiting for the opportunity to spring the papers, rescinding Jean Baptiste's governorship. Handing the sealed papers to him, he said, "The King has recalled you home knowing of your close ties with the Austrians. He hopes you will petition help for him. Here are the papers making me Governor until a time when you can return." Pierre's train of thought was shattered, because at that moment he saw the bright white sails of the Defiance coming into the harbor. Baptiste opened the letter and shortly acknowledged Pierre as Governor of the port of New Orleans.

"Congratulations, DeBois." Shaking his hand, Pierre thought Baptiste was a little too happy to be going home and it surprised him. Pointing towards the waterfront he replied, "It seems your ride home has just arrived." No one had noticed that Pierre's forehead had beaded up with great drops of sweat, but it had and his mind worked frantically on a way out of this mess. The men quickly disappeared from the house as Baptiste peered out at the French ship. "It looks like we are to have more guests, Jonathon."

Bebai had hurried to get the clan and their supplies on shore. His thoughts were on breaking loose the ropes with a blast of the cannons and turning the ship out to sea for home. All the slaves were poised for the break as the last few stragglers exited the plank. He was focused on the passengers. No attention was being paid to the Defiance slipping up along side. It wasn't until the shadows of the long masts broke across the deck that Bebai realized the war ship was dashing all his hopes of escape.

Captain Trouin's crew was quick to lash the two ships together and board the San Felipe.

"Where is your captain?"

"He's gone into the city," Bebai replied.

The privateers, brandishing their weapons, swarmed onto the deck. Bebai could see Sabotha's whitewashed eyes staring from the group of Gypsies gawking from the shore. Trouin saw her, too; he also was afraid of the witch. "I'll wait for him; he can't be too far." The group of people on the shore suddenly stiffened and Pierre magically appeared amidst the black capes of his men. "Captain Trouin! I am so pleased to finally reconnect with you again, especially after the unfortunate actions of Mr. Fuquay," he announced as he bounded up to the deck in front of the furious captain. Holding tight to the handle of his cutlass, the intrigued captain decided to see what type of story Pierre would come up with.

"What unfortunate actions would that be?"

"Well, it seems Fuquay and this fellow here," he said, pointing at Bebai as his men grabbed him, "had conspired all along to cheat you out of the gold that, I must admit, was rightfully yours. The pirates you placed on board took control of the ship and forced us to go along with their plan of sailing in early."

Trouin didn't believe a word of it, but he still acted interested in the tale being told. "So they did? Fuquay and the king of the slaves here were trying to steal my gold?" He drew close and Bebai stiffened in the grasp of the Gypsies. "What has become of my first mate, then?" the captain asked.

"After eluding you for days, the mutinous pirates grew tired and careless until one night we took the ship back. Your first mate, I'm afraid, was killed along with the other mutineers. We only saved this fellow and his people to sail the ship." All the while they talked, heavy crates had been relayed to the deck from below and stacked close by. Trouin scratched his chin and everyone there knew he didn't believe anything DeBois had said, but before the captain could speak DeBois continued, "Would you like to see your prize? Waving a sweeping hand towards the crates he motioned for a box to be opened. The bars of gold seemed to shoot rays of blinding light in all directions. Trouin seemed appeased, but he still had questions. "I thought there would be more," he said running his hand over the bars.

"Fuquay was a pirate, but no one ever said he was a good pirate. You surprised him coming through the fog and I'm afraid he left most of the gold floating in the bay with the governor. Besides, I claim no part of it! It's all yours." Trouin read between the lines and he knew DeBois was saying to take the gold, but don't tell the King.

"I accept your story and the gold, Pierre, but I have one last question. What does a man have to do to get a drink on this ship?" With that, the ice was broken and as the bottles of rum appeared, no one noticed the proud Africans being herded off to the slave cages. The men of Fulani and their king blended in with the sea of black until they disappeared once again as slaves.

Chapter 11
The Company of the Indies

The sight of the Defiance dropping her sails and heading out of the harbor with a full wind made a large smile appear on DeBois's pale face. It had been easier than he had hoped to get rid of Trouin. All he had to do was give him only what he had planned on giving him from the beginning. On the other hand, he thought he was never going to get rid of Jean Baptiste Le Moyne.

Pierre had spent the entire morning being introduced to a long line of officials who were to serve under his direction. All the way from the Sargeant-at-arms to the slave master and none of their names mattered to him anyway, because as soon as the good governor was on that boat, everything would change. He played along knowing he must, but in his mind he was thinking of which one of his men would be best suited for each particular job.

It wasn't until noon that Le Moyne excused himself, satisfied he had done all he could do to help make a smooth transition of power for DeBois.

"Bon voyage," Pierre said from the balcony, as he watched the ship sail away.

"Bon voyage, indeed," Sabotha echoed from behind him in an almost sinister call. So much so, it startled Pierre and he jumped forward. "Ahh." DeBois gave a cold shiver as he turned to face the witch.

"I've cast the bones. The bones don't lie and all is well. Put your men in their proper places, but call on the man named Chepart, commandant of the soldiers; he will be helpful to you. His heart is the same as yours." Then like always, she disappeared in a mist and was gone.

Pierre turned to Jacques who had a strange look on his face.

"I know the feeling. It's very creepy to me, too and I've seen it a hundred times." Not missing a beat or waiting for a response, he continued, "Antoine, my friend, are all the Sinti ready?"

"Yes, my king, the gypsies are ready," he replied.

"Then take control of the city and if anyone resists you, feel free to take care of them. Send for the commandant."

Without a response, Jacques followed Antoine out into the streets.

Pierre demanded his supper and repositioned himself on the balcony in order to view the streets below. A shocking quiet, cold rush of movement attacked the streets below. The strange sounds of glass breaking, people yelling and dogs yelping reverberated throughout the city. Over and over again the noises echoed as the cold dark rush gnawed at the city until, finally, all the sounds stopped.

It was so quiet, Pierre paused from biting his chicken leg to stare out onto the silence. It was as if all life had ceased to exist.

"Wait, wait just a moment more," he said holding his drumstick, as if he were leading a great orchestra.

"Now." He brought his hand down and without warning the laughter and the music came back.

"Ta-ta-tum-te-dum, ta-ta-tum-te-dum." He directed the mighty reorganization of New Orleans life.

His skill as a director was somewhat limited by the half-eaten drumstick that he waved vigorously to the silent music. On one of the down beats, a piece of chicken broke loose and went sailing through the air and landed at the feet of Sieur de Chepart, who had entered the room unknown to DeBois.

"Pardon my interruption, sir. I was told to come up by the servant below." Chepart was a tall, rugged-looking man. His goatee gave him an air of authority and Pierre was certainly startled by the entrance.

"I am Sieur de Chepart, Captain of the Guard, at your service." If first impressions were to be basis of their relationship, then this could be the most unusual relationship of all. *So this is the King's cousin*, Chepartt thought.

"Come in, sir, come in." Pierre could see the shadow of Sabotha standing in the dark room beyond them. "I have been told you were a man to trust with special duties commanded by the King himself."

"You have been informed correctly, Governor. I am, foremost, the King's servant." He picked up the piece of chicken and approached, placing it on the table.

"Here, join me. I insist. The night is in its beginning and we have a lot to discuss."

Chepart was willing to listen to the King's demands. He was just hoping to be asked to do something more dangerous than policing the city.

"How are things in Paris? It's been six years since I last saw the city."

"Not good, Captain. The commoners have driven the King out of the city on rivers of blood. All who are for the King are taken to the gallows." Pierre played to the sympathy of the Commander.

"I knew things were not well, but I had no idea the city had fallen to the rebels. These special duties you speak of, what would you have me do?"

Pierre continued, "Our King is in need of money. He has plans to buy the Austrian army to take back his beloved France. We are looking for ways to produce a profit in this New World without the excuses of the acting Governor. Any ideas you have will be of special interest to me."

New food was set before them and Chepart filled his plate.

"Of course, I don't expect you to do this business without proper compensation. I feel we all should be entitled to a fee of some kind for thoughtful obedience to the King."

Chepart liked where this conversation was going. He had come to New Orleans after the wars in the North of France against the Moors hoping to use his position to further his fortune. He drank in the intoxicating wine of this new Governor.

"You know, you will never get rich by skimming money off of every vice offered here. The real money is in slaves and tobacco."

"Slaves and tobacco? That market has been thought of a long time ago." Pierre wanted new ideas and it disgusted him to hear this.

"I can tell you are thinking like most men here," Chepart said, "but let me speak. So far, the only land available for plantations has been allotted close to the city. The treaties have been in favor of the Indians, letting them keep the fertile lands north along the river and confining our French farming to a strip of land next to the swamps." Standing, he approached the map. "I propose we build a fort twenty miles up river to control the Natchez Indians and take control of the lands between here and the fort. Two large plantations can be placed between the fort and the city. I've privately given both plantations names. Here above the lowlands close to the White Apple village is St. Catherine and twenty miles to the north is Terre Blance."

Pierre rubbed his chin. "I like it," he said, standing and joining Chepart at the map with two wineglasses.

"Let's have a toast, Captain. To St. Catherine and Terre Blance. May they make lots of money."

"No, sir! I have thought upon this for a long time. Let's toast to the beginning of a new company called the Company of the Indies."

"It appears you have thought about this, sir. To the Company of the Indies it is."

Chepart responded, "To the Company and the profit it will bring."

The two men drank in the wine and became intoxicated not only in their blood, but also in their minds with the possibilities.

"We will need lots of workers if we are to build two plantations at the same time," Chepart said.

"It would be worth your while to visit the slave pens in the morning. I hear they have some strong new workers available," said Pierre. He was thinking about Bebai as he tossed the captain a small pouch containing gold coins.

The commandant lightly tossed the pouch in his hand and responded as he turned to leave the room. "I will make sure this is spent well, Governor."

Pierre couldn't contain himself. He waltzed around the room as if dancing on some great ballroom floor. "I control the city, I control the army and soon I will control large plantations sprouting gold from the earth." He stumbled forward over what he thought was a table leg and being drunk he was unable to break his fall coming to rest face down on the floor. He laughed and began to pull himself up until he realized the object that caused his fall was Sabotha's stick.

"Come, my witch, will you dance with me?" He continued to get to his feet, but Sabotha waved her arms in the air. A mist appeared in a great swirl. Pierre rolled his eyes and said, "Here we go again." Sabotha scattered the bones across the floor smacking the wall with a hollow tone. Then, in a flash she was above them eyeing each position.

"*Ah tori tu nu ah tori tu ek.*" She turned her spiteful eye towards him. "Be careful with this bargain you have made. Don't let it be your undoing, Pierre. I feel a great presence coming together against this alliance you have made." He pushed forward eyeing the bones himself at close range.

"I don't see great danger. I see gold and lots of it. How can you see danger? You just said all was well and that I should take possession of the city. Now, danger is all that you see and my undoing." The room began to spin as the drink began to push him towards unconsciousness.

"I see gold," he said as he grabbed her arm. "Do that burnt candle and the blood of a toad thing you do to get your way." Then he passed out.

Red splatters flew outward as Sabotha began to chant. *"Sa tel to nori deminni. Deminni ju sori."* Her cries filled the night.

Chapter 12

Sishu

The winter blasted at the earthen lodges of the Arikara, but Manez had a certain peace about him. Whether it was the soothing looks cast his way by the beautiful young Neesuunu or just the feeling he belonged here for some reason, he weathered the cold. The nights were as frosted as he had ever seen. Perhaps it was because he was so far north or maybe it was just the distance he was from home that made it seem colder than normal. No matter what the reason, because of the weather, he knew he wasn't going anywhere for a while.

His father Onotsa had mentioned the powerful magic of the Arikara. In fact, he had told about the Shunuwanuh in one of his stories. He told about their belief of a great one that looked over all the people from above and could enter the body through a window called Sishu and then live there. The Sishu was a gift from Nishanu Natchitak, the one who rules the world, like part of the body, but more of the spirit body. This Sishu interested him and that was another reason to stay.

One day, Manez had been hunting along the river when he noticed a young boy who had edged too close to the river while trying to snag one of the great paddle fish hidden in the mud. As the leather line was drawn in, it caught between two large rocks. The boy, thinking it was a fish, yanked too hard and lost his balance, falling into the freezing water. The white slave was gathering wood close by and was the only one to see the boy go in, so he bravely dove into the water to save the child. Frantically, he beat his arms against the currents while the cold water attacked his body. Turning almost blue, he reached the unconscious boy, threw his arm around the child's neck and began to pound his way back to shore. Manez rushed to help the white one by taking the limp, lifeless boy into his arms. He tried all the things he had learned about drowning on the boy, but there was no response. Several villagers gathered close to watch, but they didn't seem to be panicked; in fact, compared to Manez, they were very calm. They checked to see if the boy's medicine bundle was still securely tied around his neck, then set off to see the Shaman.

To Manez, the boy seemed dead and as he helped the white man from the water, he gave him a look that told him it was too late for the child. The slave broke into uncontrollable shivering and Manez gave him his hide coat. The white slave was withdrawn and sad as they walked back to the village. Here was a slave destined to serve a people he didn't belong to for the rest of his life and he cared about them. There was a deeper side to this man than anyone suspected.

The village was alive with activity when they arrived. The boy's body had been placed on a bed of sticks covered with blankets close to the fire. All of the women were chanting while the men played the drums and danced around the boy. The movement of the people caused the smoke from the fire to whip and swirl all around the center of the camp except where the Shaman stood over the boy. That space he occupied with the boy was calm with no smoke, just clear air. Everything in the Shaman's space moved slowly as if in heavier air and Manez caught himself focusing on that space instead of all the distractions around him.

The drums beat to a feverish pitch. Then, as sudden as a bolt of lightning, it stopped; all was quiet. A long walking stick covered with hawks' feet and pieces of bone was waved above the body.

92

Then the Shaman snapped the stick like a whip and pointed it at the bag still tied around the boy's neck. A bright flash of light shot from the end into the bag causing it to glow, then the glowing slowly encompassed the body. With a shout, they all cried, "Sishu" and the light faded as whiffs of smoke entered the calm circle then spiraled upward away from the boy. To the amazement of all present, the boy's eyes open and then he sat upright, causing a sudden rush of the tribe toward the white slave. Manez took a defensive position. Because the man was standing so close to him, he grabbed his arm in preparation to defend him. The people grabbed the slave and began tossing him in the air.

"Walks Far is a man of honor. Let him walk as one with us," was yelled out by one of the Arikara men.

"Neishanu has given him the eyes of the hawk and the strength of the bear today," called out another man.

"Let us celebrate the return of the one that was lost," echoed yet another.

Then they paraded him around the camp and prepared a feast for all.

Manez suddenly realized he had given his coat to the white man and he should be cold, but to his surprise, Dawn had slipped up behind him covering his wet clothes with a blanket. Grey Eyes had a place prepared for them at his side. He just nodded as they arrived and continued watching the festivities. The white man wasn't prepared for the sudden attention; though he was uneasy as his clothes dried, even he warmed to the enchanting Arikara. Since their arrival, Dawn had kept Manez at arm's length, but something changed this night. She snuggled close, clasping his arm as the fire burned brightly, not only in the center of the camp, but in his heart. The night went on forever.

The next day, he woke to the sound of chopping wood and took a peek outside of his lodge where the white man was busy chopping firewood.

"I thank you for building a fire, but I'm sure you have better things to do."

"No, I do not. I have been given to you," said the slave.

Manez looked at him curiously, then he looked up the hill towards the Chief's lodge. So he had been given a helper; the one called Walks Far. He could speak, but he chose his words carefully and only answered to specific questions.

"Walks Far is a funny name for you, I would have called you Pale One or Winter's Son."

Walks Far did not respond to Manez's attempt at conversation, but he continued to make the fire.

"Have you always been called by this name?" Manez pressed him for an answer.

"No, I was once called James Knight."

"Ja-mes, uh, Ja-mes Ni-ght is hard to say. Walks Far is a better name for you."

Once again, the white man became quiet and continued with his fire. Manez could see he was a broken man, taught to be only a slave. If the Arikara believed in Sishu, then this man called Ja-mes should be treated like he belonged to Neshanu Natchitak.

"You have been given to me as a helper and I say I will call you Ja-mes."

The bearded man paused and gave a crinkly smile from beneath the beard.

"Does that please you, Ja-mes?"

"It's been such a long time since I've heard my name spoken, it sounds strange to my ears."

Manez stood and directed the man to sit on the hides.

"In my village, it is required to tell your story before the fire for all to hear. So Ja-mes, what great story do you have?"

He looked at Manez, as a child in disbelief, then began to stir the fire as his long hidden thoughts came alive again.

"I come from a land of rain far away. So far away, past the mountains and the waters, you could not go there even if you spent your whole life traveling to it. Some of my people thought I was foolish to leave, but I was in search of a precious yellow stone. A stone called gold that was worth many hides in my village. I took two big canoes that could hold one hundred warriors called the Albany and the Discovery. Captain Berley and Captain Vaughan paddled to the north along the big lakes and just like you, the winter tried to trap us."

He stopped and pushed a small smoldering stick back into the fire.

"Berley and Vaughan took the Albany and went back and took refuge on Marble Island. I chose to continue on the Discovery and became trapped when the deep river became shallow. The cold drove my men crazy and some of them attempted to walk back across the frozen water." He looked out over the Arikara at the sky. "We never saw them again. I remember eating roots and hoping I wouldn't starve to death. All but twenty-five of my men died. We thought about eating the dead, but we couldn't because we knew their wives and children. We just waited to die." He paused, not moving the smoldering stick.

"Spring came at last, but the ice in the lake had pushed in the side of our canoe and broke holes making it impossible to go back home the way we came. I decided we would try to walk south towards the Missouri and hope that we could find more white men like us.

"The land was much bigger than I thought, rough steep hills covered with trees and thorn covered vines blocked our every step. We found it was easier walking at the bottom of the canyons, but at the same time it was better for the Crow to track us. Manez made a wave of his hand in the air then spit on the ground before he said, "Dirty, sneaky Crow."

"They hid in the bushes and attacked without warning. I was the third man back when they came, the two men in front of me fell to their arrows. I never saw what happened behind me because a large, brightly colored man clubbed me, knocking me out cold."

He pulled up his shirt and exposed the long jagged scars on his chest and stomach. "I was there a long time."

Manez examined the man's face and he could tell by reading his expressions the Crow had broken him. Ja-mes stopped for a long while staring at the gray sky with his steel blue eyes. He placed another log in the fire then began again.

"Maybe three years," he said, as if talking to himself. "It seems more like ten years now. The Crow had many small battles with Grey Eyes and one day he decided to put an end to the troublesome tribe. The Arikara nation attacked them and killed every man, woman, and child. All that were saved were the slaves from other tribes. I became the property of the chief and now your property." Manez was surprised at what he had said, but before he could respond, the man continued. "I think about my home across the sea sometimes and it picks at my heart, but I have been here so long I realize this is where it will end." Walks Far stood once again. "So with no way to find my way home, here I am, James Knight, servant to Manez, bear fighter of the Cheyenne." He finished his fire and quietly walked away.

Manez was right. Ja-mes had a Sishu. It was broken, but it was just the same as the Arikara Soul. *What of my Sishu?* he thought as he gazed across the snow covered camp. *Will Neshanu Natchitak find favor in me?* This was a great question that only time alone could answer.

Chapter 13

St. Catherine

Sieur de Chepart had a certain pep in his step as he accompanied his men along Charlain Street towards the slave pens. He tossed the bag of gold Pierre had given him several times and then snatched it from the air with a hard, quick snap. His thoughts were on the orders he had been given the night before and all the things he must do to get his land concessions started. "Sergeant, make sure the men understand that the Chaouachas are the first to go. We need them taken and the land cleared before I get there."

"Yes, sir," he said, before rushing off with several soldiers.

"Pierre says there should be some fine specimens available today," he told the rest of his company. "Walk the pens and pick out every strong body you can find." They rounded the corner to the slave sale just as the auctioneer yelled sold, then pointed to a well-dressed gentleman on the front row.

"I guess they started without me." He eyed the muscular frame of Bebai who had just been purchased from within a group of African slaves. He made his way close to the man who had bought Bebai.

"Now, that's the kind of worker we're looking for," he almost yelled as he bumped into the man.

"Excuse me, fellow, but did you just buy that fine specimen there. Oh! I'm being rude." He extended his hand. "My name is Captain Sieur de Chepart. And you might be?"

It was all a very sudden action catching the man off guard and making him flustered. "I'm Francis-Rene de Chateaubriand and this is my sister, Lucile."

"Francis, if I may call you by your first name, what possible use would you have for a man like this? You being what I perceive as the city type."

Francis was not one to be bullied and it was a sure indication Chepart was attempting to push him.

"Being an educated man at the college in Dunn and having served in the Knights of Malta, I'm not in the habit of being bludgeoned and ordered about. As a matter of fact, I'm the one used to giving the orders."

Chepart was surprised, but undaunted in his quest. "The Knights of Malta and a college man to boot! Well, Francis, what will you take for this man." He tapped the slave on the shoulder with his riding whip.

"I'm sorry, but this man is not for sale. I have a special need for a man to transport my equipment up river. You might find what you're looking for in that group he was accompanying." He pointed in the direction of the pens. "That bunch seems to be eager for something, the way they're carrying on."

Some of Bebai's subjects were standing on the cage rails yelling towards their king.

"If you don't mind me asking, what possible reason could you have for going up river?" He eyed Lucile in a lustful way. "I would think an educated man would think more of the welfare of this beautiful creature than to take her off into the wilds."

Francis stepped forward a step. "I've come to chart a passage across the northwest for king and country." Another gentleman arrived. "This is Nicolas Chamfort, my associate. He will be heading up the expedition."

Chepart extended his hand. "Nicolas Chamfort. The same man who served with La Harpe and the Parisian men. I am Sieur de Chepart, Captain of the City, at your service."

Chamfort's reputation was made during the Persian campaign and Chepart knew to give him no reason to dislike him.

"It's a pleasure to meet you, Captain, but we must be going. Our ship is heading upstream. It's imperative we excuse ourselves and proceed with our expedition. "

That's a shame, because the new governor would love to have a chance to greet you and perhaps help you with your quest."

Francis peeked over his wire-rimmed glasses at Chepart. He always enjoyed a party and one with the governor might lead to more recognition.

Chamfort chimed in once again bringing Francis back to earth. "Give our regrets to the governor, but we really must be going." He turned, almost pushing them towards the river and dragging Bebai along with them.

In an instant, Chepart was focused back on the slave sale. "That one there and I'll take those two."

Joseph Malgamont, a local plantation owner, pushed in front of him. "I'll take all those black fellows."

"No, we'll take them all," Chepart said gruffly. He was still frustrated that a man like Chamfort could get into the city without him even knowing that he was there. "I'll buy the rest." *I can't afford to do that again,* he thought and then he barked at his men. "We're late! We must be on our way, get them going; Pierre will be waiting."

Pierre's feeble attempt to go to bed was interrupted by the banshee type wailing of Sabotha. He popped up, eyes wide-awake as she cried out from an adjoining room.

"Why does she always do that? Couldn't she just once gently tap me on the shoulder and say Pierre, my boy, would you kindly wake up? No, she can't, She just has to scream bloody murder."

He was interrupted by another cry. "O shedee a wantoo bomba."

By the time the sound echoed off his wall, he was entering the next room with her.

"I'm going to..." His words were cut short by the sight of the old woman lying on the floor on her back swimming in a pool of blood. Not hers, of course, but from the body parts that looked like goat.

He stood there amazed. "Sabotha, old girl, you get wilder and wilder every day."

"The way has cleared for this new venture, but you must do it yourself with the anointed ones from the Dark Wind. Do not leave it to others to do. Go now. Take this land from savages," she said as she slid into a shivering fit before passing out.

"Oh, my God, she's really overdone it this time." He bent down and leaned way in over the blood to see if she was dead, but just as he was about to touch her, her eyes popped open. She grabbed at him causing Pierre to be repulsed from her in shock. The sudden reverse motion caused him to slide to the floor on his knees close to the blood. "Go," she cried. "Now."

Pierre was up in a flash and running for the door. "Ahh," he yelled, as he ran away.

"Make the call for the men; gather the men. We're leaving at once."

Pierre pushed the men as if the devil was hot on his tail and they arrived at the Chaouchas village before daylight.

It was a cool, early spring morning. The light was hanging between reality and the distortion your mind brings when you see things that perhaps are not real. The Indian guards at the White Apple village were in doubt at what they saw. The shadows seemed to grow and come alive along the tree line above them. The wind blew through the trees moving the shadows that clung to the last remnants of darkness. As the shapes extended into the valley, death came with the shadows. It waved slowly back and forth, like the arms of a great river, to the screams, cries of terror and the blackness until there were no more sounds at all. The Chaouchas hadn't stood a chance against the gypsy clan. Pierre hated to admit it, but he loved the fighting and the killing. He couldn't see himself not battling against someone somewhere. It heightened his senses and he knew he could never sit on his behind like an aristocrat.

Taking in a deep breath of morning air, he barked orders to his men. "Stack the dead there for burning." He pointed to an open space. "Anyone healthy enough to work put them over there and tie the old ones with the children here. Move!"

Jacques appeared suddenly. "Some of the stronger Indians escaped into the forest and some of our blacks ran away into the swamp."

"Take twenty men and you go after the Indians. Send Louis and his men into the swamp after the slaves," he ordered, almost perplexed that he had to give an order for common sense. "As soon as the old are ready, march them away. The Osage traders are waiting for them."

Jacques's group looked like ants frantically doing what they were told to do and moving in all directions.

The sun had been up for three hours when a cry from the clan announced the arrival of Chepart. Pierre sat in the shade of a large oak tree waiting for the Captain's arrival.

The conversation was cordial, but strained. "I thought we agreed that I would take care of the Indians living on our land."

Pierre pulled him close and pointed to Sabotha who was hiding beneath the shade tree.

"My witch conjured up a vision and in it she saw our venture becoming a disaster unless I came to take this village myself." All the while Pierre was talking, Chepart was eyeing the witch and in turn she was giving him an evil gaze while scraping her long finger nails up the tree trunk. With that look, any anger he had wilted away and he cowered next to Pierre. "Can she really change men into animals?" he whispered.

Pierre's answer made him turn white. "Yes"

"I think I'll get the slaves to work," he said and then he hurried away.

The whole adventure unfolding in the valley was total chaos at first, but Chepart's leadership proved to be equal to the task because after three hours the group began to make headway on St. Catherine. The line of wagons unloading supplies was a mile long. The log and mud huts were quickly converted into housing while the land was cleared for the fields. All around the valley, plumes of black smoke circled hundreds of feet into the sky.

"I see you've had a hand in this kind of work before, Chepart," Debois said, nodding him approval.

"Yes, I learned how to deal with these heathens the last time I was stationed at the fort."

Pierre changed the subject a little. "Chepart, I suspect a little trouble when tomorrow comes." He paused and rubbed stubble on his chin. " I want you to take twenty men and go on to the fort tonight, have a look around for yourself. If you suspect anything from the Indians, take care of it before we arrive."

"I will assume 'by taking care of it' you don't care how." Pierre didn't answer, but the look in his eyes was the answer Chepart wanted.

"It's done then. I'll see you when you move to the fort." The Captain exited and Debois heard him pulling out of camp.

Not far away, hiding on the crest of a rocky knoll, the Natchez braves of the River Nation watched as the foreigners demolished the land below. They were the personal guard to the Grand Soliel, son of The Great Spirit. The Soliel had dispatched them after survivors had come from the south of his kingdom telling of the great disturbance there. The scene below them played out as the shadow of darkness descended upon the valley. Their watchful eyes traced the steps of the slaves being driven to the south and the lashing on the backs of the all the strong who remained. A watchful eye was cast on cruel Captain Chepart marching to the north. They stared, taking it all in until they could only hear the screams in the dark, then they ran as fast as they could up river where the Grand Soliel waited.

During the night, Sabotha was awakened by a sudden cold shift in the spirit world. A sweat appeared on her forehead and she began to cast the bones with cries of anguish. "Domini par se hata." Her cry echoed across the camp. "Domini par satri sema." She screamed and cast the brown bits of human remains once again. All who were there couldn't help but be frightened at the screams she made. "Domini ske trada sush," she yelled at her highest screeching. Then all was quiet, but no one slept, especially Pierre. He knew something was wrong. Periodic looks up the hill told him she was brewing up something bad for someone and he hoped it wasn't him.

Morning came too quickly for the whole camp after the witch's terrifying screams in the night, but as Pierre stumbled from his lodging, he noticed all eyes in the camp focused on the ridge to the north. At the edge of the cut tree line stood a grove of sycamore trees and tied to each tree by their feet were the headless bodies of Jacques and his men.

Chapter 14
Stones of Gold

As winter began to loosen its icy grip on the upper Missouri, Manez found himself longing for the people of his tribe. He wanted to go home and even the sweet Dawn that he had come to care for couldn't keep his thoughts from drifting to Piney Creek. "The water must be pouring through Piney Creek this morning," he said to James. "The beaver and the bobcat should both be prowling on a day like this." He fumbled with the claw hanging around his neck and thought about the long winter's wait of the bear, Four Claws. Manez stretched himself to the morning sun. A terrible thought crossed his mind, *They will be preparing for the Dog Warrior ceremony soon.*

James spoke more these days. "The tribe will be going to the great pow wow. You can go then." He looked at the sky. "Maybe twenty moons from now."

"Twenty moons are too long to wait." Manez started towards the Chief's lodge. "Pack what we will need; we're going home today."

The village was stirring and he met Dawn at the fire with her father, Grey Eyes..

"Great Chief of the Arikara, the time has come for me to go. I could not have hoped for a better time than this has been. My people will celebrate many things soon and I wish not to miss these things."

The old man thought for a moment then said, "I knew you could not stay, even though others said you would stay." He cast a faint look at Dawn. "You have straightened my world, bear fighter, and restored my life to me. Take what you need and be blessed in your going. Take this pipe as a gift and think of us when you smoke it." The chief handed him the tribal ceremonial pipe.

Manez moved away pulling the beautiful girl a short way from the others. He said, "I will regret going soon, but if you will come to the pow wow with the others, I will not be sad for too long."

He hugged her with his strong arms and then she said, "Yes, Manez of the Wolf Band, fighter of bears, I will come." He hugged her harder, then he turned away ready for home. By the time he returned, James had packed everything they hoped to need for the journey. The news of them leaving traveled fast and as they wandered down the path away from the village. The Indians lined the way waving goodbye and tossing a variety of objects considered good luck at them. James paused and took a long look back at the home he had shared with the Arikara. Then, as quick as the feeling of regret had come into his mind, it was gone again with the cool, spring wind.

Manez was thinking about the trip home and charting a path back home as he walked. "We will cross the Moreau River at Thunder Butte, then we will go west to a place called Elm Springs."

James looked terrified and didn't respond to Manez's talkative attitude. He was afraid of what might come next. After so many years being a captive, he didn't feel comfortable alone, away from the tribe, but Manez was planning a surprise for his slave.

The end of the day found them at Elm Springs and that's where they camped. "I don't want to seem confused to you, but we have been going west most of the day and if I recall from your stories, your village is southwest of here," James said, after camp was made.

"Yes, it is, but I have a surprise for you tomorrow. Just wait and see." The water coming from Elm Springs this time of year was more like a fountain. It spewed blasts of water up into the air three

107

feet high. "The ice is melting very fast. Tomorrow we must hurry to get across the river." Large trees covered their campsite and a dirt embankment protruded overhead to hide their fire.

"I think it will be safe to light a fire," James told Manez. The wood was gathered and soon a good fire warmed their bones. Some of the buffalo jerky was produced and the two unlikely companions chewed at it slowly. The stars were bright and after a long time of silence Manez spoke. "It would be a waste not to tell a good story at this fire. You spoke of your home Ja-mes; tell me more."

"My home is a distant memory, as hazy as the winter's sky. I had planned to go back; several times, when trouble came to me, I made promises to mend things I had done wrong. I think all men do that when they want Neshanu Natchitak (God) to listen."

Manez grunted and shook his head. James continued, "To the east are villages as large as the whole Arikara nation; the paths are wide and are covered in stone so it is easy to walk all the time. Each path is lighted at night by an oil flame. Water runs inside every lodge and all the windows are covered in glass, not buffalo skin." Manez threw him a funny look. "Glass is like hard, clear water. You can see through it, but nothing can come into your lodge."

"Glass sounds strange. I wish to see this glass someday," the boy replied.

"Perhaps you will, Manez, perhaps you will."

Nothing more was said. They stared at the stars for a long time before going to sleep.

James Knight dreamed about his feather bed, so soft and comfortable, waiting at his home in upstate New York. He dreamed about all the faces of the men he buried along the way he had traveled, then he slept hard with a comfort he hadn't felt in a long time. No nightmares like nights before. Tonight, all the dead rested and no matter what would happen, he knew he was finally at peace with himself, a forgiven man. "Thank you Neshanu Natchiak," he whispered to the twinkling stars.

Manez was waiting when the peaceful dreamer finally open his eyes. "We must be careful and very quick as we pass through Apache lands. It won't take long for the Shamans to feel our presence here. Follow me and do as I say." Manez didn't wait for a reply, he ran off to the west around the springs with James right behind him. Up the wide valley they ran towards a rock cliff. They were almost sprinting, and then suddenly Manez slowed down as the valley began to narrow. The shapes of burial poles rose in the distance while an eerie calm perforated the morning air. Quietly, Manez spoke. "Don't touch anything; stay on the path." James nodded in response. They continued to the cliffs now looming above them. James became light-headed, almost toppling over onto a burial site, but at the last moment he regained his balance. He had forgotten to breathe in his excitement. The flat wall of the rock suddenly had an opening in it and the two ducked into the crack, but Manez began to move quickly again. Through the narrow cut they ran. The sun was behind them throwing bolts of light on the rock walls before them. It was all a flickering treat for the eyes as they both looked up at it. Then suddenly they were blinded by sharp rays of golden beams bouncing down from the walls above. Manez suddenly stopped and fell to his knees. Picking at the stones at the base of the crag he said. "Are these the stones of gold you seek?" James moved close enough to pick up a rock that had fallen from above them and hold it in the sun's blistering rays. Shards of glistening gold shot out making funny shapes on the walls around them. "Yes, Manez, these are the stones of gold."

Manez produced a hide pack and the two of them began to fill it. With his eyes bigger than his strength, James dug at the stones. Finally, Manez said, "Enough. We must be able to carry it."

James shook the bag, dumped some of the gold out and then checked it again to see if it was light enough. "It's good," James said.

"Time is running out we must go." Manez led the way back through the narrow crack until it opened once again to the burial grounds. It had only been minutes since they had passed that way but an eerie change had settled in among the Apache dead. The air was still and very thick. Some dust had caught in the air, suspended indefinitely until they had passed several feet away. Manez slowed to a walk, carefully maneuvering each step close to the ones they had made earlier, hoping to not disturb the dead anymore than they had already. The wind suddenly whipped around them causing a tattered spear to fall from its high perch of the dead above them. The two thieves stopped, frozen, as if waiting for the ground to open up and drop them to their deaths. It became calm once more and they stood there waiting, but for what, Manez wasn't sure until the wind whipped up once more.

"Mestaa'e asesta'xestse!" (Boogeyman! Run!) he screamed and without hesitation the two bolted forward. Something moved behind them, perhaps a wisp of dust or the shadows distorted by their fear James thought, until it took form and began to follow them fast. A fanged black mist whirled about, collecting bits of rock, dirt and leaves, then eeking out pained noises as it came for them. They fled back through the sacred places and along the jagged cliffs away from the growling ghost until James could feel the creature's hot breath on his neck. It was the Apache's Unske, protector of the dead places. To James, it was the rotting corpse of a Crow brave running him down.

110

"Don't let it catch you, don't let it touch you!" the boy cried out as they sped toward the opening to the valley below. *How could I have been so stupid to not know the Shaman would have put the Unske in this place?* Manez thought as he ran for his life. "Don't let it touch you, Ja-mes. He can steal your heart," he called out, but the sound of the slave stumbling behind him told Manez that James was falling. A large rock had tumbled in his path, tripping him and causing him to fall into Manez's heels. The force of the hit made them both roll to the ground, just past the rocky cliffs. Manez clung to his medicine bundle chanting, "Ka den ra mori, Natchitak Neshanu Natchitak. (Don't let him take us God, Neshanu God)

The Unske swooned back and forth at the entrance of the burial grounds taking great cuts in the air with its clawed hands. The spirit cried out at them seeming unable to come any closer. The Unske made one final howl, then it turned back into just a dusty shadow and spiraled back to the dead.

Manez quickly helped James up. "They know we are here. We must go and go fast."

They ran back past Elm Springs and across to the rock edges of Thunder Butte, then they turned southeast. Manez hoped to reach the safety of the Missouri River basin and he hoped it was far enough away that the Apaches wouldn't follow them. The day was long and by late that evening their bodies were so numb, Manez led James into a hole caused by the uprooting of a great oak tree. "Naese-kahaneotse," (I'm tired) Manez painfully cried out. They collapsed under the tree to nurse their separate fears and waited for the next surprise that was sure to come their way. The sound of a distant drum kept Manez's ear turned to the wind. It grew louder and surrounded them.

Chapter 15

Grand Soliel
(The Sun God)

Unseen, Chogah (Large Rabbit) had watched Jacques with his men run out of the village in pursuit of the runaway Chaoucha Indians. The killing of the defenseless tribe didn't set well with him. The Natchez rule of only killing in self-defense had prevented him from deliberately destroying the intruders. The memory of what he had seen tormented him and he knew what had to be done.

"Hatugha, run to the temple and report what you have seen in the village and only what you have seen there, nothing else," Chogah said. As Hatugha ran away, Chogah said to Gidi (The Cat), "Choose for us a path that will not be safe." The thin Indian smiled knowing the path would lead them to the intruders and danger. He slipped into the woods and the group followed.

Jacques and his men were city dwellers and if a mouse could be found in a darkened alley in Paris, they were the men to do the job, but this place was foreign to them; crickets chirping, flying spider webs wrapping around their heads and the hollow sound of someone knocking high up in the trees. A lost soul feeling began to overwhelm some of them after they had traveled deep into the woods. *DeBois would never know how far they chased the Chaouchas*, they thought, *and none of them would ever tell*. Slowing to a walk, one of Jacques's men spoke. "This place is creepy. We are all thinking the same thing. Let's just tell Pierre we couldn't find them and turn back."

Jacques stopped suddenly; something strange was planted in the middle of the path. It was a tall pole. On the bottom of the pillar, a great horned beast with four hooves frowned at him. Above the buffalo was a bear, strong fierce and menacing. A great Indian chief was carved above the bear. He was wearing a full-feathered headdress and his eyes were painted green. A large sun sat above the chief's head and two hands entwined with snakes were above that. Twenty feet in the air at the top of the pole was an eagle, its wings throwing strange shadows on the men below. Jacques stood frozen staring at the strange sight, wondering what sort of sign it was. He started past the pole only to have a sickly feeling turn his stomach, so he stopped. "Let's make camp here close to this stream before it's too dark. Simon, gather some wood for a fire." The others were happy to stop because a sense of dread filled their hearts as well. The fire was a great fire. It was soon sending rolls of smoke and piercing rays of light into the canopy of trees surrounding the stream. The day of killing had made the group tired and even though they were frightened, the warmth from the fire pushed them into slumber. Even the watchman could not keep his eyes open and slowly succumbed to sleep.

Chogah and his braves had cut to the same path just a few yards from where the men were sleeping. Darkness consumed every thing except the places the flickering fire exposed. Gidi and those who followed ran into the smoke-filled path of the Frenchmen, surprising the guard and causing him to pull his pistol. He fired wildly into the air. Hatchets and knifes flashed and the Cat tossed his into the chest of the guard. One of Jacques's men rolled to his feet brandishing his cutlass. Chogah rolled headlong on the ground under the Frenchman's first thrust and jammed the knife up under his ribs into his heart. Jacques and another Frenchmen turned to run, but a hatchet in the back of one's head killed him and Gidi cut into the legs of the other causing him to fall. Jacques rolled to the ground begging for his life, but Chogah took the sword from him and cut his head off. The Natchez screamed chants of victory that filled every crack and cranny of the forest. The victory was swift; all of the intruders were dead.

A smirk appeared on Chogah's face. "Take the bodies. We will hang them from the trees of our enemies. These foreigners will know fear after this night. Scalp and behead the intruders." The heads were then placed at the base of the totem pole as a warning while the headless bodies were hurried away. Night was ending and they had a lot to do before going home.

A large grove of sycamore tress stood guard on the ridge above the St. Catherine plantation. It was a fitting place to hang Jacques and his men as a warning to these invaders. "When the sun comes, fear will fill the hearts of the white men. This is our revenge for the Chaouchas. The Grand Soliel will not see them come any closer," Chogah said. "Let's be gone before the light comes."

The Natchez evaporated into the trees on a dead run. Much was to be done and the Rabbit knew in his heart this was only the beginning.

As the flickering beams of morning broke through the shining, maple trees, Hatugha had run to the stone road that cut into the center of the city. His heart swelled with pride as the daylight bounced off of the rock houses and stone gardens, all of which encircled the great stone mounds. He paused as he entered the River Nation where two giant totem poles stood sentinel close to the entrance of the Grand Village of the Sun God. He bowed down upon one knee and rubbed the carving of the great eye in the stone highway. The carving was a scalloped circle bordered by two snakes. The top one a white snake for goodness and the bottom a black snake for evil. An open hand with an eye in its palm was in the center. "Oh, great eye, look not with misfortune upon the bearer of evil news, but see me only as a messenger today," he said, then he hurried into the plaza. There were three stone mounds surrounding the plaza. The Grand Soliel's mound was on the north side of the plaza and on the opposite side was the Temple mound where the Great Spirit had come to teach the Grand Soliel how the people should live. He granted the Soliel the status of a living god before ascending back into the heavens. The White mound stood halfway between the other two on the outer circle and the White Woman, his mother and advisor, lived in the house at the top.

The White Woman had sensed the disturbance in the south and she had prepared the way for the Grand Soliel to greet Hatugha. The Spirit Men were called to make sure no laws of God were to be broken. The Table Sacrificers were in place at the alter just in case blood needed to be shed. Mumblers came to interpret language heard, but not known. The Pipe Carriers, who were entrusted with the war pipe, peace pipe, and the pipe of prayer, were also present. All honored people were gathered, watching for the Hawk to appear.

Hatugha raced to the top of the mound and then came to a halt to bow down before the Grand Soliel. The White Woman asked. "I feel a disturbance in the south. What news does the Hawk have for the Soliel?"

Hatugha gasped and gulped down chunks of air. "Forgive the lowly warrior who brings bad news before the Grand Soliel. Chogah has sent me on an all night run to tell you the Chaouchas are no more. The Osage brought an evil presence to the valley below the rocky cliffs; dark skins, Indians and the whites. All that weren't killed were taken away by the Osages."

The mumblers slumped to the ground and began to interpret the voices only they could hear. "Our world is broken; only the Soliel can fix it," cried a mumbler. The Spirit Men threw flaming dust into the fire causing it to burn bright blue and the Sacrificers brought forth a young girl, ready to place her on the table. It was pandemonium atop the mound, loud enough to cause a large crowd of the Natchez to gather below.

The White Woman, who had been whispering in the Soliel's ear, suddenly screamed and waved her hands. "Nehetaae" (That's enough). Then the Soliel stood before the people.

"Aahtovestse." (Listen to me) he said, then paused.

"Weep for the Chaoucha's. They were a proud people. Burn herbs, smoke the pipe and pray that the spirits that went before them takes them in. We have long been at peace with the French, but there will be no rest for the ones who have done this thing. We are a blessed people, but we can't live with these killers so close. Send runners to the Emerald Mound; call out their warriors. Take the news to the Crystal Mound and tell them to send us their bravest for battle. We will meet this evil before it comes to us in our sleep." The drums began to pound the morning air as runners went west and north to gather the Natchez fighters. The commotion atop the mound began again. The Mumblers cried in a strange tongue never before heard. "Tommi ne nac, tommi ne ta toie." (Sabotha's language) They fell down in fits crying on the ground.

The Spirit Men rushed to their side.

"What are they saying? What's wrong with them? Someone answer me now," the Grand Soliel said.

"A powerful force disturbs the spirit world and it is not of the Great Spirit. It is the black magic controlled by center earth," the Shaman replied.

The mumblers continued their writhing on the ground as all eyes watched.

"Emao mae (It's red blood), emao mae is all they can say. They are terrified of things to come from this black magic controlled by the whites."

The Soliel could see that the actions of the Shaman and the Mumblers were upsetting everyone, so he stood, arms extended above the Natchez. All that were present became quiet and bowed to one knee.

"The Great Spirit has taught me the way of our people. Because of this we have lived many moons beyond the blackness found in center earth. A blackness that has no power over our Great Spirit. We will not cringe in fear, but we will pray and smoke the prayer pipe."

He lowered his arms and the chanting to the drums started as the pipes were brought forth. A loud revelry summoned the day back to life and the drums played on.

Off to the side, away from the others, the Soliel called for Moeha. "Go meet Chogah and tell him to shadow the ones to the south. See what he can of their Black Magic and perhaps we can use it against them." The Soliel retreated to a private place where he fell on his knees in prayer to the Great Spirit.

The Rabbit hadn't gone far to the south before Moeha (Badger) met him on the path. Moeha was a short, stout man who had received his name when he was young because he went down the holes after the coyotes.

"Greetings, Chogah my friend."

"Moeha, what news do you bring from the Grand Village?" the Rabbit asked.

"There will be battle and soon. The warriors gather from the Grand Village, the Emerald Mound, and the Crystal Mound as we speak," replied Moeha "I see fresh scalps hanging from your belt and from the count, you must have dealt a blow to the Vehoe. (White men)

"It was a short battle close to the totem poles. We cut off the heads and hung the bodies in the trees above the Chaouchas village. What makes you meet us, my friend?" asked Chogah.

"There is Black Magic in the Vehoe camp and the Soliel wants you to find where it's coming from. It might be useful to use against them."

Chogah remembered the strange cries that had come from the Chaoucha village and he also recalled the outline of someone hiding in the shadows. This was surely the one with the black magic.

"The Vehoe have found the bodies of their men by now. They will have put extra guards in place, so we must be careful on our return there." He pointed at Vekeso (Bird) to lead the way back to the south. "Be careful," he said as they all followed.

It was hard for even Pierre to gaze upon the cold, stiff bodies dangling from the trees and his men were reluctant to cut them down for fear of disease. "Cut them down, now! All of them."

Thomas Arnold appeared along with an Osage scout and five other men carrying several hide packs. "Pierre, I think you should see this." DeBois looked inside the packs and winced a little before exploding.

"Where did you find them?"

118

"Deep in the woods, piled against a carved pole," said Thomas.

The Osage began to speak. "Onestanotse Metseha."

"Open the bag and give me the head," Thomas translated.

"Vehoohtotse meonanevehoe Enohtsenotoho."

"Look at this head. The road builders did this after they stalked them," translated Thomas.

"E-nanouoho Chogah Natchez e-momataehe Eehoho."

I know this warrior Chogah of the Natchez. He is very mean and angry. I am afraid of him. You should be afraid too."

Pierre had seen enough and he proceeded to push the Osage aside. He turned as if he were yelling at the trees deep in the forest.

"I'll show you what being afraid is, Chogah of the Natchez. Double the guard tonight and send for the rest of my men, now."

DeBois's voice echoed along the ridge and deep into the forest where Chogah was hiding. He didn't understand the words, but he heard his name as clear as day. He had his men take positions on a cliff overlooking the intruders and the path to the next valley where the Natchez burial grounds were. In silence they watched and waited for what they knew would eventually come. The Chaoucha valley was a long, narrow, fertile strip of land holding layers of black, rich soil and they could see the earth being turned for crops. The Natchez had long been familiar with growing corn. That's why they knew the whites would come to the Natchez valley. It was three times the size of Chaoucha land and they would try to possess it.

Pierre hurried away to where Sabotha had taken refuge in a hut from the bright sun.

"You told me not to worry; you said go ahead, take the land, the bones will it. Now I've got this Chogah native running around in the woods chopping off the heads of my men. If the bones 'will it', then perhaps you should get some new bones because your old ones aren't working very well." She had her back to him and throughout his ranting she hadn't moved or said a word. He moved close to her and leaned around so he could see her face. She didn't move, but her eyes were wide open. She was frozen. He turned her around, but she stayed stiff, staring straight ahead.

"Now, this really does it, Sabotha. I'm finally right about something and you freeze up on me. Come on, snap out of it!" He slapped her cheek gingerly, but she stayed locked in a trance.

He became aware that Thomas had stepped in behind him and after a quick look at the old hag he asked, "What's wrong with her?"

"I'm not sure...the way things are going around here this morning," he said giving Sabotha a puzzled look.

"Thomas, I want to deal with this Chogah character very swiftly. I think it's the right thing to do." He looked at Sabotha for a sign, but not a muscle twitched.

"Bring up the full garrison from New Orleans. With our overpowering numbers, we should end this Natchez thing quickly, don't you think?" His eyes flashed another look at the witch; she was still locked up.

Thomas was always ready for a fight. "Yes, sir! Their bows and hatchets shouldn't be any match for our rifles."

"Well, then it's settled. Bring up the men, We will march to Fort Rosalie as soon as they get here." Pierre shook her violently. "We're going to fight the Natchez. Is that a problem?" She didn't say a word. "Ok, then, we're finished here." Thomas exited the hut. Before Pierre followed, he reluctantly extended his pointing finger and softly touched the large, black wart on her nose.

Chapter 16

Des Natanapalle
(The City of Slaves)

The hot air hung thick around Louis's dry mouth. It was his first look at a swamp and he hoped it would be his only look at it.

"Ben, cut those marks deep in the trees. We want to find our way home," Louis called to the back of the group that had been snaking their way along. A few hours out of DeBois's sight and Louis was beginning to feel his loyalty waver a little. He was wet up to his knees and mosquitoes gnawed at every exposed piece of skin in sight. His thoughts were interrupted by a large splash and the sight of one of his men being pulled down by an alligator.

"Kill it, kill it!" he screamed, as muskets belched balls of fire at the water. Then all fell silent and calm as if nothing had happened. The water suddenly swirled causing chaos among the men and all of them headed for an island fifty yards away. "Head for high ground," called Louis.

The waters opened wide, and again another man was pulled down and with musket blasts, all the men raced for dry ground in panic.

With everyone on shore, Louis took stock of who had gone down.

"Who's missing?" he asked.

"Nathan and Ben are gone," replied Areo.

"Does anyone see the marks on the trees that Ben was leaving?"

All the men craned their necks looking for the marks, but in the confusion they weren't even sure which way to look.

"I think it was that way, but I can't be sure. We ran farther than I thought," Areo said.

"Would it be too much to ask for a volunteer to go back and look for the marks on the trees?" Louis knew the answer to his question before he even asked it. All the men's eyes turned away pretending they didn't hear him and Louis cursed them.

"Cowards are we? A little lizard in the water and we become cowards. All of you stop shaking in your boots and build a fire. Tomorrow better bring new courage to you or we will never find our way out of this miserable place."

He was met with muffled enthusiasm from the group as they prepared a place and began to build a fire. It was hard to tell what time of day it was. The thick trees were clogged with vines that blocked most of the suns rays, but it had to be getting late because what little light they had was fading quickly. The coming darkness was a bad thing for all of them. The swamp was even more terrifying as the darkness settled in. In the distance some kind of cat cried out. A strange bird thumped against a tree and the mosquitoes never stopped their assault on them. Hours passed and at the brink of exhaustion, the group finally began to relax, huddled in groups around the fire. Areo had gotten so warm next to Louis he unconsciously pushed back away from the fire during the night. He wiggled close to the water's edge, sound asleep.

"Areo, I can take the buzzing of the mosquitoes, but I won't listen to your loud breathing," whispered Louis.

"I swear it's not me, Louis, it's…..." Areo turned to see who was sleeping next to him just as the giant jagged-toothed jaws collapsed, crushing his head.

"Alligator!" cried Louis and the small island exploded with activity. The gypsies ran screaming in every direction, one by one disappearing into the dark, dangerous swamp.

Only John and Seth remained with Louis and they ran until they were exhausted. They stopped and leaned against a tree. The swamp quieted until only bugs were heard once more. Somewhere in the distance there was the scream of pain, a call for help, then silence reigned once more.

"We mustn't flee in fear; our only hope is to use our brains to get out of here. Settle down, find high ground, then wait for the light of day. Here, come this way. I can see higher ground," Louis said. They splashed along another forty minutes until Louis pulled himself up a small outcropping covered with trees. They slid in among the closely grown tree trunks for protection. No sleep could conquer their fear, so they listened to the bugs and stared at the terrifying blackness all around them.

Back at Terre Blanca, Pierre was pacing back and forth in front of the hut where Sabotha had taken up residence. He was worried about the whole affair. Terre Blanca and St. Catherine should be the crown jewel in what, so far, had been a dismal business enterprise. New Orleans was overrun with prostitutes, bars and drugs before he arrived and even though he taxed them heavily, the money was slow in coming. News had come to him that it seemed the city had begun to grow a moral consciousness under the disguise of becoming a modern city and without his presence, the local clergy had been using the pulpit to denounce the new governor. He needed to see results in the form of cash now.

"All dead," Sabotha said on one of his passes.

He seemed to not hear her and continued his march.

"All of the slave chasers are gone," she repeated to him.

Pierre paused and an absent minded look appeared upon his face.

"What did you say?" he said trying to figure out if she was talking to him.

"Louis and what few men he has alive are lost in the swamp."

"Lost in the swamp?" he repeated angrily.

"You told me go ahead, take the land, kill all the poor, helpless Indians. The bones don't lie, do they? Louis is lost; Jacques has his head cut off and you've been in a coma unable to talk for two days," he finished, almost yelling at her.

"There is a power in this place," she said as she tossed the bones in the turtle shell. "Ah dita fom ekta," she started saying. Then, with her eyes bulging, she cried, "White Magic... stop it, stop it!" Then with a shiver, she passed out with her eyes rolled back into her skull once more.

"Sabotha, wake up! I have to know if I should battle tomorrow." He shook her violently, but there was no response from her, only an occasional shiver.

Pierre could hear the garrison from New Orleans in the distance and the face of Chepart suddenly appeared in the doorway.

Pierre turned the witch away from him and continued to talk as if she was listening.

"OK, then I'll do that." He patted her on the back as he took Chepart outside.

"Sabotha says we should move out as soon as it is light. Give the men a rest until dawn, then we will march.

"Yes, sir," Chepart said as he saluted, then retreated.

Lord, he loves to play soldier, thought DeBois.

Louis thought he was dreaming when he saw a light moving quickly through the trees. It flickered as it passed between the many swamp trees, but it moved steadily towards him. He rubbed his eyes, but it was still there only to disappear for a few seconds, then reappear even closer to them. He thought about calling out, but the chilling image of Jacques with his head cut off strangled any words before they could be formed. The light passed close to them and it seemed that it would disappear, but another man with a torch met it on a strip of high ground very close to them.

" Eeva-nanovahtseo'o," the torch bearer called out on the arrival of the brave.

" E-a'xaoto," he said, as they shook hands.

A sudden yell echoed through the swamp. "Exanenestse!" (Get ready!) As the cry reverberated through the trees, another torch was lit. A few yards away, another was lit, then another. Over and over the torches took flame until a thousand flames turned the night into day. The light exposed a rickety city perched on an island in the woods. It was a rough-looking place made of old tin, broken boards and rope, but it was a city just the same. It was Des Natanapalle, the city of slaves. Things were stolen, men were murdered and all the evidence just disappeared into the swamp. Another call rang out into the swamp.

"Estaxestse!" (Come quickly!) and the city came alive with slaves and Indians. They crowded into the walkways until every path was filled. A hush settled over the mass of people at the appearance of a muscular black man.

They called out to him. "Samba, Samba, Samba," they chanted until he held up his hands.

"Freed slaves and red brothers, the French garrison has left the city and our spies say it is defenseless. They have gone to fight the

Natchez, who this very day have declared war on the French. You know the terror the French have brought us; we see them in our dreams. They try to turn us against each other; they put the bounty hunters on us. We hide here in secret at Des Natanapalle hoping things will change, but that change never comes. We must make the world change; we must put injustice on the plates of our oppressors. It's time the people of Des Natanapalle stop hiding and return the fight to the French. I, Samba, chieftain of the Bambara, say we join our brothers the Natchez and fight them."

The town erupted in wild jubilation. Anyone who could fight gathered weapons and torches and forming a lighted snake two miles long moved out into the swamp.

"This is our chance," Louis said, as he slipped out from behind the tree trunks.

"We will follow them out, then find our way back to the city," he whispered.

John and Seth reluctantly followed him down the small hill to the trail. It was easy to follow the torches and within the hour the three gypsies found hard ground and slipped away from the swamp into the woods towards New Orleans.

Chogah watched the Vehoe from above on the ridge and from all the activity below, he guessed they intended to march north to Fort Rosalie.

"Moeha," he quietly called. His friend appeared among the rocks.

"How do your feet feel; do they beg you for a little run?"

He laughed. "Even if they didn't, you would send me anyway, Chogah."

"Go to the Soliel and tell him the Vehoe will march to Rosalie at daylight. We will pester them along the way to slow them down, but the Natchez must beat them there."

Moeha cupped his fist into his friend's.

"Don't worry. I will hurry even if my feet are a little unhappy about the distance."

With that he ducked into the brush and was gone.

Chogah motioned for his men to follow him.

High atop the Temple Mound, White Woman had been locked in mental battle with the Black Magic of Sabotha for two days. Her cries echoed out over the Soliel's kingdom. Upon the arrival of all the warriors, she made her appearance at the side of her son.

The nation, two thousand strong, stood before the Soliel. He pointed at his mother.

"The White Woman has fought the darkness and produced a spell over its power. It can't see us anymore. Aeeeeeeee." The Natchez cheered with him. "It's time for us to drive the French back into the sea. Our spies tell us even Samba and the Des Natanapalle are preparing to attack the city to the south. It is our time. Let the drums call out to our brothers; tell them the Natchez fight the Vehoe today." With a wave of his arm, the Grand Village emptied towards the South.

As quietly as the breeze pushes through the leaves on a cloudless summer day, the Natchez moved into the forest. It wasn't far south to Fort Rosalie. The Soliel wondered himself why he had ever let the French build a fort so close. Perhaps he thought at the time they were as honorable as the red man, but the years had proved him wrong. At one time he had hoped knowing them would help his people survive, but the lasting thirst of the French for more of everything pushed the two people far apart. He had given them the tall bluff and surrounding flat land near Bent Springs next to the Wide River (Mississippi River). Tall pines grew in abundance and the springs provided plenty of water for the French. The land had been cleared around the fort. Several farms had sprung up, relying on the fort for comfort and safety.

The West and North walls of the fort had been constructed by burying ends of logs at an angle towards the outside and the other ends had been sharpened. All the Osage camped in the shadows of the West wall. The South wall was the exterior of the stable, barracks and officer quarters. A large warehouse containing trade goods dominated the complete East side of the fort. The warehouse was the Natchez's goal. If they could reach it, they would split the Osage from the French and be fighting them down the bluff.

The Soliel didn't wish for battle, but the line must be drawn. All the signs indicated that the French intended to attack them next and here at Rosalie it would stop. He felt it in his heart that nothing would ever be the same.

It was a fog-covered morning caused by the temperature of the water clashing with the warmer air. The smell of cedar smoke filtered out over the Natchez who had walked unseen within sixty yards of the fort's bridge and gates.

A well fortified fort stood just beyond the fog. The scouts reported that Chepart and his army had marched all night and upon arriving at the fort, he had captured four Natchez braves hiding near the fort. On advisement from the Osage, he tortured them, hoping to get the Soliel's plans, then left them tied to poles just beyond the wall. Occasionally a guard peered out over the wall at the four Indians in front of the fort.

"Good morning, La Fleur," Gaspard called to the watchman.

"I don't know why anyone would consider this cold fog good. Damn Indians whined all night. It gives me the creeps I tell you; I can't see anything. Well, I've got my morning orders. 'Go out and check the prisoners', so I have to go out whether I can see anything or not."

Down the hill near one of the farms, a dog began barking; the sound echoed off the rocky knoll. La Fleur turned and strained his eyes out into the cloudy mist once more, but there was nothing he could see. "Sounds close to Fertin's Farm." He rubbed his eyes making them water. "Damn fog," he mumbled. "Open the gates," he called to Jean Delon.

The gates slowly began to open. The four giant hinges moaned as if the weight of the world swung on them. At the height of the noise, the unseen dog's barking stopped with a sudden yelp. With every inch of the gates movement, the Natchez began to overpower the farms below the fort. First was Francis Fertin, caught coming from the outhouse; they cut his throat, then shot an arrow into his brother-in-law's neck. His two children were hacked to death in their beds. Next was the Tilly Place, where five family members including his two children were killed at the breakfast table. On it went; farm to farm. Grimault La Plaine and all he loved. Guerin was killed along with his wife and two children. Des Charante and his four children were shot with arrows while going to the river fishing.

It wasn't uncommon to see Natchez Indians close to the fort, but from where Antone Jouard sat in his tree stand, there were unusual numbers of Indians moving about in the woods. He slowly slipped down from hiding and started working his way towards the fort. Jouard had seen Fertin go down and then he stumbled upon the body of one of Charantes's children on the path; the child's liver had

129

been cut out. He met a woman named La Miette, covered in blood, running down the path towards him. Two Indians were chasing her. As she passed, he pushed her to the ground and with the same motion, he pulled his pistol from his belt. The first Nathez brave looked shocked when the bullet entered his forehead. He fell to his knees, letting his hatchet slowly slip to the ground. The other brave charged Jouard. With his rifle ready, "Ka boom," he blew a hole through the chest of the Natchez.

"Close the gates," La Fleur screamed, but the battle cry of the Natchez drowned out his orders. A thousand braves charged from the fog into the fort. The battle tested French scrambled into action, but the Indians hacked and cut them down, one by one, as they came from the barracks. They finally bolted the doors and began to shoot from the slots in the windows. Across the courtyard, Chepart had been admiring a map of Terre Blance when the battle began. When he opened the door, he met the knife of Hatugha. It ripped through him, from his stomach to his heart. The bloodstained map and his lifeless body fell to floor. La Sonde, the surgeon, died trying to drag Pierre Le Blanc to safety.

Everyone who was still alive ran to the warehouse and barricaded the door. The men in the barracks could see the onslaught upon the warehouse and in a futile effort rushed from the barracks with muskets blasting, only to meet the sharp pointed weapons of the Natchez.

Five, ten, then fifteen solders went down before they reached the doors. They stood in the gap, firing away until the last man perished. The doors were beaten down and blood splattered the walls as the French women with their children were killed where they stood.

As suddenly as it began, all was quiet. There was no cheering, no glee in what they had done. It was a ruthless way to defend themselves, but it was the only way the French would understand. The weapons were taken and the Indians faded into the woods, like the mist fading into the morning sun.

Antone Jouard had battled his way to the water's edge with La Miette and just as the Indians had used the fog, they stayed shrouded by the tall reeds until they no longer heard fighting. It was almost noon when Jouard decided to return to the fort. All along the way, the bodies of his friends lay thrown down. What he found inside the fort was worse. The blood of one hundred and fifty men, thirty-six women, and fifty-six children stained the ground.

La Miette's screams of anguish echoed off the walls of the rocky knoll when she found her daughter. Far away, deep in the woods, the Natchez paused; her cries stopped them from their retreat. Hatugha looked back towards the sound waiting for the command to go finish them, but the Soliel, realizing it was the sound of a woman's deep grief, shook his head no. He moved on to find the black witch.

Chapter 17
The Giving of the Shield

Walks Far found rest after his big scare, but Manez could only listen to the drums and watch for the Apaches that were sure to come for them. So many conversations were going on he sometimes didn't understand exactly what the pounding was saying, but one thing he did know for sure was that a great disturbance was taking place among Mother Earth. Far away to the south, the Natchez were going to battle with what the Mandan drums called 'the darkness'. Manez looked around, scanning the tree line once more. The cool night air slowly soothed his racing mind and allowed him to settle down. *I should have been home by now,* he thought. That crazy bear chasing me and the beautiful Dawn have all been exciting adventures, but I am worried about my people. I must release Ja- mes and send him home. The sound of a limb breaking fired his mind into action. He rolled towards where the noise had come from. Walks Far also heard the noise and scrambled to his side peering into the morning twilight. Manez motioned at his eyes then pointed towards a large broken down cottonwood tree. Four silhouettes could be seen creeping along. "Apache?" James whispered, but Manez shook his head no. "No Apache would make a noise." The two hid and watched the figures settle in beneath the old tree.

The shadows talked softly, but it was only strange words to both of them. Ja-mes listened more intently and a sudden fog lifted from his mind. "English," he whispered. "It's English they're speaking. It's the Vehoe." Manez listened to the strange tongue.

A strong voice was speaking softy. " I don't know why they stopped chasing us. It could have something to do with the drums

132

pounding all around. Check your powder and reload every gun that's empty. You there, Francis, stop whining about the savages getting your sister and help reload." A man poked his head up from the tall grass and he looked straight at James. Walks Far tried to duck, but Manez held him still until the man stopped looking. Then James ducked down, giving Manez a frown.

"In this light and time of morning, only movement can be seen, not shapes in the shadows." The young Indian looked at the sky. "It will be light in one hour. We must not be close to the fire sticks when daylight comes." The boy gathered his things to go, but James held his arm and listened to the old, new words.

"Captain Chamfort, I know to some extent I can be useless, but I dearly loved my sister Lucile and the thought of leaving her behind with those Apaches, well, I would rather die trying to save her," a small light voice said.

"I'm sorry, Francis, to sound so insensitive about your sister, but the best way to help her now is to regroup and get reinforcements. Fort Rosalie is close by, remember. We passed it by on our way upstream. The Captain we met at the slave sale, Chepart, has his men stationed there." Chamfort poked his head up once more and took a quick look. "I wish the slave hadn't run away. Did you see him fight?" he asked. "When the Apache charged, he grabbed my sword from its sheath and his first blow was so powerful he cut through the first man into the next, killing them both. The blade broke, but he deflected the hatchet of the next brave, then stuck the stub of the blade in his eye, killing the fighter. I just knew he would perish, but he picked up a tree limb that had a spike protruding from the end and began to battle his way towards your sister. The spike went into the back of one brave, then another one's head was crushed. He wielded the club as if it were a great weapon, killing a dozen Apache. When they dragged Lucile into the woods, I lost sight of both of them. What was the slave's name?

Chamfort looked at Francis. "Bebai Fulani," he replied.

"Yes, Bebai. We probably owe our lives to the slave. The Indians were so intent on killing him, they let us slip away." He took another look, but this time he stayed below the tall grass blades and looked through the stems waving in the breeze.

With out a word, he raised his rifle, poking the barrel between the blades, and fired.

"Boom."

The ball whizzed past James' head. "Noxae Enanotse Vehoomestse!" In his mind, he had said what he intended, but his mouth cried out in Arikara.

Another puff of smoke and a steel ball wedged in the tree next to him.

Confused, he tried once more. "Wa-it! Put...put it d-down. Look at me." Then he stood up. Manez tried to pull him down knowing a sudden fiery blast would make him bleed, but Walks Far kept his balance.

"Wait! Put it d-down. Loo-k at me!" he repeated, much bolder this time.

The blast Manez expected didn't come. Instead, the small group of men stood and stared at the thin, blonde white man, much like Manez had done the first time he had seen him.

"My god! It's a white man dressed like an Indian!" the startled Chamfort declared.

Realizing they weren't going to shoot anymore, James cried out.

"I'm James Knight! James Knight. I'm English."

"Good god, man, I almost shot you! What on earth are you doing dressed like that?" Chamfort called out to James, as he came closer to the thin man.

"Goodness gracious, James, it is you!" He extended his hand and expected to be acknowledged. Instead, James had a look of uncertainty on his face.

"I'm Captain Chamfort. You remember, sir, Queen's brigade...we fought the Dutch."

James didn't have any idea who this fellow was, but he acknowledged him.

"Oh, yes, Cap-tain. I do re-mem-ber. Sorry, my English, long time no speak." He desperately tried to think about the words.

"Are you out here alone? the captain asked looking around.

"No, this is Manez," he said, pointing to the place where he had last seen the young Indian, but he was gone. Several hundred yards away, Manez stood in the shadow of a pine tree and with the sun coming up at his back, he could not be seen. James stared into the bright morning light, covering his eyes with his hand. He couldn't see the boy who had given his life back to him, but he knew he was watching and with a closed fist, James touched his chest above his heart. In the blink of an eye, Manez vanished over the hill.

The forest laughed at the morning. Small animals darted about in front of the young Indian as he soaked in the almost forgotten senses from the summer before. His feet stepped lightly as he crossed back along Oak ridge, making sure to stay clear of the area where he thought trouble was.

The trees thinned enough that in the distance he saw two birds headed south. One of them was a monstrous, black Crow, while the other one was small like a Magpie with white tuffs of feathers under the wings. "What a strange pair to be traveling together. "Kaw,

135

Kaw," he called out to them. He loved the crow birds. He had always felt they had special powers. Legend says some mighty braves can change into a crow when they want to, so he watched them cut the air, hoping to see the magic.

The two birds suddenly split apart and took a wide birth around something far ahead in the woods.

"Smart birds, but what did you see?" Manez slowed his assault towards home and began to read the signs along the trail.

"One, no, two people passed by here not long ago, but they are not alone. Four others follow cautiously behind them."

He continued on west. He hoped he could reach home by dark, but it seemed every time he did something for himself, it bled over into an adventure like the one with Dawn, Walks Far and Four Claws.

"Snap." He froze when he heard the noise just short of crossing Stony Creek. He stood still, watching the tree line on the other side. A good ten minutes passed...nothing. He thought, *It probably was an old, rotten limb falling down to the rocks in the creek bed.* He stepped half into the open, then froze. Like a lizard, he moved back into the safety of the trees. Something black was weaving between the trees on the other side of the creek and something white followed the black movement closely.

He looked out at the blue sky through the cluttered limbs for the two birds and smiled to himself. He knew it was the magic of a great warrior.

A sudden war cry broke the calm of the forest and an Apache brave charged from the tree line. The tall, black man wielded a large limb like a club above his head. The club had portions of deer antlers tied to its end and he had an oval-shaped shield made from a piece of leather tied between two tamarack limbs. The shield was painted with black dots and white wavy lines. His face was cut and scarred, but the cuts made a beautiful, fierce design around his eyes and his mouth.

The Indian, wanting to 'count coup' first, had raced in before his brothers were ready. That was a deadly mistake, because the black brought his oval-shaped shield up into the ribs of his attacker, knocking him backwards and at the same moment, he brought the deer antler down on top of the brave's head, driving it into his skull, killing him. All was quiet; even the insects became silent. Then, arrows flew at the black. He shoved the white one behind a tree and caught the first arrow in the hide of his shield. The second arrow stuck in the fleshy part below his chest. He was so quick with his club that he pulled it into the path of the third arrow, making it stick in the wood. The Indians rushed in at him with hatchets in hand. The black took a wide stance with his club raised high in the air and as the first warrior charged in close enough to him, he drove the club into the brave's side, flinging him twenty feet away, dead. He tried to regain his stance, but before his weight was balanced and his club was raised, the third Indian wildly swung the hatchet and took a chunk of skin from his leg, causing him to go down on his knees. The black, with a sweeping motion, took the feet from under the brave with his club causing him to fall away. The fourth Indian arrived at that moment and pinned the club to the ground with his foot, then proceeded to hack at the small shield with his hatchet.

While all this was going on, Manez wondered why the white one didn't charge in to help the black, then he noticed the long, golden hair of a woman hiding in the brush. The third Apache saw her too and ran for her. In that instant, before he realized what he had done, Manez's long knife was rolling end over end through the air at the Indian until it buried deep in his side, killing him. The sudden death of the brave caused the fourth Indian to look in the direction the knife had come from just long enough for the black to pull his club free. With a low circular motion, he brought the full weight of the club into the leg of his attacker, breaking it. The dark man stood above the Indian ready to crush his skull, but he hesitated. The man was in great pain.

"Noxae! Nehetaae, nehetaae!" (Wait! That's enough, enough!) he cried out holding his hands up towards the champion. There was no more fight in the Apache and killing him would not accomplish anything.

The dark man turned to cast his gaze upon the young Manez and said, "Wati to hati." Then without another word, he gathered up the white woman and stumbled back into the tree row along the creek bed.

Just as they disappeared into the sea of green, the crow, with the magpie in tow, flew out from the top of the trees. The Cheyenne brave and the Apache were astonished at the sight of the birds emerging from the place that the dark man and white woman had just gone. Manez clutched his medicine bundle, knowing he had just seen big magic. The Apache mumbled something, but Manez didn't understand what he said. They both watched as the birds flew south, but before they were out of sight, Manez called out once more. "Kaw kaw." He loved the crow birds.

As Manez approached, the hurt Indian recoiled in anticipation of being killed by the young Cheyenne, but Manez placed his palms down towards the ground, a symbol of calm. He brought a limb and set the broken leg by tying it to the limb, all under the gaze of the mistrusting Apache. In a matter of minutes, the wounded Apache stood with the help of another limb as a crutch that Manez had provided and gave him a puzzling look of wonder.

"Taana-asestse," ("Go,") Manez said, motioning at the Indian with his hands. "Taana-asestse," he repeated.

The Apache gathered himself, placing all his weight on his crutch, and moved away from him. Before he was very far away, Manez retrieved a knife from the body of a dead Apache. He moved towards the wounded man once more, only to have the brave almost fall down from worry, but at the last minute, Manez placed the knife in the Apache's belt.

"Nahkoheo'o" ("For bears"). Manez shook his bear claw necklace as he said it. The Apache smiled weakly and began to make his way back up the stream to the north.

It was almost noon as Manez turned toward home once more. A lot of time had been wasted, but he was pleased. The day was beautiful and he would have a great story to tell about the black magic when he returned home. Back down the western ridge, keeping well out of the way of the Crow camp and up the steep valley, he ran. At the mouth of Round Springs, he knelt down and drank from the cool, clean water, keeping one eye on the mouth of the cave where his whole adventure had started. Of course nothing was there, which was a relief, but in a way, he missed the bear. As he continued down Piney Creek towards the camp, he wondered if Four Claws had made it through the winter, but his thoughts of the bear disappeared when he topped the hill above Round Valley. There it was; he had made it home.

The camp was just as he had remembered it, nestled along the stream in the valley. The painted tepees offering up the colorful deeds of the Hotamimasaw who lived in them. Small groups of women were hammering at the corn in the stone bowls. Several men were practicing shooting with their bows and not very good shooting, either. An arrow bounced along the ground almost hitting the women working and they reacted by throwing stones at the men.

"Let's see, that has to be Laughs Plenty. He's still the worst shot in the camp."

A big, black dog barked at the ridge, then it let out a long reverberating howl that bounced off the valley walls. All activity and time stopped as everyone stared at the ridge and the young brave standing there.

Onotsa appeared at the entrance of his teepee, gazing long and hard at the figure on top of the hill. A rider on a white pony came from behind the teepees. It was Kanan, his brother.

"A yee, a yee," Manez called, making it echo so many times it sounded like a hundred warriors atop the hill.

"Manez!" Kanan called as he charged up the hill on the pony. "Father, it's Manez! He's not dead!" The tears collected in the corners of the old man's eyes and he stumbled, almost falling.

The horse came to a stop just a few feet from Manez and Kanan dove into him with his body, causing them both to tumble to the ground laughing.

"I knew you were alive," Kanan said as he picked him up and started down the hill. "When your horse came back without you, we went looking for you, only to find the bear tracks mixed with yours in the cave. Where have you been?" Others ran in and patted him on the shoulders.

"Well, it's a long story, brother, one that will have to wait." He paused as the group separated, making an opening for Onotsa. "Father," he said, throwing his arms around the Chief. Cheyenne warriors weren't supposed to cry, but a watery eye or two could be seen among all who witnessed a lost son returning home.

"Son," the old chief replied.

After awhile, he stepped back a bit, then touched the pipe hanging around Manez's neck and looked at the Arikara weapons.

"I can see we shall hear a great story around the fire tonight." Then turning to the village, he said, " My son, Manez, who was lost is found. Tonight we dance and hear the stories."

The Indians scattered to prepare a suitable feast for his return. An old woman chased a lazy dog away. Onotsa laughed, then looked at the pipe and escorted the boy home. Manez was overjoyed to be home, but he caught himself thinking of how much more joy Grey Eyes must have felt when he saw his daughter returned. Then, deep down inside, something stirred. It was a feeling that perhaps he would never have a home or at least not without Dawn. He wondered what she was doing and he touched her with his thoughts.

A group of young boys chased the horses, sending trails of dust in all directions while the women resumed their corn pounding. Laughs Plenty coaxed Kanan and Manez into joining him shooting arrows and for a while their faces beamed with joy at just being boys. Large, black clouds floated by, all the while thunder rolled in the distance bringing a fresh, clean breeze. It tried to rain, but the sun shone through the curtains of water making a sun shower. Overall, the day was beautiful. A man called Crooked Hand came with a large buck he had killed for the feast. Onotsa beamed as he watched the village burst into a joy that he hadn't seen in many moons.

Manez could see Onotsa sitting in front of his teepee, so he excused himself from the arrow shooting and joined the old chief. They sat for a long time. Onotsa chased the clouds with his eyes while Manez fiddled with the Arikara pipe.

"My son, you are the only survivor of the Sutaio. I told you I would speak of these things when it was time and this is the time. You went away a young brave, but now I see a warrior before me."

Manez knew this was not the time to talk, but a time to listen; so he sat still, thinking on the chief's words. "The Sutaio were the first to live in this valley. They were looked on with hatred because of the good hunting and fresh water found here. Their magic was strong, making many tribes afraid of them for a long time." He looked out past the horizon as if waiting for more words to come.

"I was a young man then and had a friend who lived there. The magic they owned was good, but their fighting was bad and after awhile the Apache tested them in a battle. It was a bad defeat for the Sutaio and the Apache took many horses along with captives. The war drums of the nations soon told the story of the battle bringing the Crow, Arapaho and Natchez against them for their valley. My friend was the last chief of these people and he had a son. That son was you, Manez." Once more, the old man stopped telling his story by playing in the dirt with a stick.

"Your father was called Nahahevoha (Wild Horse); a tall, strong and fast brave just like you. He was the first to capture one of the four-legged dogs left behind by the metal-headed Vehoes. Don't think I shame him talking about his fighting. It was only because they had so few in their tribe that they couldn't stand against the plains Indians." He looked straight into the boy's eyes. "I've told you of your father's life, but now I must tell you of his death." He shook his head for a moment. "The Apache came on a cool Fall day just before the shadows turn into real things. Our scouts found signs of the war party moving past us and so I sent a runner to your father while we prepared for war. I had planned to be sneaky, to catch them off guard from behind. We followed them on both sides like a fox hunting a rabbit, not trusting them at all. You know down the valley where it narrows close to the wall of sand stone?" Manez nodded his head. "The Apache turned back on us. It had been their plan all along. We weren't surprised at that. They think they are sneaky, but no tribe is as sneaky as the Cheyenne. Our arrows filled the sky killing many where they stood. We charged from all sides, running through them, cutting at their arms and legs. It wasn't long until the Apache ran away. We began to gather many scalps, but our rejoicing was short because we saw smoke coming from the Sutaio camp. I told everyone to hurry, that we had been tricked and we must go. So we ran as fast as we could, but we were too late. Another band of Apache had attacked the camp, killing many and taking the rest captive. Your father was lying on the ground surrounded by twenty dead Apache. He fought bravely. Only you were found alive, so I took you to be raised as a Cheyenne, but in truth, you are the last of the Sutaio." He stopped with tears in his eyes, then said, "Tonight, after you have told your story, I will ask for the Red Shield Ceremony. I am proud to call you my son, Chief Manez, bear fighter." Talk was over. He stood, then patted Manez on the head and walked away towards the sweat lodge. Manez sat still and watched his father move away. The sun was flashing its final bolts of light. Far away to the north, the thunder still rolled while lightning dashed across the sky and with each jagged strike, a feeling of great pride swelled inside his chest.

Kanan called out to him and he joined them to prepare for the evening ceremonies.

Not far away to the south, Bebai and Lucile came close to the burning Fort Rosalie. They stumbled over the dead bodies hidden at the edge of the forest.. He checked the signs on the ground and could tell the Natchez had been here because of the hide shoes. "Come." He pulled at her and she resisted a little, causing him to give her a serious look.

"I'm tired, really tired." Her voice broke and she took two short, funny breaths. "Too much d-d-death," she stammered, then began to cry for the first time since her adventure had started. Bebai took her arm and guided her beneath a large oak tree where he piled up some leaves between two large roots. There he sat down with her nestled under his arm and as night chased the flickers of light to the tips of the leaves, she cried herself to sleep.

A full moon cast a light glow down the valley and for the first time in two days he could see the river glistening below them. He thought, *Follow the river, Bebai. It will take you home.* He didn't know how it would take him home, but in his heart he knew this pretty, white woman would play an important part in his escape home. *Keep her safe, slave; keep her safe,* he thought, then he too fell asleep.

A shadow moved on the water; it crept along the shore quietly floating with the current. Chamfort, Francis and James along with their other two companions had found two canoes hidden on the shore of the river. It seemed an easy thing just to wait until dark and then slip down stream to Fort Rosalie, but now as they came around the bend the sight of the burning fort caused a knot in their stomachs. Several bodies lay close by on the shore.

"Pull in close and tie up to that tree," Chamfort whispered.

"Stay here. I'll have a look." Without a sound, he crawled up the bank and disappeared into the underbrush.

He was gone a long time. In fact, it had been long enough that Francis grew uneasy, then said way too loudly,"He's been taken. Let's push off and move on."

James covered his mouth with his hand. Then shook his finger at him. A twig snapped, causing the group to grab at their weapons

144

and point them at the brush. Several tense moments passed until Chamfort called out softly, "It's me. I'm coming in and I'm not alone." His silhouette slid through the grass followed by two other shadows. Without saying a word, he placed a distraught women in the second canoe, then helped Jouard into the boat beside her and the group slid back out into the dark safety of the river.

A long time passed before Francis asked, "Who are they, Chamfort?"

"That's Antone Jouard. He worked at the fort as a hunter. He was up in the trees hunting for deer when the Natchez came. He said they attacked without warning, killing everyone they saw. That is La Miette, a soldier's widow living outside the fort. Her children were killed trying to hide in the fort."

All was quiet again as the canoes slipped further down the river. The current was slow and after two miles, Chamfort pulled the two canoes together. La Miette was still grieving, an occasional sob slipping from her swollen face. Even in her condition, she was an attractive women in her prime at thirty-one years old. She was a sturdy-boned, working woman with dark hair and an outdoors complexion.

"Is she going to be alright?" asked Francis.

Antone replied, " Give her time, just give her time." He patted her on the shoulder.

Chamfort shook his head in agreement then asked, " What do these Natchez want and where have they gone?"

"We had rumors that last week Pierre Debois moved onto their burial grounds in the south. It would seem that's the case, because they moved off to the south after...you know."

La Miette sobbed once more.

"I believe if we stay on the river and only travel at night, we can slip past them."

Chamfort motioned downstream and pushed a paddle hard at the water causing the canoes to slowly disappear from the light of the burning buildings along the shore.

The showers from earlier in the day had moved far to the north, but traces of lightning could still be seen in the distance pointing their icy fingers across the sky. The light showers left a refreshing scent along with a cool breeze. All afternoon, the small girls had gathered dark stones from Piney Creek and scattered them twenty feet wide around the campfire. The rocks were to hold bad spirits in the flames and not let them escape into the shields. Wood was gathered, venison was cooked over the open fire and maidens danced to the native drums.

"Aahee, aahee," Crooked Hand cried out, announcing the arrival of the honored guests. Kanan and Manez had been standing just out of the light of the fire and when the appropriate time came, they entered the circle.

"Great Onotsa, leader of the Wolf Band, two stories told, two shields to give." He stepped away from the boys leaving them in front of their father and the elders. The drums stopped, the maidens became still and all was quiet as Onotsa continued chewing on a meaty bone. Somewhere in the dark, a dog growled. It seemed like hours that they stood poised in their finest buckskins until finally, Onotsa tossed the bone towards a pack of dogs and addressed them."What acts of 'counting coup' do you claim Kanan? The people will judge your story."

A lot had happened in Manez's absence and with all the excitement of the day, he felt bad he hadn't even talked to his brother. Manez gave him the 'I'm sorry' look, then nudged him forward to tell his story. Kanan had a hard time getting started. His voice was strained and he cleared his throat many times, but all around the fire heads lifted, eyes grew intent; they were ready for his story. Several old men shook their heads in anticipation of what was to come.

"We all saw my brother's pony come home alone. We all searched Piney Creek and saw the bear tracks cut deep in the dirt. Some gave up hope and after many suns stopped thinking of him. I saw the color begin to leave my father's eyes and I knew that Manez must be found, even if I had to cut him from the belly of the bear. I searched. I read the signs and saw the footprints running to the trees then disappearing. I remembered the story of the Kiowa Chief's daughters chased up a tree so high that they went into the sky and now they shine down on us. Could Manez have joined them there? I wondered about that many times while searching the woods. Farther and farther I went, even searching hollow logs for a door into the other world where he could hide, but no sign could be found. Many times I didn't come home, causing me to become a stranger here." He looked at his father, then cleared his throat. " It was on the night of the full moon, when spirits prowl the sacred places, that I let darkness overtake me. I took shelter at the bottom of a hill beneath a cottonwood tree. The wind blew while strange shadows from the moonbeams darted all around me. I built a small fire and settled down for the night and I had almost fallen asleep when a branch fell on the hill above me, causing it to roll down into the fire. I stared at it, but not for long, because a large rock came rolling down behind the branch hitting the fire and sending bright, burning embers everywhere. It looked like rain and as I looked at it, I saw the smoke-filled shape of Manez cross in front of the moon with the bear still

147

chasing him. I then knew he would come back to us." He paused as the village voiced their approval of his story so far. He asked for some water and afterwards he began once more.

"The face of an ancient one appeared on the trunk of the tree and said things to me." A sudden gust of wind whipped the campfire, causing all of them to believe the same spirit was there now. The children clung to their mothers and the dogs whined as the wind swirled through the camp. Even Kanan was surprised at the entrance of the breeze, so he too stopped until the cold air bounced off the teepees and disappeared into the dark.

"The face was cut deep into the bark. It had wood eyebrows, lips and a limb stub for a nose. He called out to me, 'Kanan, son of Onotsa, Chief of the Hotamimasaw. You waste your time searching for your brother. Even you know his life is linked to the bear's life and the spirits have always looked over him. Go home now; your father needs you.' Several small fires broke out around the tree as the spirit disappeared. Stunned, I stood a long time watching the leaves burn, wondering about what the spirit had said. Suddenly the wind stopped, causing the full moon to glow bright as day and I knew it was time to go. I ran back along the valley and the hollow log. I ran until the morning light pushed down on the top of the trees lining the ridge above our valley. The morning birds sang, a mountain lion cried like a baby somewhere atop the ridge, but all the sounds suddenly stopped and I fell to the ground, watching for the cause. I lay still, listening. Not far away, I could hear pony hooves clawing at the steep ridge, making small stones tumble down below. I parted the grass with my bow and looked up in that direction. Apache ponies could be seen, maybe six of them, winding slowly up the ridge. I crawled forward through the grass to the safety of the trees, then I made my way up, making sure to stay just far enough away not to be seen. I had seen the Apache many times as a boy from a distance, but now that all the nations were crowding each other. They had begun to come closer, willing to risk defying the magic of the Wolf Band. The Apache dismounted at the top of the ridge leaving their horses there. I crawled to the top as the Indians made their way down towards our camp. Now that they were quiet, I could hear more ponies. Looking to the south on the valley floor, I could see a war party hiding behind the tree line. With no time to waste, I pulled my bow and shot an arrow through the neck of the closest Apache. He fell unnoticed by the others. I moved farther down the hill, sneaking up on another from behind and stabbing him in the back. The other braves called quietly to the ones I killed and when they didn't answer, another Apache stood up to look. I shot him in the head with an arrow. Then I gave out a war cry so all in the valley would hear the alarm. It was so loud, it echoed off the walls of the ridge and bounced over and over again. It even scared me. As the camp below me came alive, I had time to shoot one more arrow, but it struck the charging warrior in the arm knocking him down just long enough for me to sink my hatchet into his chest. The last two braves charged at me running, twenty yards apart. I met the first one and locked tomahawks with him, flipping him on his back just long enough to throw my hatchet into the stomach of the other attacker. Then I quickly pulled my knife out and drove it into the heart of the man on the ground. Out in the valley, the Wolf Band met the Apache charge driving them into the ground. Many were killed; it was a great day for our people."

Manez looked at his brother and held up six fingers while shaking his head. The drums pounded and the pipe was passed all around while the tribe celebrated and the old men huddled together for a long time until Onotsa held up his open hand. All became quiet.

"We talked about the things you have said and believe that was a good story." He stopped short, took the pipe and blew a large puff out into the clear air.

"Manez, we see the sacred pipe of the Arikaras you carry." He leaned forward and touched the polished buffalo horn shaft. "What magic helped you take this prize from them?" he asked with a twinkle in his eyes. Now, Manez had told his story many times around the Arikara campfire and he had learned to tell a good story. He winked at Kanan and then began to shake the bear claw while waving the pipe high above his head. He danced around weaving his way through the tribe making a full circle and even the drummers got involved pounding out a beat for every step he took. He gracefully found his way back along the black stones, then suddenly stopped in front of Onotsa.

"I was told by a wise man, once, that because I took the claw from the bear, I would be linked to him in this life. I wasn't so sure of this truth. I just thought it made me look older."

Several laughs came from all around the camp. "I went on a hunt up Piney Creek trail; the leaves were falling fast and it was a good day to hunt, a day much like today. It grew dark quickly from a storm. The fingers of light, along with the rain, chased me into the cave close to the burned pines. You all know these things because of the signs left behind." Most of the hunters shook their heads in agreement. " I built a fire with what wood I could find, but it was wet, causing puffs of smoke to roll out the front of the cave. It was a lazy day and I thought of many things...the Ghost dance, giving of the shield. My eyes could not push back the dreamer and he came to overtake me. He pulled me out into the open plains; I was running through the tall grasses chasing the buffalo. Closer and closer I came, faster and faster I ran, until I thought I might go so fast I'd disappear. A bull suddenly stopped, throwing his head to the side and tossing me down on the ground. I lay there face down, dazed, feeling his hot breath on my neck. Suddenly, my horse bolted from the cave, waking me to the fact that the bear was there. The hair on the back of my neck stood on end and my hands began to tingle."

Two small children on the front pulled closer in their mother's arms letting Manez know his story was good.

"I had just enough time to scramble up the wall to a ledge as the bear attacked the fire, throwing it in every direction. It was the second time I had seen him tear into a fire. I remembered the Arikaras back on the Little River trail and I realized it was the fire he hated. Its smell drew him to it and the men that made the fire were just victims of his wrath. I watched for a long time and didn't realize I had gone to sleep until I hit the floor of the cave. I lay there stunned, looking at the ledge above me and in that instant, I ran. I ran for my life, because deep in the black crevices of the cave, the bear stirred. I flew as fast as my legs would carry me with Four Claws churning the dirt on the path behind me. The path winds through the woods and with every turn the bear came closer. I could see the river down below the path about thirty feet and just as I could feel the earth tremble beneath the steps of Four Claws, I jumped, crashing through the trees into the water below. Popping to the surface of the water, I could see him standing on the ridge, knocking chunks of rubble everywhere in his disgust and I decided to go downstream then get out on the other side.

"The spirits caused me to go home the long way. I traveled through places I had never been, coming close to a large Crow camp."

He paused as the whole camp spit on the ground at the mention of the Crow. Then restarted his story." I intended to just slip by their camp, but from the top of the cliff, I could see a young, Arikara girl tied to a pole in the center of the camp." Several women moaned, but Manez continued his story. "My feet said run, but my heart cried out for the girl. So, I made a plan to slip down at dark and release her, but all that changed when I felt the hot breath of the bear on my neck. I knew it was him. The hairs on my neck stood on end and I panicked, collapsing uncontrollably down the hill with the bear right behind me.. I scrambled into the camp and jumped over the fire, to the surprise of the Crow." The Cheyenne mumble in disgust at the mention of the name once more.

"They were about to kill me when Four Claws broke through the brush, attacking the fire and anyone connected to the fire."

He told about the bear attacking the camp and his escape. He repeated every detail about how the girl was Grey Eyes's daughter and how he aquired a white Indian for rescuing her. The white Indian was from along way off, who had frozen water for windows and his fires burned without wood inside every teepee. He told them he had seen an Unske and how he prayed to Neshanu Natchitak to save him. (Not even Onotsa had seen an Unske)

Just as they thought his tale was going to end, he told about the black crow turning into a warrior and then fighting the Apache. He repeated it firmly and with a scared respect in his voice, so all the people would know this was big magic he had seen.

Then just when they all thought he would never end his story, he stopped. Standing very still and quietly, he lowered his head to signify he was finished. A whooping cry was heard from Silver Hair and the drums began to pound out the beat of every dance step around the black stones. Manez raised his head, then looked at Kanan, giving him a wink and a grin.

Back out over the top of the big ridge, a wolf began to howl. His cry was barely heard between the beats of the drums until his pack joined in. They made a terrifying noise as they ran along the highest point of the ridge on a hunt. All the Cheyenne stopped and listened to howl after howl echoing down on the camp as the pack chased their prey. Young and old Cheyenne felt a chill in their blood from the lonely cries of the wolf, until a lingering bolt of lightning threw its sharpened fingers across the sky and the thunder that followed broke even the hypnotic sounds of the wolf.

Onotsa called, "It is time. Bring the shields." He had been sitting with the elders, smoking the pipe and as the young girls danced into the light with the willow rings covered in buffalo hide, all the Cheyenne stood in honor of the making of the shields. Everyone close enough to touch the leather-wrapped rings rubbed on them to symbolize the tribe's unity and to give some of their magic to them. Then the rings were taken to the Shaman, Cripple Elk.

"Nenaasestse,"("Come here,") he said, as he motioned to them. When the two boys were close enough, he reached out for the rings. "Ne-asetanotse." ("Pass them to me.") "Tse-vohpenovatse." ("The one who paints.") His words boomed out as the people opened a path for the painter Blue Eyes to come forward.

The painter rubbed the rings and then touched each boy's shoulder. He rubbed his paint stained hands across their face, as if waiting for a sign so he could begin his work. Then, with amazing skill and grace, he began. A black circle was placed on each shield symbolizing the camp of the Wolf Band. White ice stones were painted along with a golden bolt of lightning that symbolized the day the shields were given. All the elders gathered around them and shook their heads with approval. Then the boys were asked to paint something on the shields. Kanan painted gray smoke circling off to

153

the side of his shield and Manez painted a bear standing at the bottom of his. The elders mumbled their approval, then all the men entered the lodge. The Elk hornpipe was retrieved, then packed with the medicine man's best smoking mixture. As they smoked the pipe, they began singing sacred songs. As they sang, Blue Eyes filled in the circles with red paint and drew black buffalo horns at the top of the rings. The pipe was passed once more around the lodge, but this time four songs were sung before the elders rubbed the rings with clay to remove the supernatural powers. Two old women came into the lodge during the songs and tied bird feathers around the outer edge with red strings. Then Onotsa stood before the tribe. The boys were expecting some sort of important speech or magic words, but he just said, "Let's eat."

They all went outside and placed the shields on a pole where the women could work on them. While the men ate, the women tied strands of black hair and yellow quills around the feathers on the outer edge. The drums pounded while the Bear Dance was performed and for a brief moment, the beautiful Dawn was chased from the young warrior's mind. He danced around the fire, dreaming of some great, defining moment yet to come. He was of the Wolf Band; a real Cheyenne warrior. *That's all I've ever wanted to be*, he thought.

Chapter 18

The King Is Dead

Chogah held his breath as the French soldiers noisily edged by him up the path towards what was left of Fort Rosalie. He kept his Natchez warriors quiet and well hidden until all the men had passed them. Then he waved his hand and all the Indians evaporated into the brush, following behind their enemies on both sides. The early morning light was invading their hiding places in the night shadows. Soon it would be impossible for them to remain unseen and safe. Chogah had his orders from the Soliel that he was to watch the Vehoe until Soliel arrived and so, he stuck just close enough not to be seen.

It wasn't the first time he had been in battle with the French. He hated them; he had lost his eldest son Nitka to the fire sticks when the whites first came to build the fort. Only his loyalty to the Soliel kept him from dashing into the midst of the French murderers to drive his tomahawk into their heads.

Not far to the south, Sabotha's eyes popped violently open. "Ahh tomak oney monke," she screamed, her voice echoing down the hill causing fear to grip the entire encampment.

"Where is Pierre? Is he gone? Don't tell me he's chasing after the Natchez," she yelled at the closest man.

He gulped his answer to the witch. "Yes, yes, he's gone up the trail towards Ft. Rosalie," replied the frightened Frenchman.

Sabotha grabbed his shirt close to the collar and drew him so close he could see the terror in her eyes.

"Go quickly, find him and when you do, tell him death awaits for him beyond the ridge." She pointed her quivering, bony finger up towards the trees. Filled with fear, he reluctantly stumbled towards the path.

"Tell him death is coming for him!" she cried out, sending chills up the backs of all who heard. The man's pace quickened as Sabotha chased him up the trail with her shrill call. "Run, man, run! Death is coming!"

With that call, he broke into a steady run up over the hill and down the path into the woods towards Ft. Rosalie.

Sabotha held her hand up towards the north as if blocking the sun as she stumbled back towards the hut. She cried out in terrible tones chanting, with her words spilling furiously over her lips. "I block the witch's spell, fe trok nori com. You have no more power here, White Witch. Leave me alone," she cried upon entering the door.

The bones she had thrown the day before still lay on the table. Something about them caught her eye, something she hadn't seen before when she was looking for a sign for Pierre. "Me, die?" she cried out. "I will die if I stay in this place!" She scooped up her belongings and scurried out the door. The gypsies left to guard Terre Blance gave her a questioning look. "I won't die today. Maybe tomorrow, but if we stay here today, we will all die." A sudden cloud of dust rose as the tents and fields emptied, following Sabotha back towards New Orleans.

The soldiers were plodding along rather slowly under the direction of Pierre. The path was narrow and with so many men, their movement was like a fat snake trying to creep along a narrow ledge. Pierre swatted at some tiny, biting thing that had been

156

pestering him for an hour. Soon after leaving the safety of Terre Blance, an uneasy feeling settled into the pit of his stomach. In the past, this feeling had been helpful to warn him off of potential dangerous situations and today it seemed to be telling him he should have waited for Sabotha's blessing from the bones.

Pierre's thought process was interrupted by De Lucus who was Chepart's second-in- command. He had pushed his way past the Dark Wind, close to Pierre.

"I don't what to insult you or interrupt your plans, lordship, but at this rate of travel, my captain will have killed all the redskins before we ever get to Ft. Rosalie."

A scheme took form in Pierre's head. "No insult taken, De Lucus, I see you share the same passion for battle as Chepart does."

"Yes, sir. He took me from the academy and personally trained me for this position."

Pierre subtly guided him to do what he wanted him to do.

"Well, I know we're not used to this type of travel so, if you wish to move your men out in front and travel at the speed you wish, you are more than welcome to do so. We will nurse our sore feet and follow along behind."

"Yes, sir." The young man jumped at the chance to lead the column into battle.

"Hold." Pierre called back to his men, letting the seasoned French soldiers pass.

After the last man had passed, the gypsy clan resumed their normal pace and in a few minutes the soldiers were out of sight.

The trail pitched back and forth up a steep incline close to the river. Loose stones tumbled down the embankment splashing into the water. Chamfort was keeping a close eye on the activities on the opposite bank. He had been hugging the east bank of the Missouri ever since the first rays of light broke. Quietly, he held the two canoes close to the underbrush because of the constant sightings of the Natchez sneaking about on the other side of the river.

"How many do you figure, Jouard?" Chamfort asked, scanning the shoreline.

"I'd say five hundred, maybe more, that we've seen along the shore. Who knows how many are back in the trees. They seem to be all gathering near that point there." He pointed at a large rock outcropping shoved up into the sky by some long forgotten force. The trail slithered its way dangerously close to the waters edge as it ascended to the crest of the hill, then it cut back sharply along the rough, rocky ridge. Large pines trees stretched their shadows over the menacing outcropping.

"That would make a good place to stay away from if you were worried about being attacked," Chamfort whispered, as if he was planning a secret mission.

A sudden war cry cut through the morning air and a Natchez brave ran from the woods into the advancing French soldiers so suddenly there was no reaction, even as the Indian drove his tomahawk into the skull of a soldier. While the men were in shock, he raised his weapon to strike once more, but De Lucus fumbled his pistol from his belt and shot a hole in the brave's chest. For a brief moment, an unbelievable quiet gripped both the French and Indians, as if they couldn't believe what was about to happen. Then the woods moved forward with bloody screams. A lance tossed from back in the trees caught De Lucus in the leg, pinning him to the ground. A wave of arrows cut into the flesh of the first four rows; they fell forever dead. Random rifles popped, causing little damage to the wave of humanity coming from the trees. The young lieutenant pulled his cutlass, hacking off the arm of a charging warrior, but before he could stand up, his neck was cut, killing him and sending a spray of blood into the air. The Indians had the high ground; their overwhelming numbers pushed the French to the edge of the cliff. One by one they killed the invaders and pushed them over the edge into the water.

Pierre, purposely taking his time, made it possible for the Frenchman to catch up to the clan.

"Pierre, Pierre, news from Sabotha," he cried out, as he bent over gasping for breath from his run.

"News from Sabotha? What news?" an extremely surprised Pierre exclaimed. The last time he had seen her, she was locked in a trance.

"She sends you an urgent message. She says death waits for you beyond the ridge."

"Oh, I see how she is. She's staring off into space for two days, then when I go off to do something on my own, death waits for me." Pierre had placed his back to the river while he was talking and he noticed all eyes were staring past him towards the water. As he turned, a soldier's body floated past; they watched it go out of sight. A few moments later, four more dead soldiers swiftly floated past. All the clan gazed upstream as the whole river began to turn red.

Somewhere up the trail, rifles barked faintly. Chogah took that as a sign to attack; so out of the shadows of the trees, the small band charged. His numerous encounters with the French had given him too much confidence as he blindly led his braves from the safety of the trees into the midst of the Dark Wind. The arrows plunged into the waiting gypsies. One buried deep into the leg of the man standing next to Pierre. Once again with sparats raised high in the air, the clan met the charge of the Natchez driving the sharp points into the heads and bodies of the Indians. Chogah wielded his hatchet, striking out at man after man to no avail. He purposely tried to divide the gypsies, hoping to kill Pierre. "Here, push them apart, here," he yelled, but the gypsies began to advance, cutting into the bodies of the Indians with their clubs, causing doubt and fear in his braves. When the other Natchez from the fort joined the fighting, causing the small road to be clogged with the battle and bringing it to a standstill, the Dark Wind began to retreat back towards the safety of Terre Blance.

Samba slipped out of the swamp just as the sun tipped its light enough to put out the torches. The only thing standing between them and the city was Joseph Malgamont's plantation. The group slowly walked past the eighty acres of tobacco, hoping not to cause a dog to bark or wake the guards tending the slaves there.

A sudden scream and a gunshot caused the group to duck into the tobacco plants. Samba looked up at the house just as the structure burst into flames. A fat, black man shoved Janee Malgamont to the ground as a skinny buck-toothed man tore parts of her dress away.

"We're gonna show you what your daddy gave to our little girls." The skinny man pulled away some of her underclothes.

The fat man pressed the gun against her head. "Your daddy can't help you now."

He began to giggle as her white flesh was exposed. He never saw Samba approach from his blind side. A kick in the head knocked him cold. The skinny man tried to hide his personals and get up, but Samba held him down with his foot.

"Who are you and what are you doing here," he asked the man.

"I'm Ditka and that's Chub; we live here. We knowed you was comin' and so when all of the guards 'cept one went into town to get drunk, we broke out and crushed his head. Then we slipped into the house and shot that animal, Malgamont, and killed his wife. We burned the house." It was obvious he was a simple-minded man. Other screams could be heard coming from the basement.

"What about the house slaves locked in the cellar?" Samba asked. Ditka gave him a strange look as Samba raised the gun and shot him in the head. Janee screamed as the pieces splattered on what was left of her dress.

"Grab the girl; the rest of you pry open the basement door before it's too late. The fat man stirred, rolling over on the body of his friend.

"If I were you, I would run away into the swamp before I decide to kill you too."

All the slaves were freed from the cellar just before the house fell.

"We must hurry. Those two idiots sent a warning to the whole city."

With that, the four hundred Natanapalle pushed through the trees, spilling into Dreidic Street, looting as they went. The mob met the city fire brigade as they turned on Basin Street and proceeded to turn the wagon on its side, spilling all the firemen onto the road.

Samba had a plan that involved speeding forward to the river front and trying to commandeer a ship. He didn't know how they would sail the ship even if they made it that far, but even dying while standing on the very instrument that had brought them to this wretched life would be a victory in his eyes. The rebels almost ran as they moved forward following Samba. The band of slaves had dwindled from four hundred to barely one hundred. Most of the castaways were only interested in stealing anything they could before running away back into the swamp, but not Samba, not this time. To him, this was to be his defining moment of defiance. As they approached the corner of Rampart Street, Samba held them back. He leaned out and took a look at Congo Square. Eight soldiers with muskets stood shoulder to shoulder on the grass at the front of the slave pens. Men, women and children, who had been caught outside, ran for hiding places like roaches caught in the light.

"Anyone with a gun, come forward," Samba ordered. Six slaves appeared with weapons they had found along the way.

"When I say 'go', step around the corner and shoot your weapons. The rest of us will charge them, wildly screaming as we run. We will see how brave the French are facing one hundred crazy, escaped slaves." The men with the guns positioned themselves and when they were ready, the order was given to charge. The white smoke from the rifles covered the whole street corner. Only one soldier fell, but the sight of a hundred slaves running out of the smoke stirred a fear in the hearts of the city guards, causing them to run away towards the Cathedral. The normally quiet slave pens erupted with cheers of joy in all languages as the bars were opened, giving them their freedom.

Sabotha with the small band of escapees from Terre Blance had made it to the alley beside the bank just as Samba's men set the captives free. So far, the gypsies had been lucky and had only encountered two or three small groups of rebels, which they quickly killed. The protection of the walled mansion was within reach, but the army of slaves stood in the way. A shadowy cloud began to hypnotize Sabotha's mind, her eyes fluttered and as she became numb, she slid down the brick wall onto the street.

"Hi tuak necamma mentas. Necamma mentas," the witch mumbled as the vision of an important man having his head chopped off washed over her brain. As the blade came down, she woke up to hear the slave leader cry out in a great voice.

"There is no time to waste! We must keep them on their heels. Let's move on." With their numbers growing back to about two hundred men, women and children, the group sprang forward. Flooding past the Cathedral onto Canal Street, they beat and clubbed their way to the French Market Custom House. The sudden exit of the slaves allowed the gypsies to advance on to the mansion. Just beyond the market and out of reach, the mast of the tall ships could be seen bobbing up and down on the tide. About fifty heavily armed sailors had taken position atop the dike that the market stood on making it impossible to advance. Several anxious tribesmen tried to charge the dirt embankment only to be shot down as they ran.

"Here we are so close, but just like always, the whites are standing in the way. It's just as well, we didn't know how to sail them anyway," Samba said drooping his head.

An African man as black as coal had moved up beside Samba. He stared out at the top of the ships and began to speak. "Toti, Fulani ketha, jamde bechi."

Samba gazed at this curious fellow, wondering what he might be saying. "Can anyone help with what he is saying?"

An old man named Nuna made his way to the front. "Jamma grne foma?" the old one asked the African what it was that he had said.

"Toti, Fulani ketha, jamde bechi." he replied again pointing at the tall ships.

"He say the Fulani sail big boats."

Samba just stared for a moment. "How many here are Fulani?"

No one moved, so the old man asked, "Jati hastc Fulani?" When he had finished, twenty-five men stepped forward. They were all the slaves of Joseph Malgamont, bought the day Bebai was sold. Samba eyed the dike with new determination. He knew everyone there would be hung if they didn't escape.

Lucile contentedly widened her blue eyes and stretched under the strong arm of Bebai. She smiled at him enough to embarrass him. His tattoos shone ebony against his red flushed face.

Far away the sound of rifles firing echoed up from somewhere close to the river.

"We must go in a hurry!" he exclaimed as he stood up, then helping her to her feet he pulled her along the ridge. All day long, as they marched through the trees, sporadic gunfire and war cries could be heard coming from the valley below.

"What do you think is happening? Is it the Apache still trying to kill my brother?" A faint quiver of hopelessness could be heard in her tone.

"I think a great upheaval is happening between the Indians and the French. I don't know if your brother is down there, but there is nothing we can do to help him. Chamfort will have to do that. We must make it to the city without being pulled into the madness that has gripped this place." Lucile found a sudden new energy and forged ahead. By the middle of the afternoon, the battle sounds were not heard any more and that was a relief to Bebai. The high ridges gave way to flower covered open meadows. It didn't seem anything like the nightmare of the past two days. This country was beautiful, but still a wild and untamed place, Lucile thought as she broke the purple and yellow flowers off. The calmness stirred her heart.

"Bebai, I'm sorry if I treated you unfairly, you know...before I knew you. If we survive this, I'm going to do everything within my power to set you free. Your life so far has probably been a nightmare. You being sold into slavery like you were." She peered at the back of his head hoping he would talk to her about his life.

"A nightmare would be more welcome than what I have seen and done these last six years of my life." He looked up sharply at the sky as he gathered his thoughts. "Six years. Has it been that long, Bebai, since you ran the antelope out of the bush in front of the slavers?" He spoke as if he was talking to himself. A great weight had been lifting from his soul the last few weeks since his English lessons with Lucile. He felt a freedom to unload all the emotions he had kept hidden inside for so long.

"Yes, it was six years since I ran across the trail of the slavers. They had a group of women and young girls tied to poles dragging them along through the tall grass headed towards the ocean. I must have surprised them, poking my body out of the bush in the middle of their horrific parade, because they froze just long enough for me to dive back to the safety of the tall grass. Then I ran for my freedom back up the Mambee. I thought putting distance between us was my only hope, but when I heard the cries of the Anteki warriors, I realized I was really running for my life." He paused as he pushed a limb away from the trail for her, then he resumed his story. " I killed my first man that day. Actually, he was just a boy." Lucile stopped on the trail surprised at what Bebai had said. He tugged at her arm making her resume her walking.

"The boy was one of the Anteki. Five of them were after me before I knew it, trying to run me down. A fast, young boy sprinted away from the others, quickly shortening the distance between us with every push of his legs. He was getting closer and I knew he was about to throw his spear. I heard his feet slide through the sand as he gathered himself to let his pointy stick slice towards me. I judged it perfectly, falling to the ground and it passed over my head. I quickly scrambled after the weapon, turning it on the boy who came so fast he ran the blade through his body. Everything slowed as dust clouds floated motionless around the boy gushing blood and looking into my eyes in disbelief that death had come to him so young. With my lungs still throbbing, I took his weapons and pushed my body along the trail towards a hill not looking back until I stood high above the valley. Great screams of pain echoed out over the Savanna. I had heard screams like that once before and I knew the sound well, a father losing his son."

A sudden breeze blew past them, pushing Lucile's blonde hair away from her face then letting it fall framing her dark blue eyes. Bebai noticed how beautiful she was; he looked on her for a long time.

"I smell the ocean and believe me, I know what the ocean smells like. We're getting closer." He pulled at her once more and she began to follow.

"If the Anteki never caught you, how did you become a slave?"

"While I was away hunting, my brother killed my father and took the Fulani throne. When I arrived home, my brother took me captive, then told everyone I was dead. He sold me to the slavers who took me to France where Dubois bought me. I did many horrible things as the slave of Dubois. Things I will never forget." With that, the conversation ended and Lucile knew not to ask anything more.

The foreboding shadows caused by the late evening sun reached across their path. Bebai was still trying to hurry along, but Lucile could tell by the defining lines in his muscles he was still tense and the dark holes created by the evening light slowed him. They traveled on another hour, ducking in and out of good hiding places until they came to a large hill blocking the path. Lucile was tired and she tugged at his arm, telling him she needed a rest. His big hands pushed dirt and limbs away from a smooth place on a log, then he helped her to sit. Bebai caught himself staring at the pretty woman. She was vulnerable and her clinging to him gave him a sense of equality. He vainly dreamed of the two of them finding a life with each other, but he knew all his dreams would change as soon as they reached civilization. He turned from his daydream to the sound of guns shooting out beyond the hill.

He motioned for Lucile to stay while he pulled himself up the hill to take a look. To his amazement, the streets of New Orleans spilled out towards the water just down the other side.

"Pop, pow." Shots rang out far away, close to the slave pens. In the light of the burning buildings, he could see the sailors on the dike shooting out at a massive group. "Slaves, it's slaves attacking the sailors!" Bebai yelled. Lucile scrambled to his side. "It looks as if the slaves are trying to make it to the big boats, but the men on the landing are keeping them back."

Somewhere down below, in one of those moments of quiet calm during battle, a voice cried out as clear as could be. "Jasira matoti."("We live to die.")

He couldn't believe what he had heard. His men, the Fulani, were down below giving out their battle cry. Emotion seizing him, tall and proud he stood, calling back across the calm.

"Bebai uti tuyedi." ("Bebai is with you.")

His voice, deep and strong, echoed off the cathedral walls. So strong was his call, even the sailors turned to gaze at the top of the hill at the mysterious, shadowy figure calling out.

The Fulani below began to chant, "Bebai, Bebai, Bebai."

"Who is this Bebai?" Samba asked Nuna.

The man was laughing and cheering along with the Africans.

"He is their king. He is the king of the Fulani!"

Samba smiled inside for just a moment, but a sharpened rake handle was thrown from behind him high in the air. He watched it roll over, cutting the air towards the dike, then piercing through the chest of an unsuspecting Frenchman. In that instant, all two hundred slaves charged the wall. Their screams were so fierce the forty-nine sailors faltered in their attempt to shoot them, just long enough for the first wave of slaves to reach the dike. With knives, axes and clubs, the slaves hacked at the armed men trying to push them back. Samba led his men forward into the strongest part of the resistance, causing the battle to split into two separate fights. The group on Samba's side consisted of mostly veteran sailors, while the other group was mostly cooks pressed into service.

Bebai and Lucile were already headed down the hill as the two sides began to clash. Random cowards running away from the fight paid little attention to the pair as they made their way towards the battle.

Back on the trail, the road ran red with the blood from both sides. All the French soldiers caught between Chogah and the Soliel were dead. The Natchez, trying to get close enough to murder Pierre and his Dark Wind, trampled bodies into the dirt. The gypsy clan had cut and clubbed the Indians all day long. Weary, the blood-stained men fought, hoping to survive long enough to get back to the plantation for help. It seemed as if at any moment the Indians would overpower them, but in that instant, the band broke through the trees and stumbled into a Natchez burial ground. The warriors immediately stopped fighting and stayed atop the ridge overlooking the retreating clan, afraid to continue without a sacred blessing from the Soliel. The warriors' taunts and cheers burned deep into Pierre's soul. Never had the Dark Wind been driven back in battle and now, with his remaining men, he would return to the plantation where he would get reinforcements and go back to finish the job.

Pierre and his band made it back to Terre Blance only to find a deserted camp. Everyone was gone. His pride was broken for the moment. "This battle is lost, men, retreat back to the city." The gypsies turned down the dusty trail towards New Orleans and as they did a great cheer went out over the valley from the victorious Natchez.

As Bebai and Lucile rounded the corner onto Canal Street, they came face to face with a group of thugs breaking store windows. It was obvious they didn't care if the city burned to the ground, as long as they got something out of it. An unshaven broken-toothed man jumped back at the sudden appearance of the large, black man.

"Well, now, what do we have here?" he said, eyeing Lucile holding on to Bebais' arm for protection. "Looks like we got ourselves a white woman that likes the darkies, boys." They all laughed and began to get set in positions around the two. "If you like that stuff, maybe all of us will have a little."

Once more, the sparat rose in the air, high above the Fulani king. His stance widened as his muscles tensed, showing all the toned lines of his frame.

The whiskered man must have been drunk, because he didn't notice the change in Bebais' body. He laughed and fiddled with the buttons on his pants.

The club came down, driving the deer antler down into the top of his head and out his ear. A quick kick by Bebai and the body fell to the ground freeing the club. Automatically, he swung it to the left, bringing it up under the armpit of the next man. The prongs on the horns pinned him to the club and Bebai in turn slung him over into two other men, knocking them down. The fourth man came at him from behind, intending to stab him, but he caught the wrist of the man with his big hand, turning the blade back into the rib cage, killing him. At the sight of the three dead men, the others ran away. Bebai urged Lucile to follow as he continued down Canal Street towards the custom house. He blocked random attacks from Frenchmen as he moved along, then he answered each attack with the sparat. The entire group containing the Fulani had pushed their way around the building and when he joined them, they broke through into the docks. Nothing stood between them and the tall ships. He turned to go, but he felt a tug at his arm. It was the old man Nuna, pulling him back around the corner and pointing back across the square.

"Samba of Bambara."

Bebai looked at the man called Samba, fighting, trying to get free to join them. Then he looked back at the tall ships. "Fulani, find the San Felipe. Get her ready to sail. Take the women and children with you; the rest of you, follow me."

He turned and with 50 men charged back into the fighting. By now, it was hand-to-hand combat. Anything you had became a weapon and the soldiers found out the empty rifles were no match for smaller sharper objects being used by the slaves. In a matter of minutes, Bebai clubbed the last man standing to the ground, causing a great cheer from the rebels.

Samba came up to Bebai and placed his hand on the king's shoulder. Looking quite serious, he said, "You know, King Bebai, you didn't have to come back to help us. We had them right where we wanted them."

Bebai's blank face scowled at the large plump-bellied man. Then, Samba's wide smile revealed the whitest teeth Bebai had ever seen and they both broke into the loudest laugh he had ever heard.

The two men clasped wrists in a handshake. The island man spoke first, "I'm Samba, leader of the Bambara." For a plump man, his grip was as strong as any Bebai had ever felt.

"Bebai, of the Fulani," he said, returning the tight grip. " I believe our ship is waiting." A great weight from years of abuse was lifted from both their hearts in that moment.

"I believe you're right, King," replied Samba.

"Then let's go home, Samba."

No resistance remained on the docks where the four ships were moored. The Fulani had already prepared the sails on the San Felipe and were rushing around, trying to get enough supplies on board to last them until they could make port elsewhere.

Samba sent his men onto two of the large gun ships and had them cut away the rigging, enough so that they couldn't be put to sea. Then he focused his attention on a small cutter called Lands End, moored between the two warships.

"Our plans and destinations, great king, are not the same, so I think I will take my one chance at freedom on an island ship."

"I understand, Samba. Good luck, my friend, and keep your eyes over the horizon."

Bebai grasped the big man's hand and shook it hard. Then Samba boarded Lands End and the Fulani King rushed to his ship.

171

The long day had turned into twilight. Pierre's wounded, weary men were glad the Natchez hadn't followed them past the burial grounds. *Not much further*, DeBois thought, as he looked out towards the horizon for familiar signs that they were indeed getting close. Something wasn't right, though, because several columns of smoke had begun to billow up above where the city should be.

"Men, don't be alarmed, but prepare yourselves once more for battle," Dubois called out to the Dark Wind. The adrenaline began to flow as the men tightened their ranks and prepared their weapons. Pierre led the army straight down Rampart Street only encountering the local citizenry fighting fires, but when they turned into Congo Square they saw a gruesome sight. A gang of slaves, set on revenge, were pulling their jailers out of the pens and bludgeoning them, then tossing them over the side. Just as a skinny, toothless slave was about to push the last guard off, a steel ball entered his forehead, tearing off the back of his skull. The shocked slaves tried to flee in all directions, but their feet were no match for the musket balls and in an instant, most of them lay dead or dying.

A sailor rounded the corner of the magistrate's office on a dead run. Then, seeing DeBois and his men, he tried to suddenly stop, causing him to stumble, then fall. A red flush began to appear on his face as Pierre helped him up. He asked him, "All the whites here ran away from these murderers. What would scare you so badly that you would run blindly toward them?"

"They're killing the sailors," he hysterically responded.

"They? Who, man? Get control of yourself!" Pierre shook him angrily.

"A giant, devil man, with scars all over his face has captured the docks. A king slave, I think."

172

"Bebai!" cried DeBois. "I should have killed him instead of selling him. Quickly, men, move to the docks!"

With Pierre leading the way, the gypsies made their way past the French Market Custom House, where all the sailors' bodies lay broken, then up over the dike onto the long, timber-laden docks. One small ship had already put up sails and was headed out of the inlet, but it wasn't the San Felipe. The San Felipe sat three hundred yards away at the end of the walkway and just as Debois suspected, the slaves on board were making ready to sail. He could see the tall frame of Bebai standing with his back to him. Pierre pointed his rifle at the towering figure ready to kill him, but a cry from the crow's nest sent the slaves running for cover just as the shot was released.

"Ah-eee, Ah-eee," the lookout called as the blacks with rifles returned the shot, killing the man next to Pierre. The clan was so surprised that the slaves shot back they didn't move until another man was killed, then they all ducked behind whatever they could find.

Bebai's eyes focused on the wooden crates where DeBois had hidden. There could be no mistaking the figure of his evil master, even in this fading light. Scared slaves rushed for the gangway only to be shot down by the gypsies. For several minutes, bullets fired from both sides, hitting their mark and killing many. Bebai was considering charging Debois when the strangest thing happened.

Several hundred yards away, the galleon Alexandria had arrived from Paris with special dispatches from the King. She was a fifty-two cannon ship and at that moment her Captain Louie Semon was surveying all the commotion through his spyglass. The only conclusion he could draw was that a revolt had broken out and with the burning city as a backdrop, he loaded the starboard guns.

173

In his jubilance, Samba paid no attention to the galleon lurking just beyond the light until it was too late. The first two cannon balls cut through the center deck breaking the main mast and bringing it down with a thunderous crash. The next two blasts ripped into the after deck bringing the ship's escape to a halt. Lands End was sinking and everyone that was still alive escaped into the bay as they watched the sleek craft break apart from the explosions.

In their race to reload, two young gunners mistakenly packed the powder twice and when the cannons were fired, the shots went over the intended target, resulting in a direct hit to the powder magazine of the Encounter moored at the dock. What followed was a tremendous explosion so large that it shook the cathedral, causing the bells to ring. Burning pieces of the ship flew in every direction causing small fires to break out all around the shipyard.

Bebai used this distraction to get everyone on the ship and the San Felipe lurched forward in the stiff breeze.

Helpless to react, Pierre could only watch as the slaves escaped. His only hope was the Alexandra.

BeBai also turned his attention to the Alexandra, now hiding just beyond the firelight flickers. He could see the crew frantically trying to reload the starboard guns.

"Get all the sails up, men, catch all the wind you can!" he cried.

The whips of the gypsies had taught the Fulani how to act quickly. With the order made, all the sails went up.

"Load the port guns," the king called out, catching many questioning looks from the slave sailors.

"We will cross over their bow to their empty guns." BeBai shook his fist in the air, causing all doubt of him to disappear.

With full sails up, the gap between the two combatants quickly closed. BeBai looked through his spy glass, anxiously waiting to fire his guns.

"Hold, Fulani, hold steady." Bebai's big hands clasped the wheel and at the last moment, he spun the ship to port. The San Felipe dug into the water, she moaned and cracked at the pressure. She leaned over almost on her side before suddenly straightening upright and cutting across the bow of the Alexandra.

"Fire, fire them all!" BeBai called out from the wheel. One by one, the cannons recoiled sending fiery blasts at the ship. There would be no answer from the wounded ship. She would be lucky to ever fight again.

It all happened in a matter of seconds, but as the San Felipe cleared the danger, Bebai stood on the side rail looking onto the deck for Lucile, but she wasn't there. Somehow, she hadn't made it onboard. He frantically looked to his far left, scanning each portion of the burning dock, hoping to see her, but he only caught a glimpse of Samba. He was at the end of the pier, standing close to the tall, delta grass with his hand over his heart and then he was gone.

"Goodbye, my friend," Bebai called out. "Goodbye, my magpie," he said softly with a twinge of pain deep in his heart. He had come to love this white woman. Then, the San Felipe disappeared over the horizon.

Two small canoes sat unnoticed in the brush at the mouth of the Mississippi River. Luckily, Chamfort had held them there when the big guns first started. Another few minutes and they would have been obliterated when the first shell came roaring in. La Miette covered her ears as Jouard tried to shield her from the blinding blasts. A twitching Francis Chateaubriand clung to the hope he

175

would live through this adventure long enough to mount an expedition back into the wilderness to look for his sister. James Knight held tight to the buckskin bag Manez had given him filled with gold, ready to give it all away for his life. No one understood what was going on. Chamfort wondered if the new American States had declared an all out war. New Orleans was a place that interested the new country. He gripped a tree branch so he could stand up, then and only then could he see the San Felipe making its run out of the harbor. Several parting shots and then all that could be heard were the bells of the fire brigade wagons as they rushed towards all the flames heaved upon the city. The weary group of travelers pushed the canoes away from their hiding place and within a short distance, they made it to a place where the muddy bank could be easily climbed.

DeBois had retreated to the steps of the cathedral and from there he was directing the clean up, locking up some captured slaves that hadn't run back into the swamp. With all the turmoil surrounding him, the presence of a group standing together looking lost did not come into focus until two men came forward asking where they could find Governor DeBois. Pierre let them know who he was.

"Governor DeBois." Chamfort extended his hand. "I'm Nicholas Chamfort and this is Francis Chateaubriand. We met your man, Chepart, at the slave sale right before we left for our expedition."

"Ah, yes, Chepart did tell me that you, Mr. Chateaubriand, were the one that bought the big slave that he wanted to help with your expedition and to protect your sister. I thought your expedition was long gone. Why are you here?" Pierre didn't notice the man dressed like an Indian, but Sabotha, lurking in the background, noticed the

176

presence of the pale one. She saw James wearily drop the heavy bags and she eyed a twinkle of gold just behind the leather flap.

"We were up river when all this started and got caught in the middle of it." Chamfort said.

"That's what I want to talk to you about, Governor. Lucile, my sister, has been taken by the Apache. We must mount an expedition to rescue her at once!" Francis pleaded.

"I realize your devotion to your sister, but look around you. What could I possibly do for her. Everyone's dead or dying from here to Fort Rosalie. Her only hope would have been..." he stopped short, thinking of Bebai. "Her only hope is that she was with the slave you bought, the African king, because not more than an hour ago, all this was his doing." Motioning at the mess, he added, "If he was here, she was too."

An awful thought began to creep into Pierre's head. Bebai knew where the treasure was and he had no way of preventing him from retrieving it. A slight shudder began at his feet and continued up to his knees. He tried to control the shiver, but when he heard Sabotha's voice right behind him, he lost control of it, sending his arms flailing about in all directions.

The group of men pulled back at the slight epileptic fit and of course, the sight of Sabotha's wrinkled face with the wart on her nose startled them more than Pierre's convulsions.

Pierre gathered himself as Sabotha whispered in his ear. "More trouble is coming; the bones don't lie. Tell them the girl will be found in the alley behind the Seaside Inn. Then hurry, you don't have much time."

He turned to ask her what trouble, but she had disappeared. He snapped his head left then right. "How does she do that? Her sneakiness is unsurpassed," he let slip out. The spectacle playing out in front of the group had surprised them, but what Pierre was about to say shocked them.

"Sabotha says the girl, Lucile, is in the alley behind the Seaside Inn. But I must warn you, although that may be true, sometimes certain facts are missing."

"What do you mean?" replied Chamfort.

"Well," he said, wrinkling his nose. "She didn't say she was alive, did she?"

The group of them hurried away.

Pierre himself shuffled away towards the mansion. "More trouble is coming, la- la -la. Where was that hag when the Natchez was killing us? The land is yours, take the land. Just take, take it!" he mimicked the witch, huffing and puffing the entire distance back to the mansion. Even if he had been paying attention, he wouldn't have been prepared for the witch's attack. Hiding behind the door, she jumped on his back with her left arm around his neck choking him. "Eeeeeee!," she screamed. He turned wildly in a circle, trying to throw her off, then noticing the knife gripped tightly in her hand, he too screamed and in a panic crashed to the floor.

"Ah, I didn't mean it! I take it back, o' wise witch."

She quickly cut the belly of a frog she had been holding in her right hand, squeezing the blood out around his neck.

"You've cut me, I'm bleeding!" He held both hands around the imaginary wounds; a stern look covered his face as he said,"You don't take criticism very well, do you, old girl?"

She was quick to pull the bits of bone from her pocket and cast them into the wet blood, as she straddled him.

"It's not your neck chopped off on the guillotine, it's someone else's; but danger still lurks here in the harbor if we stay. No time to waste, we must go!" she exclaimed.

"You mean I'm not dying?" he said as he gathered his feet under him. The blood ran down his shirt. "This is by far the most disturbing thing you've ever done. I'm not quite sure how I feel about your actions. Yes, I do know how I feel. Violated, to the core of my being. I've been violated." She exited the room barking orders to all her clan.

"You, Louis, hide for awhile here among the enemy, then bring us news. We go now, tonight! Gather what you can; bring the carts."

Pierre called after her, "Can we talk about this? We should talk."

Like rats soon to be exposed to the light of day, the Sinti scuffled down dark empty streets. Louis backed into the shadows to do Sabotha's commands.

Then they escaped out of the city into an unsuspecting land.

The inexperienced slaves tried their best to handle the San Felipe. It had seemed much easier when they worked along the whites, but the big ship had a mind of its own, chasing every breeze crossing the Gulf of Mexico. Dodging every sail they saw slowed them tremendously.

Bebai wasn't worried by the lack of the slaves' ability in handling the ship, but he was worried about how, in their haste to escape, the necessities to stay alive hadn't been put on the ship. His hope was to skip all the Caribbean Islands. Any stop would bring suspicions from the local government, but five days out it was evident they had to stop and restock supplies. With no money, their only hope was to land on some uninhabited island and take what resources were available. The men were scared.

A man named Ta Loolu had taken a position of leadership among the slaves and Bebai had placed him in charge of navigation.

"Ta Loolu, my friend," Bebai called out clasping his forearm in a traditional shake. "You have done the best, moving this big ship, but I must call on you to do a magic for us."

Lucile had taught the English to him well, but his words were still broken.

"We can't stop in ports to get food and water without the troubles. We need find a place where no whites and get us to it."

The old man understood and began pulling out the maps. One by one he studied them and placed them aside until he came across the map he was looking for. "On the crossing of the big water, a storm forced us to take shelter here." He placed his finger on a fat, little island that had a big bay on the eastern edge. "Dominica, it's called. You can't see, but there is another island in the bay, Bahia, where we can get food without being seen. We just have to make it two more days."

"Two days without water for the Fulini is nothing," Bebai replied and the slaves all cheered. The great pride of the tribe swelled with Bebai's words and once more they threw their bodies into the work. The ship suddenly seemed to sail easier and the wind blew harder making the next two days pass quickly.

"Land, I see land," came the call from the crow's roost sending the Africans to the side of the ship to look. The Spanish war ship rounded the tip of the bay just as the sun escaped below the water's edge, then they dropped anchor off Bahia Island.

"Clean the storage area, scrub the water barrels, get skiffs ready," Ta Loolu called out.

"In the morning, we find food and water." Bebai moved close. "Put your best men on guard."

Not too far away, in the early morning hours, Jean Batiste, having been reinstated as Governor, made his way from the war ship Alexandra to the steps of the Cathedral. "A proclamation by the Third Estate. For his acts of treason, Pierre DeBois is to be arrested along with all his men and transported back to France. Bla, bla, bla. All previous orders and provisions establishing Pierre DeBois as Governor of New Orleans is rescinded by authority of the new government. The King is dead, long live the Third Estate!"

During the night, a thick fog had covered the San Felipe making it impossible to see and as the men aboard prepared for their trip ashore, an eerie clanking sound could be heard in the distance as each wave rocked the ship.

Staring out into the fog Bebai asked, "What is that I hear? It can't be from the island. It's over there." He pointed across the boat. "It's out on the water."

Mystified, the men clung to the rail of the ship staring out to sea.

"I don't like this. Get your weapons ready," Bebai whispered.

Just as he said it, a light breeze began to push away portions of the fog revealing a Spanish galleon with all guns run out, alongside. The ship was similar to the San Felipe.

"The Santiago." Ta Loolu read the name. "It's Spanish, but it flies no flag of nationality, Bebai. What do you want us to do?" the small man asked the king who stood tall along the rail.

"Nothing, we wait, but have your weapons ready," replied Bebai.

A slender man on the Santiago called out. "Por que es un barco del rey espanol aqua?" ("Why is a ship of the Spanish king here?")

Ta Loolu didn't understand what was being said and no one answered, making the crew fiddle with their weapons.

181

"Pourquoi est un navire du roi espaqnol ici?"

Bebai understood the French this time and replied, "Nous sommes seulement desireux de troiver dela negritude et de leau pour notre long voyage."("We are only wanting to find food and water for our long journey.")

"Long voyage, you speak pretty good French. Who are you and where are you going?"

Not wanting to divulge any important information, the African replied. "We are simply free men bound for home."

"A Spanish galleon is hard to come by in these waters, especially one that belongs to the governor of New Orleans."

Bebai gripped his weapon as the air became thick and stale.

"Although, I must confess I have no use for the governor myself. Rumors abound that he will be replaced soon, very soon."

"If this is a trick, sir, I must warn you, we are prepared to fight to the death for our freedom," Bebai said proudly.

"My friend, this is no trick. I hate the French! They're egotistical and the Spanish think I am dead; I wish to keep it that way. You look like a man who can discern the truth. Am I trying to trick you?"

Bebai thought for a moment. "No, I believe you speak the truth."

"Then raise the anchor and follow us to our hideaway. There we will be glad to stock your ship for your long voyage, wherever that may be." As quick as it was said, the Santiago raised her sails and headed back into the bay.

"You heard the man, follow him," Bebai commanded.

The harbor was littered with the rotting hulls of many ships, giving fair warning to unwanted guests. Whoever this man was, it was evident he was particular about who he let come into the harbor.

A short sail away, the fog began to lift revealing a sturdy, wooden dock that disappeared into the trees. The two ships gently bumped against the dock, bobbing up and down as they were moored securely to the bollards. A large makeshift fort could be seen protruding through the top of the trees and after a short walk the freed slaves arrived in the compound.

Bebai was expecting a large force of Spanish soldiers guarding the fort, but to his surprise, there were only about sixty actual veteran soldiers supervising all the bustling activities inside the walls of their sanctuary. The other workers looked like slaves.

The commander, a slight, wiery man arrived, bowing slightly and waving his hat towards the ground, he officially introduced himself. "Juan Leon, commander of Bahia, at your service," he said rising to his full height.

"Bebai, of Fulani," Bebai said as he awkwardly made an effort to slightly bow.

"I have heard of your ship and the African king who sails her," Leon blurted out as if he wanted to hear more. "The privateer, Jean Bart, has been snooping around these waters a long time. My spies tell me he was tricked by Pierre DeBois and quite a bit of gold was taken."

Bebai hadn't thought much about the gold Pierre hid in the cave, but an idea now developed in his head.

Leon continued, "Your fame precedes you Bebai; you have been resilient in your will to go home."

"My brother killed my father and betrayed me by selling me to the slavers. There has been nothing else on my mind for six long years."

A fierce sadness overcame his face, causing Leon to interject. "I have a deep sympathy for the slaves. Living here, I have seen the brutality inflicted on them and I have tried my best to help when I can. That is why I am going to help you, on one condition."

Bebai knew there would be conditions; there were always conditions when dealing with the whites.

Feeling uneasy, he wished he hadn't left his sparat on the ship. "What condition would that be?" he asked, hesitant of the reply.

"Look around! As you can see, most of the men and women who live here are slaves we freed from the broken ships you see in the harbor and just like you, some of them want to go home to their families. I want us to take them home." He let his statement settle in before continuing. "With our two ships, there will be enough room for everyone. I've been waiting for just this opportunity." Holding his arm out to the King, he said. "Deal?"

Bebai aggressively clasped his arm just blow his elbow. "Deal," he repeated and his big smile appeared.

"I have one condition, too." Bebai almost laughed. "We must make one stop before we cross the ocean."

Leon gave him a mysterious look.

Chapter 19
The Gathering

The lazy, warm spring days hypnotized Manez. The hunting was plentiful. Even as he sat by the stream, a rabbit bounced by close enough to grab with his hands. He had planned on spending the day trying to catch a few ciwahts (fish), but watching life unfold around him, fishing even seemed hard to focus on.

Two small girls had made their way down by the water and began cutting cattails; their giggles and glances towards him diverted his attention away from the fishing line. The girls were cute and he decided to ask the tall, older girl a question.

"How old are you?" he said, motioning towards the oldest girl.

"Nooxini na sihux (Fifteen)," she replied.

"And your age, little one?"

"Nooxini naaxkux (Eleven)," she answered. The girls laughed once more.

"Why do you pick the cattails? Surely you would rather chase the saawiitakaa (butterfly). Or chase the arikaraanu (buck)."

A bashful glow appeared on the faces of the young girls, causing him to remember the glow in Dawn's eyes and how enchanting everything about her was. He bashfully asked the girls another question.

"What time of year is it little saawiitakaa?" They were even more embarrassed because he called them butterflies.

"It's spring, Manez."

"I know it's spring, but what time of spring do you cut the cattails?" he persisted.

"We cut them for the Gathering in the Round Valley."

Manez's heart leapt in his chest. He had forgotten that Dawn would be coming soon. It was time for the tribes to come together for the gathering and trading.

A white whooping crane clumsily flapped its wings, then took flight as the two girls stumbled onto its hiding place.

"That's a good sign, butterflies, when the crane is surprised. You will have good luck today."

A big catfish suddenly jarred his string finger. "Maybe I will have good luck, too."

Over the next few days the Cheyenne camp bristled with activity. Since time began, the Wolf Band had been the host to the great gathering of all the tribes during the first full moon. The ancient ones had erected a great circle of stones that pointed towards the many distant tribes. The big medicine wheel was thirty-eight feet around and had twenty-eight spokes radiating out from the center. Six other cairns lined up with the rising and setting of the sun. These spokes were adorned with flowers and cattails. Alongside the medicine wheel, a space large enough for drumming, singing and dancing was also decorated for the grand entry. Every tribe had a place in the big valley to pitch their teepees.

The Oto, or the 'fish eaters' as they were called, were the first to come. It was a long journey from the Platte River, their ancestral home. They brought dried fish and last year's seed corn to trade. These were carried in woven baskets that were stacked on hides tied between two long poles pulled by dogs. The Spanish pony was a luxury that hadn't been acquired by the Oto.

It was only fitting that the Arapahos came down the Piney Creek path next. No tribe had been as close to the Cheyenne as the

Arapaho. Manez knew the young men of the Wind River tribe well. They played a game using a ball and nets, often challenging other tribes at it. He nodded to some of the boys as they passed by. They, too, hadn't been able to find a way to have the pony and dogs pulled their teepees on poles. The Arapaho name means 'trader'. They were given this name because they were the first people to see the white man come up the river. The dogs pulled hard at the sleds covered with fox, beaver and muskrat furs to be traded. Manez could tell it had been a good winter for the Wind River tribe.

The Ponca came from the Niobrara River country. Their strange haircuts made him glad he was Cheyenne.

Surprisingly the Snake Shoshoni, enemy of the Cheyenne and Arapaho, came from Bear River. The elders said they were in need of tools and fire sticks. They camped just inside the valley by themselves, on the other side of Piney Creek.

It was always exciting to see the Mescalero Apache. They were the most feared group in attendance at the gathering. Many times they had battled the Vehoe (white man) and won. The ponies they rode were a testimony to their fighting skills. They were one of only a few tribes that could chase down the buffalo to kill it. Many hides of the beasts were brought to trade. A pile could be seen tied on the skids behind their horses.

The Blackfoot came along with the Hidatsa, Teton and the Iowa. Manez was glad to see their Chief Grey Snow was still alive.

The second day, the Kickapoo, Pawnee and Kansas tribes of the Platte River also arrived.

Even a few of the hated Crow men came to trade, but they kept their distance from the other tribes.

A group of Wichita came from the Antelope Hills; their tattooed faces and bodies were among the discussions around the campfire. The dotted lines around their eyes gave them the nickname 'raccoon-eyed people'. Their women wore elk teeth dresses, making them the envy of all the Cheyenne women. They brought maize and buffalo jerky to trade.

The Southern tribes were slow to gather, but the Paducans, Tawakoni and Kichai finally arrived.

Chief Cituta arrived leading a small group from the Cane River Caddo tribe.

Manez had just about given up on the Arikara, but just as the sun was hanging low enough in the western sky to shoot dusty sparkling beams of light into the air, he heard a disturbance above on the ridge. Grey Eyes stood alone for a moment; letting all who observed below see him with his full set of buck skins, headdress and beaded breast plate. Then slowly the rest of the tribe came to the edge of the ridge. The sun cast glistening beams of light on the group, then a cloud dimmed the light. Manez strained his eyes trying to see Dawn, but to no avail. Perhaps the old man, fearing the love of a Cheyenne boy, left her at home. He was about to give up looking for her when suddenly the clouds moved away and she walked into the light. Her smile called out to him as he remembered how much he cared for her.

It had been a long time since the Arikara had joined the gathering of the tribes. It was told by some of the old ones that the bad blood between the tribes had begun over a wild, black pony. The pony had belonged to a warrior named Five Arrows. He was a very good fighter, this Five Arrows, and his people made him chief of the tribe because of it. One day, while he was leading a raid on a neighboring Osage village, a group of Comanche attacked his camp, killing his beautiful wife and new son. Upon his return, he was so distraught that he cut himself and made sacrifices to the spirits. His grieving was so violent that not even the Shaman could control his outbursts. Five Arrows climbed up on the black pony and proclaimed to the tribe he would ride into the spirit world after his family and that everyone should wait in the valley until he returned with them.

Many moons passed with no sign of their leader, until one day, the black pony was seen running wild through the meadows. It was decided that Five Arrows was still fighting with the spirits for possession of his family and that his horse should be left to run free until the brave warrior returned. The buffalo left and the food played out causing the Arikara to move out of the valley.

Soon after they left, the Wolf Band of the Cheyenne, led by Onotsa's father, Nutkaris (Bull Snake), came into the valley. The black pony was too big of a temptation for the chief of the Cheyenne and he caught it to make it his own pony. The Arikaras believed that the Cheyenne Chief had doomed Five Arrows to spend his life in the spirit world, caught with no way to return to this world.

Like all Indian lore, whether true or not, it was a good story told with equal enthusiasm around both the Arikara and Cheyenne fires. Manez didn't care; he was just glad the Arikaras had decided to come. The air was thick with formality as the tribe was escorted to their place to camp. Manez was quick to realize the warm welcome he had enjoyed while being the hero of the old, gray-haired Chief would not be so warm here among his peers. The Chief just nodded as he passed by. To his amazement, the young girl he had fallen in love with had undergone a dramatic change. The boyish figure he remembered had been replaced with that of a woman. She smiled at him, but any other reaction between them wouldn't be possible and they both knew it. The night cast its shadows, reaching far across the round valley. As Manez gazed up at the moon, a creepy feeling dug

189

deep into his heart. Something wasn't as it should be in his world. Kanan and Onotsa joined him, their eyes fixed on the shining ball hanging in the sky and before Manez could say a word, his father said, "Something is coming, my son, and it isn't the bear."

The countryside was wild with renegade Indians. The drums had announced that a war had started against the French and every tribe seemed to want to fight.

Pierre knew the road back to the north would be impassable, so he stuck to the hills and ridges to the west. They traveled at night, cautiously making it unseen to the woods above where Ft. Rosalie once stood.

"Raphael, take seven of our best men and scout all around the clearing. Make sure we are here alone," ordered DeBois.

"I will see it done, sir," said Raphael, as he left. "Dominic, Sebastian, bring your four cousins. We are going." They disappeared into the line of trees surrounding the outpost.

Sabotha sat on a log, humming to herself while Pierre paced back and forth, frantic with worry about being discovered by the Natchez. He was especially leery of the one called Chogah finding them hiding there.

With his nerves fading, the witch's noises finally brought him to the end of his rope.

"Now what, ole wise, wrinkled one? What part of your foreseeing gets us run out of the city and hunted, not only by the French, but also, by every Indian in the countryside?"

The witch replied, "Not all things come to pass in da way we see dem. Sometime, we must pause. Den take a little look an' see how to push it all along...back into the order of da bones."

"That does it. I thought you were crazy, but I guess it's just me losing my mind, because no one here understood a word of what you just said." He turned to some men standing close. "Is it me? Am I crazy? How about you two. Can you explain what that gibberish was?" There was no reply from the men. "See, I thought so. You've lost it, old girl."

"May be so, may be so," she said, casting the bones on the ground and then beginning to laugh. "Come morning, we see. We see who get da bones back on track in da morning, Pierre DeBois."

Quite frustrated, he grabbed a bottle and chugged himself into a sleeping stupor.

Raphael was early to return and as daylight barely broke, he shook Pierre conscious.

"What, what... oh, ok. I'm up, I'm up, Raphael," he mumbled from his daze.

"The settlement is clear. We went deep into the woods and saw no sign of the Indians."

"Ok, then, let's go down and see what we have."

Raphael placed his hand on the leader's shoulder. "Let me warn you. What you will see is not a pretty sight."

The light breeze from the east was already pushing the pungent odor of decay up the hill into their nostrils, but Pierre led the way down.

Bodies of women and children lay scattered where they had been overrun. Some were naked, but all were scalped. Pierre's focal point, as he marched through the clearing, was the fort. Partially burned but still standing, he led the clan right into the center of the structure and the sight he beheld was shocking even to his eyes. Piles of tortured bodies, some tied up and others tossed on fires to burn, littered the ground. Even the crusty, old witch had to cover her eyes

191

and leave. Pierre was never one to show sympathy. No one really knew anything about him before he was the gypsy King. He had kept the death of his wife and child a secret from even the witch. If they had known the whole story, they would have understood his hatred for the Gitanos and even his levity towards life. As a young man, he had been a clerk for the National Assembly; a job with a good title, but poor wages. Poor but happy, he and his wife, Isabella, had a son, Deton, and as the family grew, the pitiful salary offered by the Assembly didn't support them. They found a place to live just across the river on the Rue De Sharmane. Most aristocrats wouldn't dream of living across the river, but not being a wealthy man, he couldn't afford anything else. After all, the people in the poor part of the city seemed to be good people. He, himself, was raised there; an outcast, a bastard son of the King's brother.

One night, while the family was walking home from the market, a group of young Gitano men started admiring his pretty, young wife. One thing led to another and the teasing escalated into touching her. Pierre plunged into the men only to be knocked out. Several hours later when he regained consciousness, he found her battered body lying dead next to their son. He became a drunk for a while, then he learned to fight and began to haunt the local hangouts, looking for the men who killed his family. One by one, he killed them and the very last one was Calonne at the battle of Mouffetard.

DeBois stood in the midst of the bodies and began to speak. "I know it's too much to ask of you because you have no loved ones here, but we must honor the dead and bury them." He found a doll in the dirt and held it as he talked. " They are our kinsmen and if you believe in going to a better place when we die like I do, then we owe it to ourselves to take the time to put all of them in the ground."

No one knew what stirred the heart of Pierre into showing a sympathetic weakness in the deaths of those around him. The story of his life was a well-guarded secret and the truth about his sensitive soul was kept well-hidden behind the face of stone. Without a word, the men scattered in all directions to bury the bodies and the morning turned to late afternoon as the last one was put under the earth. During the process, Pierre noticed the arrival of Louis and his men, with them a stranger bound in ropes.

"Da bones begin to shake. Ha ha ha," said Sabotha, laughing.

"Louis, I hope you bring good news from New Orleans," DeBois said.

"I have the news you seek, but I am afraid it won't be to your liking."

"After this day, even the bad news will be nothing to our hearts." He tossed the doll to the ground.

"Hundreds of soldiers have landed. Lafayette himself, at the head of the army, has orders to avenge the deaths of all Frenchmen, but he also has sworn on his life to find you."

"Is it possible to take a ship from the harbor?" He knew the answer to the question before he asked it, but the thought of Bebai taking all the gold infuriated him. Louis anticipated Pierre's question and retrieved a strange man from the group behind him and pushed him to the ground.

DeBois eyeballed the white man dressed like an Indian then asked, "Who is this and what does he mean to me?"

"This is James Knight. He has something you will be interested in," said Louis.

Sabotha whispered to him, "Da bones knows what come next, da bones know."

Louis handed the bags full of gold to Pierre.

DeBois smiled slyly as he helped poor James Knight up, then he said, "James, if you wish to live another day, you will take us to where this gold came from." Pulling his knife from hiding, he continued, "Would that be something you'd like to do for me?"

Despair had settled into James' heart. It was fate that kept pulling him back towards death. Kidnapped from New Orleans only steps away from being able to go back home. All his faithful companions that had died because he had convinced them to take the journey with him through the great lakes. It was only fitting that fate would keep him until he joined his men in death.

"I will try to take you there," he submitted.

"Good then! We're good; the bones are dancing." He turned to Sabotha. "They are dancing, aren't they?" She gave him a pitiful look. "What? No dancing bones! Gather what we need. We will move in the dark," he said, as he stepped away.

Traveling in the dark was hard for a group the size of the clan, but a full moon helped them see and after two nights of pushing northwest they could no longer hear the war drums of the Natchez. Within the safety of a small canyon, the clan took shelter after eyeing the morning light.

"Our supplies are running low," Pierre confided with Sabotha. "You, James, how much farther to the gold?" he whispered to Walks Far.

"Maybe three days, four if we keep going at night," he said, but he wasn't sure. Manez was the one who knew the way. He wished he were with the young warrior now.

"Louis, bring the Osage scouts."

Louis quickly retrieved them. "We're getting low on supplies. What do they know about this country?" he asked.

Louis turned and for several minutes conversed with the two Osage scouts.

"It seems there is a Quapaw village that we will pass one night's walk from here." Pierre shook his head with satisfaction. "It is a well-defended village, nestled between two rivers and no one has ever defeated the Quapaw in this place."

"We will see, we will see. Daylight is coming. Set the guards and get some sleep. You all will need it."

Pierre slipped away to where Sabotha was resting in solitude. As he came close, she had her eyes closed so he approached her cautiously, wondering if she might cast some disgusting thing at him and scream that infernal Latin gibberish. Instead, she sat still, looking almost dead. It wasn't the first time he thought she was dead; he had expected it for years. He never could tell with her pasty white, wrinkled skin. Closer and closer he moved towards her until he was a breath away, then he stuck out his finger to touch her on the face. Her eyes popped open and they both screamed, disturbing the camp.

After she had recovered from her scare, Sabotha said, "You shouldn't scare old ladies by sneaking up on them. You could kill them."

He jumped back. "Really, I scared you? That's a first." He kept looking around, not believing it. "When do the slimy things jump out and get me?" She didn't laugh.

"I've looked at da bones and even though the White Witch still fights me in my dreams, it looks as if our new path is safe. A well-planned battle will bring you success." She turned away, fast asleep once more and he also went to lay his weary body down for rest.

195

The Quapaw guards were relaxed, enjoying the cool evening despite the fact that Eagle Horse, the Chief, had postponed the tribe leaving for the gathering. He had seen an ill-fated wind in his dreams. The warriors had become lazy at their duties; after all, they had never been attacked by anyone. Nestled on a strip of land between a branch of the Mississippi River and the mouth of the Missouri River, they were surrounded on almost all sides by water. The only way into their camp was through a fortified ditch to the southwest.

It was one of those evenings when your eyes can play tricks on you. The light was hanging just between reality and the distortion your mind brings causing you to see things that aren't real. Several times the tribal watchmen thought there were more shadows clinging to the hiding places than usual, but nothing to alarm anyone about. The wind began to blow causing an even bigger distraction for the guards; the leaves scattered while small branches broke free and then clamored to the ground. With every fading flicker of light, Pierre moved his men a little closer. After living in the slums of Paris and being able to conceal themselves among the buildings, the wide-open spaces this country offered made it harder to slip upon any unsuspecting prey. The ever-busy wind distracted the watchmen until the clan was among them. The horrifying screams cut through the windy night, causing even Sabotha to jump every now and then and so it went...on and on, until all was silent. Pierre thought it was funny how utterly quiet it had become as he surveyed the defeated village. Eagle Horse, the Shaman and several warriors had made a stand in the back of the village next to the sweat lodge. Only a few captives and the Shaman were left alive.

"What do we have here?" Taking the headdress off of Eagle Horse. "One thing about our native friends, they do know how to dress," he said as he placed the feathers on his head.

The group had a laugh, but the laughter was cut short by the appearance of Sabotha.

"How do I look? Not only am I the king of the gypsy's, but chief of the Quapaw."

She wrinkled her nose and squinted in disgust. "What do we have here?" she said poking at the Shaman with a pointed stick.

The medicine man was clutching his leather pouch as he chanted, "Cee Kataria." Then he began to sing the ancient song.

"Bring him to me inside and we shall see if we can discover dis man's magic, then maybe we can keep him."

There was an Indian named White Wings. How he got his name, no one knows, but he took great pride in trapping beaver. Every night, he went into the wide creeks lining the Missouri to check his traps and the night of the attack was no exception to his routine. A large bear had been raiding his traps. The Crow had told stories about the bear attacking their village and he was very uneasy on his walk back home. White Wings hated the wind; it made all the signs really hard to read at night. Even as difficult as it was, his instinct told him danger lingered on the path ahead, so he slipped off the trail making his way through some willow bushes. He was looking for bear signs, but he found the hard track of Vehoe shoes instead and after a few minutes of following, he slipped up behind the white man. His elk horn knife slashed across the man's neck, but to his surprise the Vehoe swung wildly backward, stabbing him with his steel blade before the Vehoe died from the neck wound. The wounded hunter made his way close to the tree line only to gaze out into the firelit night at the horrifying sights of his people being slaughtered by ghostly figures. His mind said to rush into battle and fight, but the pain from his deep cut throbbed, sending survival messages to his head. White Wings faded into the underbrush, thinking if he could just make it to the Round Valley, the Cheyenne would help.

In the middle of the Quapaw village, Pierre made plans. "The night will be short, Louis. Tell the Osage to take the prisoners they want and from the looks of some of them, I will expect top dollar for them when we meet back at this place James calls Thunder Butte. The ones that are left, get rid of them." Louis turned to leave. "Oh, by the way, if you see something I might be interested in, bring her to me." He smiled as Louis left him.

Sabotha, hiding in the shadows, mocked him. " 'Bring her to me', he says, 'something he might like, that is interesting'. It is this kind of thing that will keep you from your dreams." She tossed the shaman's medicine bag lightly in her hands. Then she went back to her prisoner.

The second day of the gathering began at dawn with the grand procession of the tribes. The Cheyenne were host to the gathering. Chief Onotsa carried the Eagle Staff and placed it in the center circle of stones announcing the beginning of the festival. One by one all the tribal flags were placed in the outer circle around the Eagle Staff. It wasn't unusual for an expected tribe to be late in arriving, but Manez noticed many tribes from the south were missing. The Quapaw, in particular, were absent for the opening ceremonies.

The entering of royalty distracted Manez's thoughts. He could see American Horse, Big Boy of the Arapaho, Blanket of the Sun,

Nez Pierce, Black Horse, Turning Hawk and Chief Washakie. One by one they marched past to their places of honor adorned in their finest feathers, beads and buckskins. Dancers representing all the tribes followed them, dancing in a circle from west to east, which included the jingle women, shawl dancers and the feathered men. Kanan liked the weapon dances best of all. At midday, Onatsa stood before the great gathering.

"People of the Earth, I greet you and welcome you here to this great celebration of life. I pray the spirits have blessed you with much and that you find what you are looking for here among the people. Bury your differences while you stay; let the dead not haunt you until we say good-bye. Celebrate!" he yelled out across the valley floor. With that announcement, the festivities began. The most exciting part of it all was the trading. Horses were traded for blankets, knives of metal were exchanged for corn seed and so on. The two brothers noticed many more guns were among the items to be bartered for as they walked through the trading camps. A fat Apache man was giving a demonstration of how to use the heavy weapons and it looked like too much trouble to the boys. They listened intently to bits of conversation and they soon realized that the Natchez in the south had won a big battle against the Vehoe taking all their weapons. Manez had never thought much about the Vehoe until he met James, but if all the whites were like his friend, he couldn't see how he could ever go to war with them. Out on the flats, some of his Cheyenne friends called to Manez and Kanan to come over. The Wind River boys of the Arapaho had challenged the Cheyenne to play against them in their hide game. The rules were simple; take the hide and throw it between the willow poles, no matter what was being done to you. Kicking, hitting and tripping were considered to be the fun of it all. Manez had learned to hold back his abilities because he never wanted to seem different from the boys his age and all was going well until he caught a glimpse of Dawn watching from the shade of the trees. He had the hide and was just about to be hit by a big Arapaho boy when he suddenly put on an incredible burst of speed, sprinting to the willows for the toss. It was so sudden, all the Wind River boys stood in amazement. Manez realized what he had done and he quickly grabbed his leg, as if he was hurt, and excused himself from the game. Kanan just laughed at him as he looked at the girl in the shade, then he took his place on the field. He hobbled a few steps, then he walked normal over to where Dawn was.

"I see you are not really hurt," she said, blushing.

"No, not really; maybe just my pride for making the Arapaho look so bad at their game."

She laughed at him and he melted in her smile.

"I'm glad you are here," he said sitting close to her.

"You know I had to promise many things to my father in order to come," she sternly replied.

"What kind of things?" he asked.

She was not quick to reply, but instead changed the subject. "Did I see you with a shield yesterday?"

"Yes, you did. The red shield of the Wolf Band. I am officially a man of the tribe now. No more games for me." He waved at Kanan as he labored on the field and laughed.

"Maybe not all games," he said throwing his grin at her. She crumbled inside at the sight of his smile.

"I have no ponies to give or scalps to offer your father, but could you wait until I do?" The seriousness of his question caught her off guard. She had known since she had run with him from the Crow how she felt about him and she knew his feelings for her.

"I told you of my promise to my father. I had to tell him I would not talk of these things until another time." Manez's heart sank. "But, I will say, if I have to wait, surely my heart will burst from sadness." Manez patted her on the hand.

He could see the teepees of the Cheyenne across the field and something was happening there. Sudden movements caught his eye and he could tell there was a disturbance. Onotsa stared out over all the activity and Manez could tell he needed them. He stood, not wanting to go and gently place his hand on her shoulder. "I must go, my father needs me. I will speak more about these things soon."

Her pretty face showed her feelings of disappointment as he ran across the field to get Kanan. His brother was quick to join him, sprinting up the incline towards their father.

As they arrived in front of the lodge, they saw a bloody, almost dead Quapaw brave being carried inside.

"Father what has happened here?" Manez asked as Onotsa motioned for the two boys to follow him inside.

"A man from the Three Corners Quapaw tribe has been found on the path almost dead. He only says one thing over and over. 'The shadows are killing my people.' This message is confusing to me. I have sent for the Shaman to tell us what it means."

Manez drew close to the Quapaw brave. "I know this man. His name is White Wings. I've seen him trapping in the woods many times."

The Shaman arrived and studied the man's wounds while talking to himself in a whisper. He brought out the sage powder and bitterroot, binding the wounds of White Wings, but before the Shaman could completely finish, he poked at the air as if jabbing at an invisible enemy; then he cried out, as if in pain.

"Oh cheeee!" All the men jumped back, frightened as the old man began to chant in an unknown tongue. "Too kee sha nanik, nanik a tinnomi ah." Over and over he said it as he began to dance around the room shaking his rattle. "Too kee sha nanik, nanik a tinnomi ah." He occasionally grabbed a handful of dirt and squeezed it tightly before flinging it into the air towards the wounded man. An hour went by and slowly the medicine man calmed down and quit his invisible battle with the afterlife. He knelt before White Wings, rubbing some of the dirt on his chest and patting him in comfort, and then he went outside. Onotsa and the others followed him outside and when they all had gathered, he spoke to them.

"Do you remember the time that the four Shoshone braves were taken over by evil spirits? The time they did unspeakable things to the people along the Green River? When they were so full of evil that they killed their own women and children?" The older men shook their heads to him. He paused, letting them take in what he had said.

"I have seen the demons once more, here, coming for this man. Their magic is great and it is protected by something just beyond what my old eyes can see. These demons are many and they are dark, mysterious things that float through the air. None of the people of earth are safe from them and they come for us." The little hairs on the back of Manez's neck stood on end as a cold shiver shot over his shoulders and down to his hands. Kanan was experiencing some of the same symptoms as Manez. You could tell that even the bravest of warriors present were spooked by the disturbing words of the medicine man.

"A great battle is coming; not only with our bodies, but a battle with the spirits. I see an old woman with great power leading the demons. Come. We must pray and smoke the pipe to prepare for these evil things that come." He chanted as he led the group away to the sweat lodge.

Onotsa held the boys back, separating them from the other men, then he spoke so no one could hear. "I know your fear, but I have raised you to only fear what can be seen." He looked sternly into both of their eyes. Manez already knew what he was going to ask before he opened his mouth. "These floating spirits must be looked on with the eyes of the Cheyenne. Take Laughing Bear and Standing Man with you to look upon these beings, then come home to tell me of their truth."

Laughing Bear and Standing Man were summoned as Onotsa continued. "I hinted at these things long ago. I told you of a darkness coming from the south and now it is time to see if the prophecy is true." Onotsa clasped their arms one at a time, then the men turned and ran along the trail. Manez looked back across the field towards Dawn, his heart filled with regret. He had hoped this would be a time for them, but all he could offer her was a small wave as he vanished into the woods.

They hadn't gone far when a small chuckle came from Laughing Bear. Something was always funny to him, but out of curiosity Manez spoke. "What brings a sudden laugh from you? It couldn't be because we are running towards our death could it?" The laugh suddenly stopped, but Manez knew he was laughing about Dawn. Laughing Bear was a large brave, weighing well over two hundred pounds, but even at that weight, he was a fierce fighter. Standing Man on the other hand was a skinny almost sickly-looking brave, but he could run all day without getting tired. All in all, the four braves were odd traveling companions.

The path was clear, but the day's activities had shortened the day considerably. Manez had hoped to get a lot farther than they had before daylight began to fade, but as the light faded, he stopped the group in a sandy wash off the main trail. The rain and wind had cupped the bank back into the hill just enough to light a fire without it being seen. They were far enough away from the Quapaw camp to not have to worry for the night. Onotsa's words floated through Manez's head. Was he the one to save his people? He had been on many adventures, but something told him that this time, this one would be different. The men built a small fire, well hidden under the bluff and watched as the night came. It was decided that each one would take a turn watching the night and with that, they went to sleep.

Not far away, Pierre's day was just beginning. He pushed away the young Quapaw girl as if she were a piece of trash, then he pulled her outside, throwing her down with the other captives. James caught her fall, then the squaws smothered her with care from the humiliating wounds suffered at the hands of DeBois. James's face showed the sympathy he felt for the girl, but it quickly disappeared as Louis violently grabbed him up to stand before Pierre.

"What say you, James? She's a fine one, isn't she? You only wish a young thing like that would look your way." Pierre laughed with all the men around him. He held one of the gold stones up to the firelight. "Where do we go from here, English?"

James knew when they found the Apache gold that he was a dead man. His only hope was that the Unske was still protecting the burial grounds and he could once more survive the touch of the demon. "Further north, a place called Elm Springs with rock cliffs."

Pierre looked at the Osage scouts. "Do you know this place with the tall cliffs?" he asked.

The scouts reacted to his question and began to talk to each other. Pierre knew fear and he could read that same fear on the faces of the scouts.

"What's the problem?" Pierre asked Louis.

"They will take you there, but they won't go to the cliffs. It seems there is a bad spirit there."

DeBois gave the scouts a whimsical look. "Why should this place be any different? The whole god forsaken country, according to the natives, has spirits. Tell them to just get us there. Now get this mess moving, we're losing the dark."

With that, the clan turned their attention to the north, but all was not well with the Osage scouts.

As the light of a new day came streaming through the trees, the four young friends were already on the move. Manez always enjoyed exploring new places and the smoking hills along the big river weren't any different. Laughing Bear along with Standing Man started a game by seeing who could read the best signs along the trail. They spotted the place where the fox and her young pups crossed the trail. They also saw the rub of a big buck on the base of a tree. After some searching, the place he had bedded down for the night was discovered and Laughing Bear claimed the buck had just fled because of the twig Kanan had stepped on with his big feet. All day, the game continued and thoughts of the Quapaw people were ushered to the backs of the boys' minds until Manez felt it. Far ahead on the trail, something passed. He didn't see it, but he felt it pass; it was more of a sick feeling riding on the breeze. He held up his hand stopping the boys. His nostrils flared as his keen eyes watched the gaps between the trees. He waved his hand over his mouth and moved forward quietly another mile until he stopped once more to survey the tall grass along the trail. "Many have passed over this trail. They stayed close to the trees and dark places."

"Could it have been the Quapaw passing?" asked Kanan.

"No, the marks are not the signs of Indians, but that of the Vehoe and they are moving fast to the north."

The other three boys had never seen a Vehoe before.

"Do we follow them?" Standing Man asked Manez.

"No, we must do what Father has asked us to do."

He turned south along the path made by the mysterious travelers. Their progress became slow, but as the forest passed beneath their feet, their boyish nature came out again. Laughing Bear had picked up a willow stick along the path and proceeded to throw it like a spear at Standing Man. The projectile hit him in the back of the neck causing him to yell. The noise startled the others and they became suddenly still, their eyes scanning the trees. The buck they had tracked earlier sprang out of a thicket and with a war hoop by the boys, the mysterious travelers were forgotten. The big buck ran down the hill towards the river. Manez knew if he ran around the hill, he could get a shot as the animal came out the other side. The speeding boy pulled an arrow and adjusted it as he plowed through the trees just in time to appear in front of the dashing buck. He tripped a little as he let the projectile fly, hitting its mark just behind the front shoulder and bringing the animal down.

"Ahee, Ahee," he cried, as the others joined him.

"There will be venison tonight," he said to them.

They all rejoiced at their good fortune and they gave no lingering thoughts to the reason they were there. The hill provided a good backdrop to build a fire. A cool breeze blew off the river bottom and the boys filled their bellies with meat, then settled in around the fire for a good story.

"Standing Man, will you tell us your father's story about the people who came to earth?"

He ducked his head a little and a red glow appeared on his face. He loved the story time, but hated to be the one talking. The boys pestered him until he relented.

"It was a time when the earth had no human beings to make laughter together. Neshanu Natchitak (God) wasn't pleased. He wanted the people to enjoy what he had made, so he dropped a hollow log as a bridge from the other side. He told the people with laughter to go through the log to the other side. The warriors went through, checking to see if it was safe. Then came the young maidens and half grown children. An impatient pregnant woman, way at the back, began to cry because she wished for her child to be born on the earth and it was almost her time. The people looked at her with pity, but Neshanu told her to wait her turn. The medicine men went through, along with many workers. The ones who work with the hides and the cooks then passed through. So many went into the log, that the pregnant squaw couldn't wait any longer. She pushed her way to the front of the line and entered the log.

Neshanu Natchitak was so displeased with her, he swelled her belly causing her to get stuck. All the humans behind her couldn't get through and had to turn back leaving the impatient woman there for all time. The people on the earth were so happy to be in this place, they ran into the tall grass never looking back and that's why the tribes are so small."

The three braves shook their heads in approval. "A good story my friend," Manez said, patting him on the shoulder.

Laughing Bear sat looking into the sky for awhile, then he said, "The stars are beautiful tonight." The other braves agreed by staring into the black sky. "Do you know where the stars came from?" he asked.

"No, but I wish I knew," replied Kanan, laughing.

"In the valley of the Wind River before there was light in the sky, a great chief called Stone Eyes had twelve young, beautiful daughters. Having no sons, the chief made the girls assume all the duties of a son. He taught them to defend themselves using the bow and arrow. So everyday, the girls would go out to hunt, collect firewood and bring water from the river. On one occasion while they were at the river, they all decided to take a bath. Taking a bath in the river was a simple thing to do. They had splashed the hours away many times, but in order to get in the water, they had to lay down their weapons. The oldest girl agreed to stand guard while the others frolicked through the shallow, cool pools, but seeing the others having so much fun, she put her weapons down to join them. Hours passed as they played, not giving a thought to the many times Stone Eyes had warned them of the dangers close to the water. The Wind River valley had many cliffs with large caves cut deep into the brown earth and a bear sleeping there heard the girls screaming. He came slowly down hiding in the underbrush until he was close enough to charge them.

Snapping tree limbs alerted the sisters to the arrival of the bear, but it was too late to retrieve their weapons, so they clambered out the other side into an open field."

Kanan interrupted the story saying, "It must have been Manez's bear." It was a funny thing to say and they all laughed at him and then he continued the story.

"They ran to a large oak tree sitting by itself in the clearing and so, one at a time, they hurried up the tree, each one climbing up a separate branch as high as they could go. The bear angrily attacked the tree over and over breaking huge chunks of wood away from the trunk. Remember, I said there was no light at night and as the pitch-blackness closed in on them, the sound of the breaking wood drove them crazy to the point they jumped, hoping some of them would survive. But the spirits weren't willing to give up any of the beautiful maidens to the bear. They took them into the heavens and their beauty immediately lighted the dark night sky."

Manez had rolled over on his back in the sand during the story and eyed the brilliant, sparkling stars. "I see your maiden, Kanan. It looks like the years haven't been kind to her, she's turned into a squaw." Kanan jumped on him and for a few moments they wrestled around in the dirt before being exhausted. The fire flared, throwing flickering light on the clay bank behind them. Manez couldn't keep from looking up at the stars. They reminded him of Dawn; he wondered what she was doing. The fire crackled and the sparks flew while everyone drifted off into separate dreams, stirred by the story of the star girls.

At the last report from the Osage scouts, Pierre and his men were close to the Wide Valley of gold. The sun poked its head up over the horizon, causing the clan to scramble for thickets to hide in.

"Louis, bring me the scouts. I need to talk to them," DeBois demanded.

"Its no use, sir, the Osage disappeared an hour ago. They were spooked by something."

Sabotha was mumbling quietly in the background and Pierre turned to look at her. She was holding what Pierre supposed were the fingers of the medicine man out and she flicked them here and there, causing some of the rot to land on Pierre's black, polished boots. He quickly wiped them on the back of his pants and gave her an exasperated look.

"There are two things to fear here in this country. One is close to the gold and isn't something I can see very well because of the strength of the magic. The one you should fear lies out there." She accidentally threw blood as she pointed this time, causing it to spray across his boots once more.

"Out there, you say," he repeated as he kicked dirt up in the air. "You're sure it's not here, but it's out there." He kicked the dirt again. Turning away he noticed James.

"Oh, my, she must be tired! You, James, do you know this place?"

James recognized the line of trees just in front of the crack in the ridge. He caught a faint glimpse of the burial ground in the distance.

"Yes, I remember this is the place, but it's too treacherous to go in."

"What do we have to fear here?" he asked James.

A flushed feeling burned across his face. He knew they would see his lie, so he told part of the truth. "The Apache protect the gold. If you go in there, you mustn't let them know you are there because they will kill us." Pierre could see real fear in his eyes and knew he wasn't lying to him.

"So, it was the Apache the cowardly Osage were frightened of. Louis, pick eight of your most trusted men to go get the gold. Here, take James with you." He shoved him towards Louis. "You won't mind showing them the way, now, will you?"

James nodded his head yes. The eight-clan members along with James slipped across the flats and into the tall, cottonwood trees along the creek bed. James wasn't sure how he was going to do it, but he knew he had to find a way to separate himself from the others before being discovered by the Unske. The small group led by James edged up the path and into the burial grounds. From the looks on their faces, James could tell the gypsy men had never seen anything like the skeletal remains laid out on the wooden platforms. Every little puff of wind caused him to jump thinking about the lurking monster he had faced before. He placed one hand on the Arikara medicine bag hanging around his neck and he began to whisper a prayer.

"Ka den ra mori, Natchitak Neshanu Natchitak." Over and over again he prayed. (Don't let him take me, God. Don't let him take me.) His heart was pure and he wasn't consumed by the stealing of the gold this time; he was only wishing to stay alive. The narrow cut in the cliff was soon reached and the men excitedly pushed past James, gathering the sparkling rocks as they rushed in. They didn't even notice as James exited the crevice and went around the burial grounds sticking close to the canyon wall behind the trees. He found a place to hide in a wild plumb thicket causing a rabbit to scurry away, then he waited.

Early the next morning, Manez led the Cheyenne braves south, staying close to the river bottom. They moved swiftly and with every step they took, a deep, resounding misery replaced the levity they had shared around the fire. Manez pushed forward. *Don't slow down*, he thought. The sudden absence of any noise caused him to stop in his tracks. All living creatures were quiet. No birds chirping, squirrels chattering or even the sound of an insect. Stillness infected the forest and they just stood there for a moment, mystified by it.

Then one by one they moved silently forward through the willow thickets to where the Three Rivers Quapaw stronghold was.

The wooden gate was partially closed, just enough that you couldn't see in. Kanan followed a blood trail off to the side of the gate where he found the bodies of two Quapaw guards. Manez clasped his elk horn knife as he opened the gate. His eyes filled with tears as he looked at the crumpled bodies scattered around the compound. Most of the dead were warriors, killed where they had met the enemy, the wounds showed the signs of the long knives. He wiped the tears from his eyes, gathered his composure and continued his search. The houses were empty; no living human could be found. Laughing Bear and Standing Man moved quietly along both sides of the encampment while Manez with Kanan came through the center of the camp. In the back, close to the river, they found the sweat lodge. A great battle was fought here where the Quapaw made their last stand. The blood pools of the mortally wounded Vehoe were found in the dirt. Eagle Horse was tied to a pole high above the camp.

"Cut him down," Kanan said.

Manez made his way inside the lodge. The Shaman was staked to the ground inside a star. His eyes were cut from their sockets and his fingers were missing. Manez yelled outside, "Don't come in here." He cut the old man loose, then he wrapped him in a buffalo hide and carried him outside.

"This is the evil of our father's dreams." His eyes were big and his face serious.

"He warned us it was coming. Don't take time to bury the dead, just make them comfortable for the after life. We must hurry! Our people depend on us."

Manez's heart was filled with fear and hate. The thought of this terrible evil reaching the valley was unbearable to him, so he pushed aside his weak legs and found a new strength down deep inside.

" Come quick," Kanan called to the others outside the gate.

"What is it?" Manez asked.

"I see where the Vehoe have gone. They are dragging the people with them."

Manez surveyed the ground, then ran down the path a little way looking for more signs and retracing the attackers movements. Close to the tree line, he found the place where someone had stood a long time watching. A cold shiver shook his body.

"Standing Man I need you to go home and tell our father about what you have seen here. The gathering must prepare for this evil. Manez had seen him run for two days without stopping and with a story like this to tell, he would run all the way home to be the one to tell such a story.

"Tell my father we must go see this thing and find the Quapaw people. He will understand this, even if he doesn't approve."

He waved his hand at his friend and Standing Man hit his fist against his chest, then disappeared into the green underbrush.

The dark path was easy to see close to the village, but further away, the spirit path became harder to read slowing the three friends. Morning turned into midday and the sunset soon followed. Kanan could see Manez was troubled by something he was seeing in the grass.

"The path has split and the light is disappearing. I can see were the Indians have gone south, but the Vehoe goes north." He stood with his hands on his knees gasping for breath.

"We have done all we can today, brother. Let's rest and start once more at daylight,." Kanan said, grasping his shoulder.

"You are right. Even if we wanted to, we can't see to follow." He pointed towards an old cottonwood tree uprooted by some ancient storm. "Let's rest there until morning." The Cheyenne men packed into the snug quarters among the roots and it wasn't long until the day was just dreams.

Louis quickly had the men fill the leather bags with gold. In all the excitement, they had forgotten about James. He could hear them deep in the crevice and they were making too much noise. James recoiled as he saw the dusty whirlwind form for a brief moment, then it didn't materialize, but scattered. Across the field, Sabotha must have felt it move, too, because she began to chant, "Akee drom beth sha- Akee drom beth sha." She stood up and peered out towards the burial ground.

"Call them back, Pierre. There is something bad there; quickly, call them back." She grabbed at the bag around her neck containing the Shaman's fingers, as if it was on fire.

"Get it off me, get it off!," she cried, running towards DeBois for help. He grabbed the pouch from around her neck, then he flung it high into the air towards the field. The men heard her cries, too, just as they were about to cross through the burial ground.

"Something is wrong. Run, men, run!" Pierre cried out.

Sabotha fell to the ground in one of her trances as the bag, as if in slow motion, tumbled to the dry, dusty earth spilling the fingers out onto the dirt. Everything was still for a moment until the whirlwind came alive. It formed, growling on the heels of the fleeing men, overtaking the first man suddenly and turning him to dust.

The panicked group of men ran faster as the monster chased them through the sacred place. It touched another one, stealing his heart and killing him. A slow, fat man broke from the group, cutting between the platforms that held the skeletal remains towards James' hiding place, but he didn't make it. The Unske flew through his body. The hit he took caused the gold filled bag to be tossed close to

214

James, but he couldn't look; he held his eyes tightly closed and cowered with his head between his legs. The hot air of the spirit was upon him for a few seconds. He could feel it studying him. Then suddenly, it chased after the escaping gypsies, killing two more before they reached the safety of the boundary. Just as before, the spirit careened back and forth, growling while showing its sandy teeth. The two remaining men stumbled out across the field to the safety of the trees where Pierre stood in shock as he stared at the beast. Then he addressed Sabotha.

"The danger isn't here, it's out there." He kicked the dirt towards the witch. Right out there, I see the danger and I must agree with you, it isn't here. My question to you, hag, is if that isn't danger, what can we expect out there?" pointing in the direction that she had tossed the fingers earlier. White with fear, she was still trembling, holding the bones in her hand. Pierre had never seen her taken by surprise like this and it shook his confidence in her. The two men with pale faces full of fear appeared with the two large bags of gold. They shook as they looked back towards the dusty spirit prowling back and forth in the fading light. Sabotha briefly recovered from her stupor to begin tossing the bones once more. Pierre's examination of the bags was cut short by her quivering voice. "There's more, Pierre. Others come to protect what was stolen. We should avoid these protectors."

Pierre looked at her not sure what to believe, then he replied, "Night is coming. We should move northwest. Let's go. We need to rejoin the others tomorrow."

Up on the hill, James had regained his composure enough to pull his head up and look around. He was surprised to find the bag of gold tossed at his feet. The thought of the Apache coming spurred his scared body into action and he grabbed the bag, then slipped over the hill out of sight. Night was upon him, so he crouched between two large rocks and waited for morning. The day's thoughts bounced around in his head until he fell asleep.

Chapter 20

Awakening

Winter hadn't been very kind to Four Claws. The scarred bear had taken refuge late after the snow had already fallen. He had gotten the better of the Crow around the fire that night, but in their revenge, they had pursued him way into the winter snow hoping to kill him. They chased him until one day he managed to just disappear. It was a smart move by the bear to go upstream along a narrow creek, then to doubled back along a rocky path leaving no tracks to follow. A great spiritual significance was placed on his disappearing and the Crow, thinking he was favored by Mother Earth, abandoned their search for him. The snow began to fall all the while he lumbered back across the rocky ridges towards the wide valley of the Cheyenne. Exhausted and yearning for hibernation, he finally found shelter in the rocky crags close to the Apache burial grounds. The protecting spirit of the place also kept him safe. The snow blew high on the small opening, shutting out any light. He was well protected, sealed in the warm sod walls of his winter home, so he dreamed. His dreams were filled with wild, red plums and pools filled with trout. He dreamed about being a young bear and playing in the clover beside his mother.

"Thump."

He dreamed about the first man he saw and the capture of his mother, as his winter sleep spilled over into late spring.

"Thump."

His fierce eyebrows jumped at the thought of the fire he was thrown into as a baby and his eyes opened suddenly as the thump came once more. It vibrated the ground and its cries tore through the silent sleeping air to stir him. The dreaded spirit he knew well was close by and it pulled life from the earth as it moved. His body was stiff and at first stubborn to move. With quivering legs, he walked towards the light. Something was there in the opening. He focused his watery eyes, anticipating the arrival of the Unske, but there was a man hiding behind the rocks.

James felt the hot breath on his neck, but he didn't move a muscle. He trembled thinking it was the Unske's breath he felt. A large puff of warm air blew into his hair as Four Claws examined him. James' legs quivered with the urge to run, but they were rubber with fear and so he sat there shaking. The bear growled softly and seemed interested in the medicine bag Manez had given him. His great feet cut deep groves in the dirt as he pawed the ground. James noticed the missing claw and thought about Manez's story. The big bear moved around in front of James, launching several menacing growls. The noise echoed down the hill, bouncing off the line of cottonwood trees and then hitting them on the way back up the hill. Great drops of sweat appeared on James' face as he pulled his body back. The echo surprised Four Claws. He shook his head several times, snorted and shot a strange look back through the trees. James had turned his head away from the bear towards the burial grounds and he too saw the dust swirl under the hanging limbs announcing that the spirit was still aggravated. Without warning, Four Claws threw his head back towards the cliffs and lumbered away. "This is surely a strange land," James whispered. "Its magic I will never understand."

James stayed hidden for a long time before he stepped from behind the big rock. The late afternoon light was fading as he gingerly made his way back down the hill. Carrying the pack of gold, he kicked his way through the prairie grass, partially brown from the winter's kill, to where the clan had camped the night before. Here he was once more, a lonely soul cast out onto an ocean of uncertainty. He suddenly wished he had never taken his doomed crew in search of the northern passage. Little drops of water appeared in the corners of his eyes as he tried to look around. The fire pit still held glowing embers of an earlier fire and portions of a cooked rabbit lay on the circle of rocks that surrounded the fire. A broken knife and a torn shirt were found on the ground close by. As quickly as he could, he grabbed them up, escaping into the woods, distancing himself from that horrible place. He dried his tears, but his heart was still broken and many personal questions loomed in his mind. How many lives were changed because of me and what good is it for me to go back? His tired, rubbery legs folded under him causing him to fall close to a split tree trunk. He couldn't go on and so he concealed himself. Tomorrow I will make a spear from this broken blade and with any luck at all, I will make it home. He touched the bag of gold once more. Maybe I can make things right, he thought, just before he fell asleep.

Ever since daylight, Kanan, Manez and Laughing Bear had been trying to run down the mysterious visitors. They had gained a lot of ground, but the trail they were following divided just beyond the grassy valley. The signs brought Manez to a stand still. As he bent down to examine the trail, he spoke to his brother.

"The Kansa live just beyond the Antelope Hills to the north," he said pointing with a flat hand. " I believe this wind is blowing in their direction and our brothers must be warned of what we have seen at the two rivers camp." The others nodded in agreement, so Manez continued, "Both of you will cut across the ridges to warn the

Kansa." He stood up while he looked far away. "This path will get you ahead of them. I will follow close to them to learn just what they are."

"Are you sure we should split up. I would feel better to have you on my side if there is to be trouble," Kanan replied.

"Look here; the path that splits shows Indian signs...soft leather. I think these are some of the Quapaw that were taken. I will see this before I join you."

Kanan could see in his eyes he was determined, so he didn't try to change his mind. "Be safe brother and remember you're not as sneaky as you think you are." Kanan laughed, clasping Manez's hand.

"We will have to have the sneaky contest when we return my brother."

With a yelp, Kanan and Laughing Bear bolted up the trail and out of sight while Manez turned his attention to the path left behind by the passing of the darkness. He was alone, moving through the landscape; his senses reawakening with every step he took. His surroundings jumped out at him and he began to move quickly through the woods. A movement out in a clearing caught his eye and he slipped into a thicket watching. Three Osage braves ran quickly across the clearing. They were headed south and always looking back to the north. *Something has scared them,* he thought. When he was sure they had gone, he continued to follow the Vehoe. He was surprised when the trail turned north towards the burial grounds of the Apache. Now he knew why the Osage ran away from the Vehoe; they were frightened by what was hidden there. Despite the fear he felt inside, Manez continued to follow the trail north towards the gold canyon. The tracks outside the burial place told him all he needed to know. The outline of brown dust of two men could be seen on the ground. The markings of the Arikara moccasin confused him. It was the footprint of Walks Far. He wondered why James would bring the Vehoe there and if James had survived the Spirit once more or was he the dirt stained ground. Night was coming quickly. He had been lucky with the Apache, so Manez put some distance between himself and the burial ground before he made his way into a plum thicket to sleep.

Kanan's progress was slow. He had hoped he could arrive at the Kansa camp quickly, but his path had been blocked all day by large trees blown down in a spring storm. The broken limbs made the morning disappear and about midday, Kanan turned his attention to the ridge above, but that, too, was a hard path. The loose, crumbling rocks and hidden cracks on the ridge didn't offer any increase in speed for them. At times, it was slower than the valley below.

Time slipped by and as it did, the two friends became careless, often stumbling about clumsily. It was so difficult that when they found a smooth place, they almost jogged to the next pile of rocks. Their system was working until a great gap in the rocks suddenly appeared, causing Kanan to stop abruptly. He would have been fine if Laughing Bear hadn't bumped him, causing him to flail at the air uncontrollably. Just as he thought he was going over the edge, Laughing Bear grabbed his belt, pulling him back. Several little rocks had tumbled over the edge and Kanan listened intently for several seconds until he heard them hit the bottom.

"I thought I was going over."

Laughing Bear moved up next to him and looked over the edge. 'I thought you were too," he replied, patting him on the back.

"Our only choice is to move back down into the trees," Kanan said, disgusted at the time being wasted. With heads dropping and the darkness collapsing on them, the two friends fought their way down the ravine into the thick brush below where, exhausted, they hid in the roots of a tree, then fell asleep.

Not far behind them, Four Claws had found a large plum thicket and although the fruit was still green, he didn't waste anytime devouring as many as he could. Winter had taken its toll on the big bear causing his rib bones to protrude through his furry sides. He moved easily along through the night, foraging on potato roots and anything else he could find. He headed west; something compelled him to go in that direction. So without even thinking, he moved closer to the valley of the Cheyenne. As light came, a slight breeze began to push from the south and the storm that had promised to come all night, finally sent lightning bolts across the sky. He stood on his hind legs, sniffing at the moisture caught in the breeze.

A sudden gust of wind threw bits of debris into the bear's face, then rushed past him. The same gust of wind that had pelted him rolled some dried grass through the fire pit the clan had left back down the trail. It then rolled it out to the other side into the dead prairie grass. It burned slowly until another blast of wind whipped at it, making it come alive. A wall of flames was instantly thrown with the wind whipping a five-foot flame across the open fields and into the trees. The heat of the fire changed the moisture in the air as it ran in front of the storm. Four Claws stood tall with his eyes fixed back down the trail and as the smoke billowed towards him, he knew it was a wild fire.

The smell of smoke in the air also stirred Kanan; he rubbed his sore back as he pulled himself from beneath the tree. Groups of birds chattered by hurriedly, gliding on the newfound wind. A sudden movement brought his eyes back to the ground as four deer and a buck eyes wide with fear danced past. At that moment, he knew it was a wild fire.

"Laughing Bear, get up!" he said, violently shaking his friend.

"What, what's the matter?" Laughing Bear asked.

"There's a fire coming, we must hurry." Kanan began to run down the cluttered trail, hurriedly attacking each fallen limb along the path. Laughing Bear lagged behind, his belly bouncing as he jogged along.

"The fire is moving fast, hurry." Kanan spurred his friend to no avail. "The river is just beyond that cliff," Kanan called back over his shoulder. At one point, he thought he would have to slow down, but in that moment, his friend began to run upon him. He began to bump and push from behind throwing his balance off.

"What's got into you? You're going to make me fall!" Kanan griped.

"Oh, you'll see," he said.

As the two reached a wide spot in the trail, Laughing Bear passed Kanan. "Hanu katariin!" he called out. (Go on, fast!)

Kanan was surprised at his friend's speed, but was even more surprised when he glanced behind them. Five hundred pounds of frightened bear was pounding along the trail, gobbling up the loose dirt.

When he ran faster, the bear ran faster and when he grew tired, the bear slowed unable to get around them. It was a funny sight; the three of them sprinting down the trail through the trees, with the two Indians making all kinds of strange noises as they ran. The fire came up behind them suddenly. The heat was licking at their hair just as the river appeared beside the trail and with a splash, they all plunged into the cool water. The crackling flames danced past, leaving the three survivors safely concealed below the water line. It was a little disturbing to have a large bear that close to them, riding out the fire and the two Indians eyed him cautiously. Thunder clapped and the long awaited rain began to pour, devouring the scattered flames, then turning them into smoke. The bear pushed himself out of the water and up the embankment and as he did, he violently shook the water out of his fur. Still quite afraid, the boys stayed in the water up to their noses, leery to expose more than they needed to the hungry looking bear. Four Claws took a fleeting look back at them, then he galloped away into the lingering smoke.

Even with him gone, the two friends stayed in the water until their skin became wrinkled.

"I think we can go now," Kanan said looking at his fingers, then standing up.

Laughing Bear moved to the edge of the river and standing tip-toed, tried to look over the bank in the direction of the bear.

"I'm not sure what just happened, but I don't ever want it to happen again." Kanan laughed.

"I didn't see you laughing when you had a bear up your..."

Kanan interrupted him. "I've never seen a fat Indian run like that before, either."

They both laughed as they cautiously climbed out of the water. Kanan surveyed the landscape, getting an idea of where they were.

"See that gap in the ridge up ahead?" Laughing Bear nodded. "The Kansa camp is just beyond it." The two friends took shelter next to the ridge and it wasn't long before the rain stopped and the sun stumbled into the midday sky. They took a few moments to worship the warmth, then jogged cautiously along the trail, still considering the bear.

This was Four Claws' territory, now. He had shared it with an old bear named One Eye for a long time. One Eye had stumbled onto the burnt ball of fur just after the Vehoe had killed his mother and left him for dead. Old male bears aren't ever very good parents, but over the years, the Indians had killed off most of the big browns. As a matter of fact Four Claws was the first bear he had seen in several years. Whether it was for his company or because he knew something only animals could know about each other, One Eye raised the small bear until he was grown. Over the years, their paths crossed often until one year, when Four Claws never saw him again. In the Spring Four Claws missed him most and this year was no different. He climbed to the top of the ridge, just beyond the round valley and looked out over his domain. Alone, always alone. His dark eyes studied the landscape around him. Something about this year would be different for him; he could feel it, this year his life would change.

Chapter 21

Sweet Medicine

Over the hill between the gap in the rocks, Kanan and Laughing Bear ran; what they saw there was unexpected. Kanan gritted his teeth almost crying, "We're too late."

What was left of the village was burning; scattered bodies of the Kansa were crumpled randomly around the camp. Two half-starved dogs barked as they approached, but then ran away into the bushes.

"Many Vehoes were here." Kanan picked up the empty shell casings as he spoke. "They go that way through the forest."

A grim look appeared on Laughing Bear's face. "That's towards the Cheyenne." Fear gripped his heart as he thought of his family in the round valley. "We must go, Kanan," he yelled at his friend.

"I know we must." Standing, he grasped his medicine bundle with his left hand and outstretched his other hand towards the dead. "Neshanu Natchitak (God), hold the spirits of these people in your hands until we can come back to this place to bury them." He turned and ran after Laughing Bear.

The day was fading fast and with the fleeting rays of light, the boys' legs began to falter. Laughing Bear was the first to stop; he placed his hands on his knees to steady the heaving of his chest. Kanan joined him, gasping for air; he too was exhausted and relished in the chance to rest. The shadows that come with a day's ending began to stretch out towards them causing Kanan to look up. He had often been amazed by the day changing to night. He suddenly grew cold and terrified that the shadows were alive. The blackness moved and suddenly they were surrounded and taken captive.

Not too far away, Manez was tracking the Osage along with their Quapaw prisoners. He had been moving slowly, staying in the shadows. The rocky canyons of the Antelope Hills began to appear around him. He remembered the red, flat plateaus from a trip he had taken with Onotsa to trade horses with the Apache.

I will be careful now, he thought, *maybe even extra sneaky*. He laughed, thinking of Kanan. Always looking ahead, he slipped down a finger-like crevice and eventually appeared next to a big cottonwood tree that stood along the bank of the river. It was quiet, he frowned, it was too quiet.

He sensed an arrow was in the air and knew he was going to get hit before he even saw it flying towards him. His sudden twist away from the projectile caused it to catch him in the fleshy meat of his side. How stupid could he have been not paying attention; the enemy was coming for him. As he grabbed for his knife, something hit him from behind and a throbbing began in his head. He fell towards the river, the water pulled him in, and as he sank he could see the shadows dancing around and around and around. His arms were flailing for a hold; he missed the tree roots over and over. He swallowed water as a whirlpool pulled him down, slamming him hard against the bottom. There he was, going to die. Manez grabbed for the leather pouch tied around his neck, but his hand only found the bear claw. He looked at it and a peace came over him, so he stopped fighting the water, letting it take him through a big hole under the bank and as suddenly as he thought he would die, he popped up into an opening. All was quiet and dark.

Kanan awoke and found himself tied to a pole in the middle of a camp. A man was yelling and waving a bloody knife at him. "What happened to the Osage scouts? I cut that Indian deep and couldn't understand a word he said."

Kanan could see his friend's bloody body just beyond the fire.

"Maybe this one will talk. Speak French there, Indian? Are there any more of you that follow us?" The language he spoke was one that Kanan had never heard and he feared he was going to be killed. Pierre drew close and asked once more. "Are there anymore of you?"

Kanan could tell the man would have an answer or take his life. Pierre poked him in the chest causing a little trickle of blood to run down his stomach. With the knife raised high, he intended to end the life of Kanan, but out of the darkness came the most hideous creature Kanan had ever seen.

"Yo nonme titca." All eyes turned to her. She outlined his face with her long fingernails, but as she rounded his face, she took a little of his blood on her finger then tasted it.

She suddenly began to gag while she held her throat with both hands. Kanan recoiled at the violent gesture.

"Here we go, again. I suppose this will end in someone's blood squirting everywhere and I was just beginning to enjoy what I was doing. It's so rare that I get to stick someone."

Sabotha stumbled around then fell on one knee to spit out the blood.

"The one that was out there is near." She took the bones from the pouch and cast them on a broken piece of tree bark. "Ha re tack to see. Tomme nuk ta," she chanted, flicking at the bones on the ground, then suddenly charging at Kanan. "This one is connected to the Indian that follows us."

DeBois came close with his knife. "I was having so much fun. Can I cut him now?"

Sabotha grabbed Pierre's hand. "No, this one will be useful to us." She patted Pierre on his cheek. "You can cut him later, when we don't need him anymore. You two." pointing at two gypsies. "Double back through the woods. See if anyone else follows." The black capes disappeared back towards the Kansa camp.

The bones were retrieved once more and as she lightly tossed them in her fingers, she thought she felt something new. It was if there was another spirit to fear, but it wasn't really a person. She tossed the bones back into the pouch. After many years together, Pierre noticed the wheels spinning in her head. "What are you thinking? His question was cut short by the arrival of the gypsies and the men who had taken the captives to the Osage camp.

"Louis," Pierre acknowledged him. "You look a little spooked, my friend."

Louis looked back at the trail."We had trouble with a Cheyenne brave back on the trail," Louis replied.

Pierre asked, "What kind of trouble?"

"He was following our tracks along the canyon, even after we had wiped them out."

Pierre looked at Sabotha and waved Louis away.

DeBois had become suddenly tired. He had an ache in his bones opening a door to self-pity. Sabotha could also feel a sudden shift in the disposition of Pierre. It was something she had seen before at Fort Rosalie and she didn't quite know how to deal with it.

He leaned against a tree and spoke softly, moving the dirt with his foot.

"I've followed your advice and looking around, I don't see a king anywhere. The pirate treasure waiting for me in the cave will never be mine." Sabotha shook her head in agreement. "The Kingdom of New Orleans will never be mine."

"I know, I know," she said.

"Even Terra Blanca was taken from me." He whimpered a little as he said it.

"Then, we chased gold into the wilderness and even that is taken by that thing, what ever it was, and I am just wondering, when do I see this kingdom I was promised?"

She drew close and he put his head on her shoulder. It was as awkward a position as she had ever been put in.

"Cheer up, Pierre, It's not all about the wealth, it's about the power. This boy that follows is the answer. The magic he possesses is beyond anything I have ever felt. We can trap him and steal his power, then with this magic, you will go back to New Orleans and be the king."

"Really?" he said lifting his head enough to get a whiff of her nasty breath and then abruptly backing away.

"Yes, really. We will set a trap for the boy and catch him. Then the bones will take his magic." She turned away throwing the bones on the ground. "Nommie ke too tak."

Manez stirred from his sleep, but as he did his head began to throb as if it could burst open. Whatever had hit him left a cut on the back of his head. He soaked the cut with water and then he tried to pull himself from the water only to wince in pain from the gash in his side. Sliding out of the water into the dark make him uneasy, but with the help of protruding roots he soon found himself leaning against the cool earthen wall in the dark. It must be a cave under the bank he thought straining to see. A small beam of light ricocheted from up above making just enough illumination to begin to see shapes. The cave extended twenty feet back into the rocks and was at least ten feet tall. He could tell that at one time there had been an entrance into the cave, but it had collapsed scattering boulders everywhere. Manez tossed a rock into the darkness. He stared into the blackness until he thought his eyes played a trick on him. He thought he saw a man. Rubbing his eyes then training them at the spot once more, he pushed back against the wall horrified. It was a man.

"He-hello?" It echoed off the walls sounding empty. "Are you real?"

Once again, the echo bounced back at him. He sat quietly, waiting for his eyes to stop watering from the strain. There in the faint light, he could see a man sitting on the ground. His bleached bones began to glow and show his outline. He still wore a headdress; Manez could tell it was Cheyenne because of the Eagle feathers tied with red leather and strung with blue beads. There was a breastplate made of buffalo bones also tied with the hide. The skeleton was that of a chief. Manez sat there hurting too bad to move for a long time.

"What brings you here, Chief? I hope you didn't meet up with the same bunch I did up there. It was pretty tough for awhile." He suddenly realized that the man had died there and he could die also. "Hun-a nua- hun a nua." He began to sing a song of life and sang it until he felt the spirit come back to him. "I'm talking to a skeleton. What kind of a warrior is afraid of a dead man?" With his strength coming back to him, he crossed the dark space getting closer to the man.

His eyes were drawn to a medicine bundle still tied to the Chief's neck. It was a design he had never seen. He thought back to the story of the Konianutqio that Onotsa had told him and he examined the bead design on the bag. A leather scroll was held close to the ribs by his bony fingers, but the strangest things were the weapons arranged around him as if he expected someone to find him there. A two edged metal hatchet made with a bone handle was placed close to his right hand. The chief had a silver bow with gold tipped arrows and eagle feathers placed across his lap, as if he was ready for war. He reveled in the spectacular fierceness the Cheyenne had even in death. "I see you were a brave to be dealt with. Your weapons are mighty." A twinge from his wound brought him back to reality and he tried to adjust himself and get comfortable once more. Manez could just reach the scroll cradled in the side of the skeleton, so he retrieved it without disturbing the bones and then retreated back into the beam of light where he gently opened the scroll. His hand followed the symbols as he interpreted the story and as he finished, he almost cried. The bleached bones before him were those of Sweet Medicine. He knew the story of Sweet Medicine well. He was orphaned as a young brave and his grandmother raised him. As a young boy, he was sent to the sacred mountain (Bear Butte) in the Black Hills of the Dakotas and as he approached, a rock door opened beckoning him to go inside. Here the spirits told him he would stay for four years to learn the power of their magic and they told him he would be the prophet of the Cheyenne. He was given the powerful medicine bundle and four medicine arrows, then taught how to use this power. Two of the arrows, when held towards the enemy, would blind them and confuse them. Another that would kill and come back to him and the last arrow would turn back time.

In awe, he dared not touch them, this was a moment to be remembered. The throbbing in his head returned and he began to black out once more. Maybe he would just rest.

Kanan could see the sun beginning to sparkle over the horizon. He had been pulled all through the night as fast as they could go. A large grove of oak trees appeared up ahead and the gypsies settled into them like bats trying to hide from the sun. Kanan had never seen such a strange group of men together before. The Osage were enemy to everyone; he knew them well, but the blacks he had never seen before. He had heard of black men being seen running in the forest, but none were ever caught. Dark drawings covered their faces, making them hard to look at. It was the French he had heard of the most; although he had never seen them, many stories were told about them trading along the big river. The witch scared Kanan and he kept a close eye on her, even now as the group stopped. Kanan noticed some young Kansa girls tied together with a long rope. It would serve them better to have died back at the camp. The men were quick to secure all the prisoners; some began to examine the trophies they had taken along the way. Some slept, while others eyed the girls closely, but the day wore long for the helpless Cheyenne brave.

The throbbing in Manez's head kept him from real sleep. He turned several times and each time he rolled onto the rocks, a sharp pain flooded his body causing him to stir. He sat up, dazed a few moments until he recalled where he was, but this time as he remembered the enemy, he panicked, causing him to hit the wall with his fist. *Why am I here,* he thought. Then realizing where he was, he also recalled the attack and his fall into the water. He stared at the beam of light and then across the cave at the skeleton once more. "I must clean my wounds." Manez crawled close to the Chief to retrieve a piece of cloth and with some water from the pool he cleaned the gash on his side as well as he could.

A variety of roots protruded from the cave's walls above his head and after a small amount of testing, he found one that tasted like potatoes. The roots were easy to break and Manez eagerly devoured them, while he kept an eye on the skeleton. For several hours, he sat there wanting to know more about the man; he was drawn to the broken bones.

The light moved across the bottom of the cave and it wasn't until about noon that Manez felt like moving. Fumbling around in the dark, he found an old fire ring that provided him with a flint and using some of the broken roots, he started a small fire lighting the cave. The light danced around the room giving him an even more eerie feeling than he had before seeing the skeleton, but for no apparent reason he was drawn closer to it. A buffalo hide scroll was wedged close to the Chief's side along with a silver tipped axe. The handle was made of bone and carved with intricate designs. A bow of equal craftsmanship and a Cheyenne headdress were also there. Manez took in every detail of the weapons.

"Friend, where did you get these things?" He rubbed the slick finish on the willow bow.

"Oh, you don't know or is it that you want to keep your secret?" The axe felt light in his hands, but as he played with it he spotted the thick leather pouch on the floor close to the body.

"Is this the dust of legends? It is, isn't it? I can tell by the look in your eyes it is."

Manez suddenly realized he was talking to himself and stopped talking. He shook the bag around, then took up the knife and tossed the point into the dirt. The continued silence caused him to blurt out once more. "I still want to know. What was your story? Where are your secrets hidden?" The skeleton's empty eyeholes followed his every move as he opened the bag and took a pinch of dust, eyeing it closely.

At that moment a spider ran across his face and with an involuntary jerk, he tossed the dust onto the skeleton and it began to tremble. Patches of skin appeared on the body and the eyes holes lit up. A ghostly glow illuminated the outline of the man causing Manez to suddenly fall back.

"Uh-e-ah. Uh-e-ah." The bones moaned as they came to life. "I'm glad you have finally come, young one." Manez pointed to himself as if he expected the bones to talk to someone else.

"Me-e-e," he said pushing himself back up.

The skeleton suddenly stood up, causing Manez to fall backwards even more.

"I've been waiting a long time. The spirits have called to me and I knew you would come."

Manez continued to point at himself as the warrior talked. "I feel trouble in this land, even at the midday a darkness overshadows the people of earth. I see the end of their days and you are needed."

Manez rubbed his stomach. "It was the roots. I've eaten poison and now the bitter roots will drive me crazy before I die. This is just my imagination and poison; it isn't real."

"Quiet!" the spirit screamed as it began to float around the room. "I have seen the beginning of all life and I have seen death. I have seen the beginning of your life and I see your death. The darkness will end all the life of the people of earth Neesuunu has shown me these things." He pointed a bony finger towards the west. "Surely, you will go save the people?"

Manez was frozen with fear as he softly replied, "Who would I be to fight this evil?"

The ghost flew face to face with him. His eye sockets contained the killing flashes of all the fighting before this time. He could feel the truth in the words of the ghost. "You are chosen, you, Manez, descendent of Nahaheuoha (Wild Horse), you are chosen and only one is chosen."

His life suddenly became clear to him. *That's why I am different from the others,* he thought. He was relieved as he accepted what the ghost said. "I am chosen; only one is chosen."

The swirling figure became even more agitated as he spoke. "The powder will give you powers beyond belief and the bag will never empty. What you wish for, you will have." He began to spin around, the room growing smaller. "I have just one warning. Be careful of the day they don't need you, because that will be the day you die."

The whirlwind figure vacuumed back into the eye sockets and as it did the eerie quiet found its way back into the cave, but not before Manez cried out. "Who are you?"

A faint whisper was heard as the ghost completely disappeared. "Sweet Medicine."

Chapter 22
Broken Promise

Standing Man's feet were light as he came up the trail and saw the twin rocks that protected the entrance to the round valley. He had made the two-day run through the night, but he didn't seem tired. The story he had in his heart made him gain speed as he trotted down the hill and stopped close to the lodge. He wasn't surprised when he saw Onotsa waiting for him, because he could hear the chant of Cripple Elk close by.

"What did you see?"

"The Quapaw are all gone. The warriors are dead in the places they fought. All the women have vanished." A group of chiefs came from inside the lodge.

" The ghosts cut the fingers off of the Shaman and poked out his eyes."

"Where are my sons?" Onotsa asked with a tone of dread in his voice.

"They followed the signs, hoping to see if they were really spirits. They are coming this way and Manez says we must prepare for them."

Several separate groups of the tribes had gathered by now and many discussions were taking place about the impending doom.

The Bear River Shoshoni, along with the Mescalero Apache wanted nothing to do with these mysterious ghosts and immediately broke camp and headed for home. The Northern tribes including the Oto, Ponca and the Hidatsa agreed to stay until morning.

"What about the Arikara. Will you stay?" Onotsa asked.

Grey Eyes looked at young Chief Hawk Eye and his men shook their heads.

"We have trading to do, so we will stay until we have finished."

Onotsa shook his head. "Set the guards. If they are ghosts, they come quicker than we think."

As the older braves discussed what action they should take, most of the young bucks began to show off for the girls, especially for Dawn. One boy in particular from the Arapaho Tribe became so daring that he did dangerous horse tricks back and forth in front of them. Another boy shot arrows into the trees close by with brightly colored beads attached to them. Dawn couldn't help see the things they did to impress her and the others, but her heart belonged to Manez and she had made him a promise that she intended to keep. All day long the young braves desperately tried to gain an advantage over one another, but as evening approached, the warriors from the Lugrand Arikara tribe chased them away and their attention was drawn towards other things.

Dawn's heart told her something was wrong, as she flicked at the dirt with a stick and stared across the camp towards Grey Eyes, her father, who had been holding council with the young Chief of the Lugrand Arikiri. She was about to go ask him if there was any news about the Quapaw village when she saw the arrival of twelve ponies and it made her heart sink. The Chief Hawk Eye shook her father's hand, then he went back to his camp. Her eyes were already filled with tears as she walked the short distance to her father.

"What have you done, Father?" She forced back the breaks in her voice.

"I, uh, I..." He fumbled for words, knowing what he had done was wrong.

"I, Dawn, your only child, was traded for these...these horses? You know my heart and it belongs to another."

Grey Eyes truly loved his daughter, but it was the custom of his people to give their daughters away only to an Arikara. He finally summoned the words he thought were the truth for her to hear. "I know what your heart thinks, but Manez is not an Arikara. You knew I would never give you to the Cheyenne boy."

In the distance, the Sandy Creek camp drums began to beat and she began to cry. He tried to hug her.

"But I made a promise," she said, as she pulled away. "That should mean something to a man whose daughter was given back to him by Manez." With her eyes filling with tears, she ran into the teepee.

The gloom of an awful day was closing in not only on her, but also on all the people of the earth. The ones who saw it felt the dread that descended upon the valley. Many, like her father, were too busy acquiring horses to really see what was coming.

Dawn was bathed and dressed in her white deerskin dress. She then waited for her world to end. She thought about running away, but the guard at the door shoved her back inside. Her tears stained her white dress and she had given up all hope when a knife slowly cut into the back of the tent. In her surprise she almost screamed, but Standing Man's smiling face followed the blade through the cut.

"Shh." He motioned for her to follow and the two of them made their way back up the trail close to Elm Springs where a horse was tied.

"Why are you doing this?" she asked.

"Do you love Manez?' he replied.

"Yes, he is in my heart."

"Then that is why I do it. He is southwest of here, but be careful." Helping her on the horse, he slapped it and they both disappeared into the fading light.

Chapter 23

The Death Song

A small girl crying somewhere in the dark caused Kanan to open his eyes. A fire had been started and the flames flickered about, distorting everything, giving the night a dreamlike atmosphere. Sabotha was sitting close to the fire casting her bits and pieces on the ground and chanting. "Tera don to me a nora, pacse sark ta tee. I will have the power from this one first, before I take yours." She took an eye from her pouch and began to shake it over the bones.

"Natowanie, let me see what this eye saw." Her whole body suddenly began to shake causing her to collapse on the ground.

Pierre called out as he walked from behind the trees. "Sabotha, I was wondering." Seeing her condition, he quickly pivoted. "Oh, never mind. I see you're busy and I don't need any of that, now, do I?"

She squeezed the eyeball tightly in her hand and as the slimy liquid oozed out between her fingers, she sucked in a deep breath as if she was taking in the smoke of a peace pipe. She relaxed as the air filled her lungs.

"I see where you get the power from now." Sabotha motioned out at all the living things around them, then stood up in Kanan's face. "You get your power from the life around you, don't you, Indian boy? I see the one who follows. He controls the magic and he will come for you." She pulled her knife from her belt and pressed the blade slowly across his chest. As the blood trickled slowly down she thought about tasting it, but remembered what happened the last time, so she just licked his face. From his position near the trees, Pierre witnessed the bizarre behavior and walked over to her.

"I will take the magic from him and when I'm finished, I will kill him, Indian boy." She pushed the point into his side. "Just like I am going to kill you."

Just as he thought she would push the knife deeper, Pierre grabbed her arm and threw her away. "Why would the boy come if his friend were dead?" he yelled at her. "All this fresh air has made you a little wild, old one. I think I like it, but we need him, don't we? I thought I was the one who got to kill him!" He gave her an inquisitive look.

"Let me stick him once more, please, just once more," she begged.

"You can stick him all you want, but not today. Now go relax, kill a frog or something."

"Louis, send the Dark Wind out."

Pierre laughed, then he went back to his Indian girl.

Penetrating cold raised goosebumps all over Manez's body. He sat up, compelled to get out of the cave as soon as possible. He pushed himself up on stiff, chilled legs looking for the origin of the tiny beam of light. He followed the speck to the wall and tried to climb up, but there was no exit there. After his eyes had focused, he ran his hand along the wall as he walked to the end where the rocks had fallen.

"I don't suppose you could help a little," he said to the white bones, half expecting the skeleton to talk. "I didn't think you would." The rocks were heavy, but he tried to move them just the same.

"If I am needed and I think I am, then wouldn't this be a good time to help me get out of here?" He dropped the large boulder on his foot and as he hopped around the cave, he spilled some of the dust on the rock. In anger, he cried out "Just get away from me."

The rock shook, then rolled away to the other end of the cave. Manez fell backwards in amazement.

"What I think, will happen? What I thought, did happen!" Manez stood back up trying to gather his thoughts. "You said I would have powers beyond belief, didn't you." He took the pouch and lightly tossed it in his hand, half expecting his mind was playing tricks on him.

"Well, even if I am crazy, it would be great imagining getting out of here." With that said, he filled his hand with the powder then tossed it onto the rocks that were blocking the cave. Then clearing his mind, he half jokingly called out, "Rocks, run away!"

The earth began to shake. As the rubble shook and shifted around, tiny cries of "Run away, just run away." began to emit from inside each rock. The small rocks moved away fast, but the larger ones only labored away a few yards then came to a rolling stop as if someone had scattered them from a pail. The cave miraculously opened, casting shafts of light back into the depths of the cave.

Manez covered his eyes as the light attacked him; a sudden rush of fresh air filled his nostrils and he laughed until his head hurt.

The bones of Sweet Medicine, the fallen warrior, were completely exposed to the light making the previous events seem impossible to Manez.

"No time to waste, great one. I must go quickly, my brother needs me." He made a pack with the deerskin and leather, then packed Sweet Medicine's weapons away except for the hatchet. *This will come in handy*, he thought.

As he stepped into the light, he thought about the open cave.

"Rocks, go back," he commanded and the rocks came to life rolling back into place until the opening was closed.

Morning was in full bloom as he trotted up the trail. It was good to be back outside, but he knew danger was still near. All morning long, he pushed his stiff, weary legs forward as fast as he could. Knowing he needed to go faster, he pushed himself harder.

Manez retraced his steps back to where the boys had parted the day before and then he followed their path, reading the signs. He ran quickly following Kanan's footprints and when the reeds suddenly appeared before him, he was forced to stop. That's when he saw the Vehoe boot marks.

"My brother, they are following you."

Close examination of the area confirmed that the intruders were following his two friends. Manez let fear take control of him as he ran once more. *What if something has happened to my brother?* he thought, carelessly cutting through the rough countryside. He was so preoccupied with his thoughts, he didn't see the leg sticking out of the bushes. He tripped, and fell grasping for air, face down into the sand.

"I can't look. Oh, don't let it be my brother." Scrambling up, he crawled back to the body of his good friend Laughing Bear. "No, no, it can't be." As tears filled his eyes, he cradled the warrior in his arms and tossing his head to the sky he sang the Death Song. He stopped abruptly. *What if they are still here, watching.* he thought. Ripping the hatchet from his belt, he crawled around the underbrush making certain he was alone. When he was convinced, he returned to the body and began covering it with rocks.

"Do not fear, friend. I will return for you. To leave you in this place would be a dishonor to me," he said was he placed a white stone on the grave. "I must go." Manez moved away trying to keep his emotions subdued intent on following the path of his brother's captors.

He moved with strength and purpose, more than he had ever felt. Down along the Pine Ridge and into Buffalo Gap. He flew past Bear Mountain above the Round Valley and as the day faded away, he smelled smoke and quickly ducked into the stubble of a plumb thicket. There he sat, listening. It wasn't long until he could hear the sounds of men. Crawling forward, always hidden by the vast stubble, he found a small, clear patch where he could see the camp. The largest oak tree he had ever seen covered the area, casting shadows with its leafy branches. Manez moved closer, always staying within the safety of the plumb thicket. As his eyes moved across the camp, he saw the Osage scouts.

He had heard of the Black Indians, but nothing he had heard could have prepared him for the strange markings on their faces. He thought of the Crow and the Magpie back in the forest and he wondered if these men could fight like the black man that had killed the Apache. Some of the Vehoe milled about the camp, but Manez knew that many more hid in the shadows. A man stood close to the fire watching an old lady casting bones on the ground and it was evident he was the leader and this was his witch. No sign of Kanan. Had he missed his body on the trail?

The witch abruptly stood and moved to the base of the oak tree. Manez followed her with his eyes and saw Kanan tied to that massive wall of wood, alive. The witch yelled at him and tapped him with her knife. She talked to the Vehoe standing close to the fire. Manez knew they meant to hurt his brother and was prepared to charge into battle, but at that moment she walked away and left him alone. The tense catlike reflexes subsided and Manez relaxed. Surprised, he realized he had crawled through the only place he could have without being seen. The group seemed content to stay right where they were and until it was dark, Manez had the same inclination.

The big, red pony made the most of the rein Dawn had given him by putting the valley far behind. She was unsure of where she was going, but she knew she wasn't about to be given away to anyone except Manez. The horse ran along the base of the ridge and then she spurred him on into the onset of night, her heart searching for Manez. The trail, at length, became less recognizable and overgrown, making it hard for her to stay on the path. Her mind wandered as she picked her way through the low overhanging branches and she questioned her sanity about running off in the middle of the night trying to find Manez. A sudden movement beside the trail startled the horse and as he jumped forward, she tumbled off the back onto her head. In a blur the horse disappeared, but as she lay there, stunned, heavy breathing and breaking limbs told her a bear was coming.

Play dead, she thought, as she let her body go limp and closed her eyes, but try as she could, she couldn't stop the goosebumps from appearing. When she felt the hot breath of the bear on her neck all she could think of was the violent bear attack on the Crow camp and that terrified her. He bumped her with his nose and pulled in the fragrance of her body, then he raised his head to growl at the stars. She opened her eyes the tiniest bit and saw burned fur on the bear's side. It was Manez's bear, Four Claws, and she shuddered as he pawed at her, rolling her over. Then tugging the neck of her buckskin dress, he pulled her under a cottonwood tree. She assumed he was going to eat her and had determined to at least make a run for the tree or die trying. But as he let go of her, instead of chomping into her flesh, he moved up the trail; then standing on his back legs, he cried out to her in an almost human voice. There was deep-seated sadness coming from the bear. He called out into the vast wilderness, then dropping back to the ground, he disappeared. A profound sense of loneliness swept over her, bringing tears to her eyes. She shook with relief, making it almost impossible to scramble for the safety of the tree.

Throughout the day, the tribes at the gathering had concluded their trading and then rushed away from the impending doom that had been predicted. The discovery that Dawn was missing had caused a stir among the Arikaras. Grey Eyes stood in the center of the camp with his back to the ridge giving orders to his men.

"I know the child is here some place. Find her." The Arikara warriors scattered in all directions bringing back reports of what they had found. The Chief eyed the Cheyenne camp as the reports revealed she had received help in her efforts to run away. The old tribal suspicions appeared, creating a rift once more between the two tribes.

"There was a horse and it went to the south with a rider."

"Was she alone?" the Chief asked.

"When she left, she was alone," the warrior replied looking over the Chief's shoulder as he spoke. An inquisitive look appeared on the brave's face as his eyes moved along the ridge behind them. Many Cheyenne had also come out to look at the ridge.

"What are you looking at?' the Chief said, as he turned to look.

"I don't know, I can't quite make it out."

All eyes squinted into the bright rays of sun cascading through the trees and down into the valley. The shadows should have been attached to the ground, but they looked as if they were suspended in the air. The Cheyenne had seen this mystery many times. It always occurred at certain times of the year, but something about this sunset was different. It took a long time for the sun to go down, but just before dark, for just an instant, they thought they saw bodies attached to the shadows.

The Shaman began to sing the Death Song and the whole valley knew the ghosts had arrived.

Chapter 24

Invisible

The sound of the crickets would have made the night seem like any other night, except for the fact Manez was still hiding among the Vehoe. The campfire flickered, making shapes dance among the cottonwood trees. The guards had come close a few times and Manez was hoping to not be discovered, while he thought of a plan. The small girl still cried out in the dark and his heart broke as he listened to her whimpers. He fiddled with the magic pouch, getting some of the dust on his hands as he tossed it lightly into the air.

"If only I couldn't be seen. I could save them all," he whispered.

A guard suddenly appeared above him. Surprised at being discovered, he raised his hatchet to defend himself, but the man just stared at the pack with the silver bow hidden inside ignoring him. He expected the Vehoe to strike at him, but as he held his arm up, he trembled at what he saw. Nothing. He couldn't see any part of his body; he was invisible.

"Anything you think," he said, causing the white man to look surprised at the voice coming from thin air. In the same instant, Manez took the golden blade of the hatchet and hacked into his stomach, killing him. He grabbed the body and when he touched it, it also disappeared. He pulled the body into the bushes and when he released it, he reappeared. Grabbing the pack, Manez quickly moved back to the safety of the brush. He was still in shock and didn't believe what had just happened. With his heart throbbing, he peered at his reflection on the blade of the hatchet. He should be looking at his face, but instead he only saw the reflection of the things around him.

The old man said I could do things beyond belief, he thought. He slid close to the stream and looked for his reflection, only to find tiny ripples of clear water. Even though he knew he couldn't be seen, it took all his courage to ease out from the safety of the thickets. Cautiously, he moved close to the tree where Kanan was tied and he could see he was not well. He considered how he could reveal himself to Kanan without making him cry out in fear, but he knew that being invisible made that impossible. So he decided to help him escape with out alarming him.

As the camp fell quiet and the night sounds grew, Manez slipped his knife between the feet of his brother, cutting the thongs; then he cut those holding his hands. Taking a leaf, he tickled Kanan's nose and he instinctively reached up and scratched the spot. Realizing he was free, he put his hands down.

Manez, seeing the witch at the fire, wanted to know what she was up to. His shyness about being unseen was slowly wearing off and as he slipped through the camp, he played tricks on the white men by poking them and making them drop things. Even braver, he moved closer to Sabotha, who was talking and drawing in the dirt; it looked like a battle plan.

"This valley is big and rich with many people. Soon we will have many slaves for the Osage."

Pierre cut in. "What should I do about that one?" he said, pointing at Kanan.

"When we know we haven't been followed, I will take care of that one. He has something I need," she replied, licking her finger.

A rustle in the brush startled both of them and two Osage braves appeared. A big warrior with a scar across his cheek began talking to the witch.

"We have delivered the slaves and here is your gold," he said, tossing a leather bag at her.

Sabotha proceeded to ask, "What took so long? You should have been back yesterday."

The Osage were afraid of the Black Magic they had seen at the burial grounds. The story of what had happened had been spread to every camp along the southern plains. The fear Scar had for the Unske was nothing compared to the fear he had of the white witch.

"We were followed by a Cheyenne. I shot him with an arrow and he fell into the river. We searched downstream, but didn't find the body."

Sabotha walked around the big Indian and as she did, she scratched him with her long, dirty fingernails. She was mad and as she scratched, she collected his blood on her fingers.

"The boy is dead?" she asked as she moved.

"He was a weak human and the waters took him down," said Scar.

Manez recognized the big Indian as the one who had shot him and now, as Scar turned to leave, Manez stuck out his foot to trip him. Scar stumbled to the ground and then jumped up, hitting the Indian walking beside him, thinking it was his clumsiness that made him fall.

Unknowingly, Manez had walked too close to Sabotha and she suddenly froze with her eyes fixed on the ground. Invisible as he was, he realized he was leaving tracks in the soft dirt. As he tried to back up, Sabotha suddenly looked up and tossed the blood of Scar out towards him. Most of the red liquid fell harmlessly to the ground, but a long line of blood struck Manez's chest. Surprised by the red line suspended in mid air next to him, Pierre stumbled backwards. Falling to her knees, Sabotha began to scream and Scar turned back around as the liquid dried and disappeared.

"Taka he dae shoo, un sa Tammie shoo." The camp came alive at the alarm and so did Kanan. With all eyes on the disappearing blood, he was up and running before anyone knew it.

Scar lashed out at the ghost with his blade, but the air was filled with more blood as his head fell to the ground. This time Manez was silhouetted in blood. Screams of terror engulfed the camp.

"The Devil has arrived!" Pierre cried, as he ran head long into a tree.

The others cried out, "En diable, diable."

When Manez turned his back on the fire, he disappeared once more causing the clan to go even wilder. They hacked at the air trying to kill the unseen intruder. Some, even in their fear, wheeled around and ran their blades into their own men, but Manez was nowhere close. Kanan ran along the path, his broken body stumbled atop weak legs and with every near fall, he felt as if he had been held up. Two guards appeared on the trail ahead, but before they could strike, a golden arrow pinned the first one to a tree and a second arrow pierced the heart of the other. Kanan stumbled once more, but Manez gave him a final shove towards home and waited for those who would follow.

Sabotha slowly uncovered her eyes as she knelt on the ground amidst the confusion. Something lay close to the severed head of Scar and reaching out she found a bear claw necklace and a lock of Manez's hair that had been cut off by the big Indian's blade.

"Now, I take the power from him, ha, ha, ha."

252

Chapter 25

Captive

Just before daybreak, Dawn found the courage to climb down from the tree. Her body was stiff from having to hug the tree limbs and as she stretched her legs, she realized she wasn't alone. Her scream was cut short by the big hands of the Vehoe covering her mouth.

She kicked at the intruders and tried to cut them with her knife, but to no avail. She was captured once more and the tortures endured at the hands of the Crow made their way into her mind. She thought about another heroic rescue by Manez, but her heart sank as the camp of the Vehoe appeared.

"They are so many," she whispered.

Everywhere she looked, the people of the Vehoe hid in the shadows of the trees. She, too, heard the death song of the Quapaw girl in the distance and at that moment she died a little inside. The white men looked to be a starving people.

The giant oak tree suddenly loomed in front of her and she was tossed to the ground in front of Sabotha. The witch looked up from her conjuring.

"Ah, what is dis dat we have here." She pushed her hair away from her face. "A pretty one now, you are, girl. Don't let that Pierre come take from you."

Dawn didn't understand what she was saying, but she knew the tone in her voice meant trouble.

A sudden gust of wind swirled around the two.

"I see, now. The wind tells me how important you are to the people in the valley." She had been fumbling with a lock of hair, but stopped when the wind died down. "You are important to our young warrior, too." she laughed. "Pierre, Pierre, I'm calling for you." The brush parted and Pierre eyed the pretty girl lustfully.

"Take those eyes off her. There are better things to do." Motioning towards the guards she said, "Put her over there with that singing girl. Pierre, the valley won't wait no more, the people are starving. Take the Dark Wind and go to the valley."

Pierre was still shaken by the ghost and as he spoke, he looked around.

"What about the, you know."

"Don't you worry bout dat boy. I got plans for him. You men, there; go chase that boy and kill him while I hold his power." She played with the lock of hair. Pierre stood a moment, then reluctantly ordered the men to move out. Sabotha tossed the bones and gave an evil smile.

The Cheyenne guards, already uneasy about what was coming, almost shot the big, red pony as it ran past them into the camp. Standing Man heard the alarm and saw the horse coming down the hill.

"Whoa there, fella, whoa." He grabbed the rope and began to rub his hands along his back.

"You've been running a long time, huh!" He hugged the horse. "Where's the girl, boy, where did you leave her?" What was left of the Arikara, including Grey Eyes, eyed him with suspicion. They knew he was the one who helped her escape. The look on the young brave's face told him all they needed to know.

"We go now. My daughter is in the hands of the spirits." He looked at Standing Man as if an old hatred stirred in his heart, then he turned away.

Most of the tribes at the gathering had already found reason to leave. A steady stream had exited the valley ever since the sighting of the ghosts. The Arikara were the last to go and they only had stayed in hope of finding Dawn. With that hope gone, they left the Wolf Clan to stand alone.

Onotsa had known all along that the Cheyenne would have to fight alone. He had made a plan and during the night, all the women and children were moved to the cave at Elm Springs. He hid fifty horsemen just behind the trees on the south side of the camp and put the rest of the men inside the teepees to wait.

A warning arrow struck the tree close to the Chief.

"Someone is coming," he said. A man came over the edge of the hill. Sliding down, he sent rocks tumbling in all directions. Onotsa strained his pale eyes. A rider picked the man up and carried him in to the chief. As he put him down, Onotsa cried out, "Kanan, my son!" He held him in his arms and looked at his wounds.

Another arrow hit the tree.

"Father, they're coming." All eyes turned to the ridge as the air filled with warning arrows from all directions.

Tall pine trees stood just to the north of the gypsy camp and as Manez made his way in the dark, he left plenty of signs for the Vehoe to follow. A mist rose up from the ferns on the ground making it hard to see, even as the morning light bounced from tree to tree. He would make his stand here and as he made ready, he hummed the song he had heard from the Quapaw girl. He cut sharp sticks from the willows and tied them to branches he had pulled back with vines, making a string of deadly traps along the trail. Then, knowing they would abandon the trail, he hid other traps beneath the ferns, deep in the woods. At the base of a tree, he put a noose and

255

covered it with leaves. He found a big, split pine tree and hid there, waiting for the Vehoes to pass.

Manez jabbed the ground with his knife. It had been only hours since he first had discovered Sweet Medicine, but it seemed like days to him. Over and over he stuck the knife into the dirt. It was something he had done a hundred times, but he suddenly stopped. He had changed. It was his arm that caught his attention. It was much bigger and muscular. He drew back the blade and peered into the shiny steel reflection at a much older, more mature face than he had expected. Manez pushed back in disbelief, unsure of the face that looked back at him. He looked down at a much larger version of his chest and legs and he was mystified by the change in his body as he shook the magic pouch, spilling more dust.

A sudden stillness engulfed the forest. The animals signaled the arrival of evil. Manez heard the first trap snap open and the sudden rush of air, as the spike flew towards its first victim with a thud, entering the flesh. Another sudden rush of air followed by another; spike breaking flesh and bone. They were in the middle of his traps and began to cry out to each other. They rushed away from the path into the safety of the trees only to be snatched up by the vines and have their heads bashed open against the trees.

Four killed. His mind raced as the remaining men clumsily stumbled along in different directions. One by one, he let them pass until the last man came close enough for him to spring up from the tall grass and drag him down, turning the grass red as he fell.

"Sergio, Sergio, where is he?" someone called out.

"He was here." A bearded man rushed to the spot, only to have his legs turn red from the blood on the leaves.

Close by, a man leaned against what he thought was a tree, only to have it come alive and cut his throat. At the disappearance of the sixth man, the group panicked and began to retreat. Manez, in a blur, ran between two men stabbing one in the heart and the other in the neck. His sudden attack caused the remaining three to fire their guns at anything that moved as they ran away. Manez watched as the last man disappeared through a sea of green. The stillness slowly returned, but as he listened, he thought he heard something far away. Something was wrong in the valley. He turned to go home, but his legs suddenly failed him and he fell on the ground, unable to get up. Numbness tingled his muscles as it slowly engulfed his body. The old woman guarding the gate to the after life smiled at him as he raised his hand to the magic pouch. He was trying to think of anything that would release him from captivity, but his limp body fell back into the green grass.

"Tor to na kee. Sa dee to no ree." Sabotha stirred the bits of hair into the blood.

"I fix em bad, dat boy with all da power. We see who come to help him now, bones."

Dawn tugged at the ropes, pulling enough slack to see what the witch was doing.

The old lady feverishly stirred the pot.

"Tor tona kee, Sa dee to no ree," she repeated as she poured in more blood.

"Now, you never wake up. Ha, ha ha." As she put the claw into the bowl, she laughed in a wicked voice, cutting it short when she noticed the girl watching.

"You turn away those eyes, girl, or I'll fix you, too!" she screamed, running at her.

Dawn quickly pushed back into the group of captive girls and Sabotha went back to casting spells, but the girl had seen the bear claw necklace. Her heart broke as she feared the worst for Manez.

The gypsies clutched the shadows of the trees as they observed the Cheyenne village below. Several warriors, disguised as women, wandered around the camp. Pierre's mouth watered as he looked over the rows of corn dancing in the breeze and the meat roasting on the fires. Small swirls of dust aimlessly rose from beyond the trees, exposing the hidden riders to him. Long pants, under the dresses worn by the women, revealed just how clever these Indians were.

"Finally, a worthy adversary. Louis, they're hiding in the teepees, divide our men into groups; concentrate the fighting at the entrance of each one. You, Jon Luke, expect the horses to charge, turn them to the side. I will bring the Dark Wind down after the charge and drive them between us. You have your orders; we go as soon as you're ready."

"Yes, sir," they replied, as they ran among the men.

Onotsa had a bad feeling and he had also seen the dust swirls kicked up by the horses. As the shapes atop the ridge divided into groups, facing each teepee, he realized his men would be trapped.

"We have been discovered. Get the men out now." The Chief swung himself up on his horse. "We will charge and hold them as long as we can." He clasped Standing Man's hand. "Don't let them take my son. Aeeeee, Aeeeee!" he cried, as he led the riders out of the trees.

Pierre responded to the charge by sending his men over the ridge. The calm morning was erased by the terrifying cries of the men rushing towards each other. The shouts bellowing from deep inside disguised the terror they felt as they rushed forward to death. Onotsa drove his horse deep into the gypsy fighters, hacking at everyone in his path. Led by his example, the Cheyenne warriors carved a path close behind him and for a moment, it looked as if the clan might panic and run. From the ridge above, Pierre's sparat tumbled end over end towards the great Chief, striking him in the chest. Onotsa flipped backwards off his horse, then crashed to the ground dead. A great cry went up from the Vehoe as they regained their courage and surged forward, pulling down the horsemen one by one to their death.

The warriors poured from the teepees and drove their picket pins into the ground, then began to sting the morning air with arrows. Five, ten men fell before the gypsies reached the line of Cheyenne fighters, but just like the horse riders, the Indians were overwhelmed by the flood of Sinti charging down the ridge with their sparats. One by one, the warriors were bludgeoned by the strange weapons of the Frenchmen, until none were left alive.

Huge clouds of dust engulfed the valley. Standing Man, watching from just beyond the trees hung his head in pain as the last of his friends were murdered. His heart told him to charge from the trees and avenge the death of his friends, but the promise to Onotsa held him back. Just as he turned to go, Pierre appeared from the cloud of dust.

It wouldn't be right not to try and kill the devil, Standing Man thought. Methodically, he slipped an arrow on the rawhide string and let it go. The arrows flint blade sliced through the thin morning air, making him smile as he pictured the look on the devil's face when the sharp point entered his chest.

Unaware of the silent shot, Pierre bent down to retrieve his Sparat from Onotsa's chest, yanking the bloody weapon up suddenly, in front of the deadly shot. The arrow pierced his hand and stuck deep into the wooden handle. All eyes quickly turned to the trees, but only shadows could be seen. Deep in the woods, they heard the yelp of the Cheyenne brave.

The great horned owl came out of the forest and landed on the limb above the now limp Manez. He gazed long and hard at the boy below him. His head turned side to side as he studied the figure on the ground. Manez was paralyzed, but he could see the owl. A rush of air and a haunting cry announced the arrival of the screech owl, who also studied the boy below. The breeze pushed little tuffs of feathers back and forth on the two birds. "Great spirit birds. If it is my time, then lead me on to the old woman; but let my spirit, like yours, come back in the form of the wolf, so I can watch over my loved ones." A sudden pain shot through his body as Sabotha pinched the hair in between her fingers.

The great horned owl twisted his head around to the screech owl and said "E-mo'ohtavo (It's a black time)."

The screech owl answered, "E-matinee? (He's alive?)"

The old owl shook his head yes. "E-etohtahe (He's afraid, though)."

"I'm afraid he can see the gate keeper," the screech owl replied.

They jerked and twisted their heads a long time, then finally, the horned owl said, "He is favored by the spirits. We should help him." He continued."If we bring him back from the gate, he will never be the same.,"

The screech owl answered, "Yes, but if we don't help him, the people of the earth will be lost along with the magic."

They rolled their heads around. Then the great horned owl said, "Then we must bring him back."

With that the screech owl called out over the forest. The note he struck echoed out of the giant oak tree and scattered out into the valley below. Over and over he called out to the earth.

"Eek, eek, eek."

It was a strange thing to hear an owl during the day, so strange, that life suddenly paused to listen to the cries.

The retreating Cheyenne stopped their flight to listen and even the Dark Wind looked back into the forest, trying to get a glimpse of where the sounds were coming from. Sabotha widened her eyes as the bird called out, but none that listened was as important as Four Claws.

The brown bear's nostrils flared as he skirted the gypsy camp. The boy had passed that way. He stood on his hind legs, listening to the spirited cries and he understood the message from the owls.

With a thunderous roar, he suddenly charged into the camp, breaking limbs as he tore at everything that moved. The shocked Vehoe stumbled, trying to grab their weapons, but it was futile to stop the onslaught of Four Claws. The first two men he met he swatted away, tearing flesh from their bodies, one landing close to the Indian girl still singing the death song. The other one tumbled into another man, knocking him down. Four Claws quickly bit into soft flesh of his neck and sent him sailing across the camp, landing close to the witch and spattering her with blood..

"Aahhhhhhh," she screamed, as the bear rushed towards her. Several men tried to raise their weapons, but Four Claws met them as if he was crazy. The first man had his sparat raised high ready to strike, but the bear clasped his arm in his mouth and swung him around like a weapon, knocking the other men down. He then dug his claws deep into his chest.

Sabotha dropped the tuft of Manez's hair into the fire and the boy's claw necklace fell from her hand as she picked up a burning stick and stabbed the bear on his side. Four Claws pivoted hard towards her, catching her with the back of his paw and knocking her ten feet back into the brush.

"Kee no sa menato! (Don't kill me!)" she screamed, as she ran behind a group of men. Four Claws lunged at the witch, locking eyes with her. He clawed at the air crazily, seeing the blackness in her eyes; then he whirled around, picked up the necklace and charged out of the camp through some men killing them as he left. The Quapaw girl pulled a knife from the dead man who had almost landed on her and she cut the captives frees. They scattered in all directions, causing the remaining guards to chase after them. Dawn turned to follow the bear as he made a path of death out of the camp, but a few steps away from freedom, a wounded man tripped her and then fell on her; she was trapped. Four Claws looked back at her as if to say 'I will help', but the barrage of weapons thrown at him held him at bay. He gave a terrifying growl, letting them all know it wasn't over, then he ran into the forest disappearing behind the curtain of green.

Manez took a deep breath; the paralyzing grip that had held him was suddenly gone. The cry of the bear bounced around the forest and Manez gazed across the mountain towards the noise, then he turned his attention towards the birds.

"He's free from the spell," the screech owl called out.

"I see. The bear did his job distracting the black one," replied the great horned owl.

The two birds twisted their heads back and forth as they talked to one another.

"What have you two been up to? I guess I should be grateful, because whatever it was, I'm free now." Manez suddenly understood what the owls were saying.

"Boy, all is not well. A great tragedy has fallen upon the people. You must take the magic of Sweet Medicine and fight this blackness that has come upon the earth. Trust the things of earth and go now." Leaping from the high branches they spread their mighty wings and dodged their way through the trees back into the deep forest.

Stiff from the spell at the hands of Sabotha, Manez leaned against a large rock, stretching his aching muscles and soaking in warmth from the sun. He wondered how long he had been pinned to the ground by the black magic.

In his head he repeated what the bird had said *'All is not well in the valley'* and it hung heavy on his heart. Slowly he regained the movement in his arms, then his legs and began to move back up the mountain towards the ridge.

Stopping to get a drink from a tiny stream, he scooped up the sweet water in his hands, but dropped the soothing liquid to stare at the stranger's reflection in the water. He still didn't recognize the face that stared back at him. He continued on into the valley.

The cave above Elm Springs was a good hiding place for the Cheyenne; one by one, women and children stumbled into the shelter of the cave. Most of them clung close to the opening of the cave, waiting for their loved ones who had stayed behind to fight. Some were rewarded when their wounded husbands came within sight. As the darkness came, the sorrow that some of their loved ones would never return gripped their hearts. The reality of death caused them to gather around the fire to sing songs for the lost warriors. They hoped the old lady at the gate heard them singing. Standing Man arrived just as it became dark and took a quick survey of the tribe. Many people of the earth had left that day, so many it was hard to count them. His heart ached and the tears welled up into his eyes. As quickly as they appeared, he wiped them away.

"Young boys, come quickly," he called into the cave. Seven reluctantly came out, wiping their tears. "Dry your eyes, my young ones. I will not chastise you for your sorrow. Even I have trouble thinking of those who lie on the ground back there. Today you become men. I need you." The boys stiffened, a surge of pride pounded in their hearts. "We need you." Standing Man knew they would do fine. "Go guard the trail; use the calls if they come after us. We will prepare a great fight for them here."

A couple of the boys mustered a yelp and they ran back down the trail.

Standing Man was glad Kanan was still unconcious, because he wasn't sure how he could tell him his father was dead. Going back outside, he looked into the sky and cried. "Manez, where are you?"

The gypsy clan moved into the captured village. All those who were always hiding far behind the men moved out into the open. The gypsy women and children that were never seen lumbered down the hill in two wheeled carts, adding more dust to the already churning thick air. The captured Dawn lurched against the thongs binding her hands as she came into the once beautiful valley of the Cheyenne. Onotsa's body was tied to a pole close to a large pile of dead Cheyenne. Sabotha played with the eagle feather headdress that had fallen to the ground. As she stared up at the old chief, other gypsies rummaged around the dead, trying to find the pretty beads and metal weapons of the conquered Indians. She cried at the horrible sight.

"Don't ya be cryin' yet, pretty girl. Pierre make you really cry and soon, ha, ha, hee."

Pierre appeared through the dust; he slapped his men on the back congratulating them on the victory and at the same time he took great pride at showing them his wounded hand. The sight of Dawn stopped his congratulatory march around the camp and his eyes on her gave her cold chills.

"Take her, there," he said pointing to a teepee. "You women, clean her up. I have plans for her," he yelled, then continued his congratulations to his men.

Sabotha poked at the corpse of Onotsa with the tip of a broken arrow. Carefully she stirred a pool of blood around inside the wound.

Dawn broke away from the guards and ran to the body, but was pulled back by the guards.

"Des boy out there is connected to da dead man here. I feel da power in em." She suddenly stiffened and put her cold gaze towards the ridge above. "Ton nammee de cray took." She threw the bones into the blood. "He still out there, powerful and strong, but I fix em, I fix em good." She waved the stick, slinging blood on Pierre's face and arm. "A dobi treene tok ta."

Pierre rolled his eyes. "I'm too close, always just a step too close. It's like you just have this uncanny sense of when you can slime me with blood or frog guts. Note to self; The witch is nasty, stay away from her." Pierre grabbed Dawn, pulling her away.

"I told you to put her in there," he said, pointing once more to the teepee.

Manez saw her too, but he pulled back from the edge of the ridge; a sudden chill brought goosebumps on his arms. He had felt this way before in the forest, when he was frozen. The power of the witch attacked his body once more and all he had time to do was throw the magic powder in the air and think 'run away'.

Back through the forest and across the tall grass in a blur, he quickly retreated until he could no longer feel the tug of the black power on his body. He found a gypsum ledge cut deep into the side of a hill and took shelter in the cool shadows of the cave.

Manez felt weak, not only in his body but in his mind. He had been given great powers, but no knowledge about how to use them.

The boy came out in him as his eyes filled with water, he thought, My father, is dead; maybe even Kanan perished in the battle of the Round Valley. Dawn is also the captive of the Veho. It was too much!

"Sweet Medicine, why did you choose me, a boy, to do a man's job? Here, I give it back to you." He tossed the weapons and pouch to the back of the cave, but the shadow in the cave stirred. His heart stopped. He had been in such a hurry to escape from the witch, he hadn't been a good Indian. He panicked and reached for his knife, but his belt was empty; the knife lay with the bow. Frozen, he watched as the shadow unfolded. It was big and its hot breath moved towards him into the light. A bear appeared, a big burnt bear, his bear. Four Claws came from the darkness holding Manez's weapons in his mouth. As he laid them at his feet, the old screech owl flew close, once more.

"There's no giving back; you are chosen. The bear even knows it's you. So do the spirits, just ask and they will come."

Chapter 26
Riders in the Sky

Sabotha's scream echoed across the camp, causing Pierre to stop lusting for Dawn and come running. It wasn't a scream of excitement like most of hers, but a scream of terror.

"I've seen our death." Her claws dug into his arm and with a quivering voice she repeated her cry. "I've seen us dying. It's, something about da boy." She dropped the bones, then crumpled into a small ball on the ground whimpering. Pierre had never seen the witch afraid before.

"Oh, come on now, just cut the head off of something. Here, how about that dog?" The old woman didn't look up at him. Grabbing the dog, he said, "Let's poke its eye out. That will cheer you up." Her voice was a faint whisper, so he leaned down to hear her.

"Dat boy will come with spirits from this place; a hot breath will be at his side. He has singled you out to kill; the girl is your only protection from him because she is special to him. Take her, keep her close; when the time comes, you use her to kill him. It is the only way." Pierre only heard the part about the girl and was quick to reply.

"I kind of like the taking the girl and keeping her close part. Here, take the bones; poke the dog's eye out and cast a spell, it will make you feel better."

She continued to whisper to herself. "The hot breath comes for me, it comes quickly."

A sudden warm gust of wind from the west pushed a dirt devil along the valley floor spooking Pierre and causing him to look up.

267

"A storm's coming, a bad one." He was finally serious as he helped the old woman up.

The day darkened as tremendous clouds formed above the valley. Giant fingers of lightning covered the sky and the rain came with the wind.

Sabotha peeked up through the rain and repeated. "The hot breath comes."

It rained all afternoon, but late in the evening some rays of light peeked through the broken clouds alerting the clan and releasing them from their hiding places.

Pierre loved the girls, but failing to convince Dawn to give him her affections, he too came out from hiding. The smell of cooking was much more interesting than her scratching and kicking.

He was surprised to find Sabotha working at one of the fires. Bending down, he took a whiff, then spotted the gutted dog close by.

"I see you took my advice about the dog; a good, bloody gutting will put you back on your feet." He patted her on the back then spotted the heart of a man.

"I know da spell of the Gitanno clan, it will drive death away." She plunked Onotsa's heart into the pot.

"That's good, I can see you're almost your old self." He covered his nose and moved on.

The witch's eyes fluttered as she chanted, "To namme sinne dochek, som toome nonak. To namma sinne, som toome noak."

Over and over she called out.

"I will stop da hot breath from takin' me down.

The wet wind pushed Manez and Four Claws back into the shelter of the cliff. The air had turned cold, but building a fire with the bear there was not something he wanted to try. He eyed the big bear with its fur on one side, gnarly and burnt. It was easy to understand why he hated the fire. Onotsa was right when he had said the bear was connected to him. He chuckled thinking about the Crow village and how Four Claws had destroyed it; he wished he could thank him. As he thought about it, Four Claws sighed and looked his way. Manez reached out and touched the fur. "Thank you, my friend, we will have a great time saving Dawn once more." Four Claws acknowledged his touch with another sigh.

The clouds lifted and Manez knew Neshanu Natchitak was looking at them both, from across that great lake. That thought stirred a deep conviction inside him, causing him to say, "Live or die, I believe my Sishu belongs to you and that all things will be done for your purpose. Remember me when it's my time to cross the lake."

Four Claws gave his approval growling at the sky above, then all was silent. Showing his approval, Manez patted the bear softly on his back. The sky became clear and the stars glistened like never before, causing Manez to marvel at the heavens above.

"Now you're just showing off, but I like it," he called out to the sky.

The cutout in the cliff was small and before he knew it, he was asleep beside the big animal. He dreamed about standing on the ridge, looking down on the village with his body glowing. There were riders in the sky from all the tribes. They rode horses of fire and threw lightning bolts down to the ground.

The bear suddenly rolled and interrupted the dream by waking him.

His nostrils flared as he pulled in the air. The witch was up to something; the bear could feel the disturbance in the air. With two short growls Four Claws said 'I will return' and moved off into the night.

Wet and shivering with cold, Manez was prompted to finally build a fire. It was a very small fire, at the opening of the cave, just in case Four Claws came back.

The flapping of wings above him signaled the return of the old screech owl. "Just ask; they will come."

Maybe it was just the warmth of the fire, the giving in to Nachitak, or the confirmation of Four Claws, but Manez felt stronger, confident and alive.

He sat before the small fire with the powder.

"Just ask," repeated the owl.

With a flick of his wrist, Manez tossed some of the dust into the fire.

"Spirits, I need your help. I ask you to come help the people of the earth and save them from destruction."

Manez retrieved the pipe that Grey Eyes had given him and lit it.

He puffed on it and called to the north. Another puff and a call to the east, then the south, along with the west. Come, spirits, from all directions to help your people.

The fire popped as the powder sent colored sparks into the air. The tiny glowing dots hung just above the flames and swirled around in the smoke from the pipe.

Manez leaned forward studying the tiny spots in the smoke, but after several minutes of nothing happening he looked back at the owl.

"They will come?" he questioned.

"Just believe," answered the bird.

One last, big puff on the pipe; letting it out slowly, he saw something.

The fire popped and tiny sounds could be heard coming from the fire. He leaned forward as the specks began to grow larger and then encircle him until they filled the sky above.

It was just like his dream.

Ghostly, transparent figures; each one representing a different tribe appeared, their horses flew on clouds of fire lighting up the sky. They sang to him and waved their weapons of death.

Manez stood in the center of the circling spirits and listened to their songs from the other side, then he spoke to them. "Sacred ones, the people of the earth have come to a crossroads. An evil darkness threatens life as we know it here. I cannot fight it alone. When I call, will you come fight with me?"

A Cheyenne brave stopped circling, coming face to face with Manez. It was the spirit of Sweet Medicine who had given him the magic inside the cave. His hollow eyes were still scary to Manez.

"It is a good thing that you have found yourself, Dog Warrior. I was thinking I might have to find another to take my place. Tonight, time will stand still for all on earth while the spirit world prepares for battle, but when the sun comes up, call to the ridge above the valley. We will come from the east."

The spirits stopped their circling, then flew away in all directions and darkness closed in around him once more, but this time it was different. He didn't feel alone.

The screech owl bounced from the tree and began to flay away. "Silly boy, I told you now, didn't I?"

"Yes, you did," Manez replied as he gathered his weapons.

The owl called back as he flew away, "Don't take the witch for granted, she has the black power."

271

Sabotha felt Manez use his magic; it made her throw up. Through her whole life, she had always been the one in control of the spirit world, but now she was terrified just trying to keep the boy's magic at bay. It was a different kind of power that came from the things around her and it made her squirm.

Suddenly she felt something coming over her in the air. Casting out the bones, she didn't look up at it, but she called out at it.

"Sek til a nos at triel." She just had time to cut herself as the rippling wave moved through the air over the camp, skipping over her, but falling on all the others. At first, she thought they were dead, even Pierre was frozen stiff.

"Pierre, wa noteka des noha," she said, slapping his face and repeated, "Noteka (Wake up)." She looked close at his eyes and felt his breath on her hand. His lips were slightly moving. They weren't dead, but time had come almost to a stop for all but her.

"I have de time; I make dat boy's magic not work foe him no more." She quickly retreated back to the wagon and began to toss bottles and bags into her basket.

"Da book about the dead, where is it? Ah, here it is!" she exclaimed, as she pulled from the wagon a large well-worn leather book with brass strapping anchoring the corners and tossed it out on the ground in front of the already boiling pot on the fire.

"Da dead dog and the heart of a man. Seven toad legs, a pinch of a pig's liver and a bat's wing." Looking away at the book she said, "Ah, don't forget the man's eyes, we must see em on the other side." She laughed as she cut the eyes from their sockets, then throwing them into the fire, she gave an evil laugh that echoed out among the trees.

Her hand touched something under the scarf tied around her waist.

"What is des hidden here?" She patted at it, then dug out a tiny wad of Manez's hair.

"I didn't lose it all, I got ya now boy. I hurt ya real bad with this here. Ha, ha, ha."

She tossed it into the pot and flipped through the old book stopping on a well-worn page.

"To namme sinne dochek, som toome nonak. To namma sinne, som toome noak."

Over and over she wailed at the book.

"To namme sinne dochek, som toome nonak. To namma sinne, som toome noak."

The rustling in the tree above him startled Manez and drawing his bow, he was ready to shoot until he saw it was a crow nestling in for a roost. "Oh my, brother, I almost shot you dead. You should be a little quieter trying to get comfortable up in that tree. Tomorrow you must be gone from here." His conversation with the crow was cut short by a sudden sick feeling coming over him. His face was breaking out in a sweat and he knew it was the witch pulling at his bones. He quickly tossed the magic powder on his head.

" I must get far away." As suddenly as the thought crossed his lips, he was flying through the night sky. Rushing against the wind, cutting the clean fresh air, he soared; but how could this be? Manez looked out at his arms to see the wings of a black bird flapping up, then down.

"I'm a bird," he called out, but the hills below only heard 'kaw, kaw'. The night above the earth was so enchanting, Manez thought about just flying away; as far as he could from the trouble below, but he knew he couldn't do that. Instead, he chose to fly to the cave above Elm Springs.

He landed in a big tree just above the entrance to the cave.

"Kaw, kaw, kaw (Standing Man, where is my brother?)"

He cried out, but his friend only heard the calls of the bird.

"Kaw, kaw (Is he here? Is he well?)"

On and on he called out, until his brother along with some others came out to see what kind of crazy bird causes such a commotion.

"Kaw, kaw, kaw (Ah, there you are; you look good. I have bad news about our father; he is dead.)"

"That bird has gone crazy. Put an arrrow through it to put is out of its misery," Kanan said.

A small boy shot an arrow at the bird, only to have it jump to another branch.

Kaw, kaw (Why would you shoot at me? It's Manez, your brother.)"

The little boy placed another arrow on the string ready to shoot once more, but the Shaman held his hand across the arrow."This is such a strange thing. This bird is talking to me. My father told of a man who could become a bird, but I have never seen it before. I will talk to him. What is it you want here, spirit?"

"Kaw, kaw, kaw (I am Manez, your brother and I bring bad news. Onotsa is dead.)"

"Our Chief is dead, killed by the Vehoe. This is your brother, Manez, telling this tale."

"Kaw, kaw, kaw (I have been given a great power by Sweet Medicine and with the help of the spirits, I will use this power to fight the Vehoe.)"

"Sweet Medicine has given him powers to fight the whites and he will challenge them."

"Kaw, kaw, kaw (When the sun comes up, I come from the east above the Round Valley along with the spirits of our fathers.)"

"When the sun rises, he will charge down the hill into the valley from the east."

"Kaw, kaw, kaw (I know you are not many and it could mean your death, but those of you who are willing, will you come with me to rid us of this evil once and for all?)"

"He calls to us to fight with him, to rid the valley of the evil that lives there. Will we fight?"

The tribe cheered as the bird jumped into flight. "Kaw, Kaw." Manez called back as he flew away.

His return flight took him back along Beaver Creek and close to the Black Hills, then back again towards the Round Valley. He was missing his Dawn. She was down there, suffering at the hands of the Veho; if only he could see her. He soared close to the camp, "Oh," he cried, realizing he had flown too close to the witch's magic. His body flashed back and forth from bird to boy until he lost control of his flight and crashed to the ground, unconscious.

At this point, everyone in the camp woke up and a little, shiver spiked down Sabotha's body. "Him got too close and I got him. I feel it all over, I got him! Dat boy be no good for long time. I make potion, make impossible for boy to kill Sabotha and Pierre. Den we walk up to him, take the magic from him and rule the world."

She giggled as she splashed the putrid mixture on the still frozen Pierre.

"He think him dead when he wake up and smell dat." She tossed some on herself.

"I think it smell kinda good."

A terrible pain shot through Dawn's heart. She knew something had happened to Manez. There was a cut in the rawhide just big enough for her to see outside. She scanned the ridge above the camp where her heart told her Manez was in trouble and began to cry out to Neshanu Nachitak.

"I've know you my whole life, Neshanu. My people have walked in your ways since their time here began. I don't understand these people who kill everything around them. The Cheyenne need your help; Manez needs your help." The flap suddenly closed making her jump back. "I need your help; hear me," she whispered.

Chapter 27
A Battle Cry For All

The gypsy women were a rough looking bunch. Dawn pulled back as they entered the teepee. She grabbed a short, fat stick from the floor and crouched low, ready to strike out at the three heavy-set women. Her stance made the intruders uneasy at first, but they soon began to laugh.

"Look at this scrawny, native girl. What does Pierre see in this wisp of a girl," one said looking at the others.

Grasping her own bosoms, the middle woman said, "She's not even fully equipped to handle a Sinti man." The women began to laugh profusely and point at Dawn's upper body.

Dawn had no idea what the women were talking about, but the Arikara in her stirred her anger and as quick as lightning, she popped the woman in the middle on top of the head with her stick, sending the woman to her knees. In shock, the other two pulled back slightly as Dawn recoiled once more into her stance.

The woman in the middle rubbed her head as she stood up, then yelled, "De terri no simmi." The other two women lunged forward, but they were caught off guard by Dawn's quick spin to the left and the leg sweep that brought the second woman crashing down close to the fire. Another pop on the head sent the middle gypsy down on her knees once more. The woman on the right ran out of the teepee screaming, as Dawn placed the stick under the chin of the woman on her knees. Rolling over, the lady on the ground also ran away.

"Na nonee, na nonee. (No more, No more.)" the women cried.

Pierre tossed open the flap of the teepee. Dawn held on so tight to the woman, her face turned red and her eyes began to water.

"Na-aseohtsetano, (I want to leave,)" she said, still choking the woman.

"I don't have a clue as to what you're saying, but it sure is cute."

"Nehoveoo estse. (Stand up.)" She pulled the captive up on her feet.

"Mo-nehetaa'e. (We will go now.)" She pushed the woman forward towards the opening.

"Oh, so you think you're just going to just walk out of here?" he said with a smile on his face and shaking his head.

Dawn took it as a sign that he meant to let her go.

"Noheto. (Let's go.)" she said, as she attempted to push past Pierre; but instead of letting her pass, he stabbed her captive, then grabbed her by the neck and tossed her into the corner.

Louis appeared with a bottle and Pierre took a big swig and turned to the men celebrating around the fire. "What a day it's been. Yesterday we were hungry, but today our bellies are full and our heads are spinning with drink. If we're lucky tonight, our beds will be filled with native women, too." He stumbled forward, away from the teepee to join the revelry of the victorious clan.

Dark shadows moved around the camp; they never rested and never rejoiced. The evening's thunderstorm rushed farther away, but something was coming; it was hanging in the air just beyond what they knew and what they feared. They could feel it coming.

The pain that consciousness brought made Manez not want to move at all. His body ached from the fall to the ground. "I was flying," he half chuckled, as he rolled over on his back. *I was flying,* he thought. He flexed his arms and legs; nothing seemed to be broken.

"What was I thinking!" he said. "What was I thinking?" He suddenly realized where he was and what he was doing. *How long have I been on the ground?* He rolled to his knees and looked out at the night sky. Morning was coming; he couldn't be late to the east ridge. He gathered his sore body up and began to run back away from the ridge where he had placed his weapons. The face of Dawn haunted his mind. "I will kill the devil that harms her." The words just slipped out. He moved quickly and soon found the place he had shared with Four Claws. Grabbing his weapons and the magic powder, he made a quick wish for protection from the witch and a speedy run. Then in a flash, he raced through the woods to battle.

After a long night of preparation, Kanan led the last of the Hotamimasaw (Wolf Band) out along the Elms Springs trail. All the painted faces of the tribe told a story. Some were sad, some were scared and some were just plain mad at the whites down below. All their emotions and more were written on Kanan's face, too, but he also had a look about him that the people had never seen. The look of a man, their young leader, was not a boy anymore. They were proud to follow him, even if he led them to their death.

"Here we will make our last stand." He pointed down into the valley. "Put the young ones with the women there, just behind the trees. If things go bad, it will be easy for them to escape back into the forest. Then gather the Hotamimasaw above the gap in the ridge; that's where we will make our charge down the hill."

Standing Man moved among the tribe, whispering Kanan's instructions and then he returned to the boy's side.

"Will he come?" he asked with a scared expression on his face. "Will your brother bring the magic with him from the east?"

Kanan stared at the beaming light beginning to glow behind the trees. "He will do what he always does."

Standing Man turned his head a little as if to say 'what's that?'

"He will make an entrance. He always does. Ha, ha , ha." They both laughed so, it made the others laugh with them.

"This will be a good day, a good day for the people of the earth."

It bothered Manez that the bear hadn't come back in the night. They had finally become friends and he had envisioned charging down the hill on the back of Four Claws. What a great story to tell around the campfire about the boy who rode the back of a bear into battle.

He smiled as he dodged through the trees.

The power of the witch was getting stronger now that he was running towards her. He could feel her pulling at his feet as he ran, but as evil as she was, her powers would be no match for the power he had with him.

He gradually slowed, coming to a stop just behind the trees. He didn't want to alarm his people. His plan was to charge at the Vehoe, first taking the brunt of their fight and maybe save some of his friends from death. He wasn't afraid of death anymore. He had seen the other side of the Great Lake and it was alright with him if it was his time, so he knelt down facing the east and prayed.

"Father, Neshanu Nachitak, have my life. Use it for good and help me fight bravely for my people. I have said all that is in my heart. Oh! If you could save Dawn, that would be a good thing."

The sky was getting brighter now; the sun would come up soon. It was time.

He took the headdress and placed it on his head, then placed the breast plate of bones on his chest. Gathering his golden bow, the four sacred arrows, then placing his knife in his belt along with the hatchet, he tossed the powder in the air and thought of all the evil he had seen from the intruders. He began to glow as he ran from the trees to the gap of the ridge. A battle cry burst from his lungs as he charged down the hill towards the Vehoe. Kanan had no time to react; the charge of his brother surprised him as much as it did the whites below.

"I told you he would make an entrance."

"Ahh- EEE!" Kanan screamed as he followed him down the hill.

The sudden attack surprised most of the gypsy clan. Still numb from their victory celebration, they stumbled around trying to get their weapons. Only one group was ready and waiting; it was the Dark Wind, Pierre's personal bodyguard. They stood poised around the teepee where DeBois slept.

Manez pulled an arrow as he ran and shot it at the dumbfounded gypsies. The shot was like a lightning bolt tearing through three men who stepped in his path, then it returned to the charging Manez. The same arrow restrung and released also sending bolts of red light through different men. The arrow zigzagged around, then reappeared back in the quill with the other arrows.

The sky above him was filled with arrows from the ridge above, falling on the Vehoe and clearing a path for him as he continued to run.

The clan shook off their shock and recovered their senses, meeting the charge of Kanan and the Wolf Band. The meeting of the two groups of men was like giant ocean waves that crashed together, then mixing together and becoming one swirling mass of humanity bent on slaughtering each other.

"The boy he come to his death," Sabotha called out to Pierre, who appeared from the teepee with a knife at the throat of the crying Dawn.

Grabbing the bones and placing them on a rock, Sabotha began to smash the bones into tiny pieces.

"Dat boy wish he never come here." The old hag spit on the fragments, then cut her hand and dripped blood on the pieces.

"I got more power dan you, boy." She found the small tuft of Manez's hair and smashed it into the concoction then began to chant, "To namme sinne dochek, som toome nonak. To namma sinne, som toome noak."

Over and over she wailed at the book.

"To namme sinne dochek, som toome nonak. To namma sinne, som toome noak."

Manez pulled his knife and hatchet as he met the sword of the first faceless man in black. Catching the thrust of his sword in the notch of the handle with his left hand, he came across the neck of the Frenchman, almost cutting his head off. Another came at him from the side, cutting his hand and causing him to drop his knife. Manez caught the blade with the notch in his hatchet and snapped it in half, then he grabbed the arm of the attacker, twisting it up, driving the broken blade into his neck.

Pierre could see the boy coming for him and began to yell at Sabotha. "Do something! Spatter me with blood, anything; but stop him!"

Pierre was within striking distance now as Manez threw the hatchet. It flew straight, but before it hit its mark, it suddenly stopped. As he watched it fall to the ground, his legs crumbled beneath him, causing him to roll at Pierre's feet spilling the arrows from his quill. The old, familiar cold sweat came over him once more and he knew the witch had him.

Pierre thought the boy was dead. He patted the spot where he should have been struck by the hatchet, then he kicked at the weapon on the ground looking strangely at Sabotha for an answer.

"I covered you with dat awful smell, no man can kill you now. It still smell good to me. You take his woman and his power, yes?"

Dawn broke loose from Pierre and collapsed on top of Manez.

"Boy, you gonna get it; you dead now."

"I knew you had it under control all the time," Pierre replied, eyeing the pouch.

Seeing Manez go down, the hearts of the Cheyenne grew faint, letting the battle suddenly turned in the favor of the Dark Wind. Louis's men regained their footing, advancing on the Wolf Band and driving them slowly back up the hill.

"Take him and kill him, so all his people can see it."

Pierre pulled the girl up by the hair, pinning her to his left side. Louis stood Manez up and as they did, DeBois yanked the medicine pouch from his neck, tossing it lightly in his right hand.

"With this, we will rule the world, and with this, pulling Dawn close, so will my sons."

Then he stabbed Manez and watched the boy fall to the ground on top of the quiver of arrows.

Manez moved as though attempting to stand up, but instead, he stuck the arrow that turns back time in the ground. The Valley began to spin and everyone's movement was in reverse for several seconds.

Everyone raced back in time, except him. He took his knife and placed it in Dawn's hand just as time restarted.

Dawn broke loose from Pierre and collapsed on top of Manez. "Boy, you gonna get it; you dead now."

"I knew you had it under control all the time," Pierre replied, eyeing the pouch.

Seeing Manez go down, the hearts of the Cheyenne grew faint, letting the battle suddenly turn in favor of the Dark Wind. Louis's men regained their footing, advancing on the Wolf Band and driving them slowly back up the hill.

"Take him and kill him so all his people can see it."

Pierre pulled the girl up by the hair, pinning her to his left side. Louis stood Manez up and as they did, DeBois yanked the medicine pouch from his neck, tossing it lightly in his right hand.

"With this, we will rule the world and with this, pulling Dawn close, so will my sons."

Manez made an attempt at Pierre.

"Don't punish yourself, boy. Even if you could get me, you heard the witch, no man can kill me," he said laughing with the witch's approval.

Dawn, with all her might, suddenly drove something she held in her right hand into Pierre's body just below his ribs, causing him to let her go. He looked stunned as he fell to his knees with Manez's knife stuck under his ribs. "I am not a man!" she exclaimed.

The medicine bag began to glow, burning his hand as it fell to the ground.

"But you said I would be k-k-king," he said, as he died.

Sabotha backed away from the girl hoping to somehow escape unnoticed, but a breath of hot air fell on her neck.

"Da hot breath come for me!" she screamed as she turned to face Four Claws. Her words were cut short as he clamped down on her neck with his giant teeth, killing her and tossing her down like a child.

Now it was the Frenchmen who grew faint at the sight of Pierre and Sabotha being killed. They froze just for an instant not sure whether to flee or continue fighting. But before they could move, the blinding rays of sunlight broke over the ridge sending glistening pointed beams over everyone, instantly blinding them. As beautiful as it was, every beam of light carried a spirit warrior, bringing death to the Vehoe and one by one the Dark Wind turned to dust as the spirits touched them.

A sudden stillness came over everyone. The only thing that moved was the dust still swirling in the air. Several moments passed; it was if they couldn't believe what had just happened.

A single Cheyenne battle cry went out across the Round Valley. "Aheeee! Aheeee!" Soon all the Wolf Band joined in echoing their cries throughout the valley.

Manez stood with Dawn, Kanan, and Four Claws holding the arrow high above his head in the middle of the people of the earth and rejoiced that the darkness was finally defeated.

Sweet Medicine hovered above them, smiling down at them. "You truly believed, Manez of the Hotamimasan Cheyenne. Faith like that is a good thing. It makes magic happen."

Manez raised his hand and the medicine pouch floated up to him along with the weapons he had found in the cave.

"I release you from your duty as protector of the people. It looks as if the young woman will need looking after."

Dawn squeezed Manez's hand.

"Someone else will come when he is needed. Remember this time and always look to the east." With that, the spirits slowly disappeared.

Manez was happy and in his heart he thanked Neshanu Nachitak for all the earth, but most of all, for Dawn.

"What a story he would have to tell!"

Far away to the East in the swamp, the air hung thick as Samba of Bambara regrouped his people after the battle for New Orleans. The slaves who had survived the battle returned one by one to the safety of Des Natanapalle. His heart was broken that he did not lead his people to freedom, but seeing the San Felipe sail out of the harbor gave him fierce determination and hope that he too, one day would be free. As he watched high above the city of slaves, he thought, *We will heal our wounds and wait for a time to come when we too will be free like Bebai, the King of Fulani.*

As the San Felipe skipped above the waves alongside of the Santiago, Bebai's mind was filled with many thoughts. The sun was setting. He knew Samba was watching the same sun go down and he wished that he too had escaped from New Orleans. The sudden appearance of a seagull floating on the wind tore at his heart. His magpie, Lucille, was also watching the same sunset. He could see her standing there waiting for a love that could never be.

"Ta Loolu, set a course for St. Malo," Bebai said. "Something is hidden there that will surprise our mysterious new friend, Juan Leon. Take us over the darkening horizon."

Darkwind 49 Media Press
darkwind49@yahoo.com

Darkwind- BOOK 1

DARK PROMISES - BOOK 2

CIBOL'S DARKEST SECRET- BOOK 3

OVER THE DARKENING HORIZON- BOOK 4

ESTEBAN'S DARK LIES- BOOK 5

LEON'S SHADOW- BOOK 6

Made in United States
North Haven, CT
30 July 2022